SO-BIZ-282

RAVES FOR BILL PRONZINI!

"Pronzini makes people and events so real that you are living those explosive days of terror."

—Robert Ludlum

"Pronzini is a master of suspense."

—*Los Angeles Times*

"Pronzini is a skillful storyteller who puts the emphasis on character without sacrificing suspense."

—*San Diego Union-Tribune*

"Pronzini is a magnificent entertainer of the first rank."

—Ed Gorman, Author of *Shadow Games*

Other *Leisure* books by Bill Pronzini:
MASQUES

NIGHT FREIGHT

BILL PRONZINI

LEISURE BOOKS NEW YORK CITY

A LEISURE BOOK®

May 2000

Published by

Dorchester Publishing Co., Inc.
276 Fifth Avenue
New York, NY 10001

If you purchased this book without a cover you should be aware that this book is stolen property. It was reported as "unsold and destroyed" to the publisher and neither the author nor the publisher has received any payment for this "stripped book."

Copyright © 2000 by the Pronzini-Muller Family Trust

Additional copyright information may be found at the end of this book.

All rights reserved. No part of this book may be reproduced or transmitted in any form or by any electronic or mechanical means, including photocopying, recording or by any information storage and retrieval system, without the written permission of the Publisher, except where permitted by law.

ISBN 0-8439-4706-3

The name "Leisure Books" and the stylized "L" with design are trademarks of Dorchester Publishing Co., Inc.

Printed in the United States of America.

For Don D'Auria and Ed Gorman
Who made it possible

CONTENTS

Stacked Deck...13

Angel of Mercy...49

Night Freight...61

Liar's Dice..73

Out Behind the Shed...85

Souls Burning..95

Strangers in the Fog..107

Peekaboo...121

Thirst...131

Wishful Thinking..141

Ancient Evil..153

The Monster...169

His Name Was Legion...177

Out of the Depths...185

The Pattern...211

The Rec Field..225

Deathwatch...237

Home...247

Tom...253

A Taste of Paradise..265

Sweet Fever...279

Deathlove...289

Black Wind...301

The Coffin Trimmer...311

Funeral Day..325

I Think I Will Not Hang Myself Today.............................331

NIGHT FREIGHT

"Stacked Deck" is solidly in the Black Mask *school (and was, in fact, first published in* The New Black Mask, *a short-lived revival of that fine old pulp magazine). It is one of the few stories of this type that I've written, despite the critics and labelers who persist in calling the "Nameless Detective" series "hardboiled." The "Nameless" series is actually humanist crime fiction, with dark-suspense overtones—or, as another labeler once termed it, "confessional crime fiction." The true hard-boiled story was born in the Depression thirties and died in the post-McCarthy fifties; everything since that has been termed hardboiled is either an imitation, an intentional tribute, or some other kind of criminous tale (usually one featuring a private detective as protagonist) that has been misrepresented so it will fit into a convenient niche.*

Stacked Deck

1.

From where he stood in the shadow of a split-bole Douglas fir, Deighan had a clear view of the cabin down below. Big harvest moon tonight, and only a few streaky clouds scudding past now and then to dim its hard yellow shine. The hard yellow glistened off the surface of Lake Tahoe beyond, softened into a long silverish stripe out toward the middle. The rest of the

13

water shone like polished black metal. All of it was empty as far as he could see, except for the red-and-green running lights of a boat well away to the south, pointed toward the neon shimmer that marked the South Shore gambling casinos.

The cabin was big, made of cut pine logs and redwood shakes. It had a railed redwood deck that overlooked the lake, mostly invisible from where Deighan was. A flat concrete pier jutted out into the moonstruck water, a pair of short wooden floats making a T at its outer end. The boat tied up there was a thirty-foot ChrisCraft with sleeping accommodations for four. Nothing but the finer things for the Shooter.

Deighan watched the cabin. He'd been watching it for three hours now, from this same vantage point. His legs bothered him a little, standing around like this, and his eyes hurt from squinting. Time was, he'd had the night vision of an owl. Not anymore. What he had now, that he hadn't had when he was younger, was patience. He'd learned that in the last three years, along with a lot of other things—patience most of all.

On all sides the cabin was dark, but that was because they'd put the blackout curtains up. The six of them had been inside for better than two hours now, the same five-man nucleus as on every Thursday night except during the winter months, plus the one newcomer. The Shooter went to Hawaii when it started to snow. Or Florida or the Bahamas—someplace warm. Mannlicher and Brandt stayed home in the winter.

Deighan didn't know what the others did, and he didn't care.

A match flared in the darkness between the carport, where the Shooter's Caddy Eldorado was slotted, and the parking area back among the trees. That was the lookout—Mannlicher's boy. Some lookout: he smoked a cigarette every five minutes, like clockwork, so you always knew where he was. Deighan watched him smoke this one. When he was done, he threw the butt away in a shower of sparks, and then seemed to remember that he was surrounded by dry timber and went after it and stamped it out with his shoe. *Some* lookout.

Deighan held his watch up close to his eyes, pushed the little button that lighted its dial. Ten-nineteen. Just about time. The lookout was moving again, down toward the lake. Pretty soon he would walk out on the pier and smoke another cigarette and admire the view for a few minutes. He apparently did that at least twice every Thursday night—that had been his pattern on each of the last two—and he hadn't gone through the ritual yet tonight. He was bored, that was the thing. He'd been at his job a long time and it was always the same; there wasn't anything for him to do except walk around and smoke cigarettes and look at three hundred square miles of lake. Nothing ever happened. In three years nothing had ever happened.

Tonight something was going to happen.

Deighan took the gun out of the clamshell holster at

15

his belt. It was a Smith & Wesson .38, lightweight, compact—a good piece, one of the best he'd ever owned. He held it in his hand, watching as the lookout performed as if on cue—walked to the pier, stopped, then moved out along its flat surface. When the guy had gone halfway, Deighan came out of the shadows and went down the slope at an angle across the driveway, to the rear of the cabin. His shoes made little sliding sounds on the needled ground, but they weren't sounds that carried.

He'd been over this ground three times before, dry runs the last two Thursday nights and once during the day when nobody was around; he knew just where and how to go. The lookout was lighting up again, his back to the cabin, when Deighan reached the rear wall. He eased along it to the spare-bedroom window. The sash went up easily, noiselessly. He could hear them then, in the rec room—voices, ice against glass, the click and rattle of the chips. He got the ski mask from his jacket pocket, slipped it over his head, snugged it down. Then he climbed through the window, put his penlight on just long enough to orient himself, went straight across to the door that led into the rec room.

It didn't make a sound, either, when he opened it. He went in with the revolver extended, elbow locked. Sturgess saw him first. He said, "Jesus Christ!" and his body went as stiff as if he were suffering a stroke. The others turned in their chairs, gawking. The Shooter started up out of his.

Deighan said, fast and hard, "Sit still if you don't

want to die. Hands on the table where I can see them—
all of you. Do it!"

They weren't stupid; they did what they were told.
Deighan watched them through a thin haze of tobacco
smoke. Six men around the hexagonal poker table,
hands flat on its green baize, heads lifted or twisted to
stare at him. He knew five of them. Mannlicher, the fat
owner of the Nevornia Club; he had Family ties, even
though he was a Prussian, because he'd once done
some favors for an east-coast *capo*. Brandt, Mannlicher's cousin and private enforcer, who doubled as
the Nevornia's floor boss. Bellah, the quasi-legitimate
real-estate developer and high roller. Sturgess, the
bankroll behind the Jackpot Lounge up at North
Shore. And the Shooter—hired muscle, hired gun,
part-time coke runner, whose real name was Dennis
D'Allesandro. The sixth man was the pigeon they'd
lured in for this particular game, a lean guy in his
fifties with Texas oil money written all over him and
his fancy clothes—Donley or Donavan, something like
that.

Mannlicher was the bank tonight; the table behind
his chair was covered with stacks of dead presidents—
fifties and hundreds, mostly. Deighan took out the
folded-up flour sack, tossed it on top of the poker chips
that littered the baize in front of Mannlicher. "All right.
Fill it."

The fat man didn't move. He was no pushover; he
was hard, tough, mean. And he didn't like being ripped
off. Veins bulged in his neck, throbbed in his temples.

The violence in him was close to the surface now, held thinly in check.

"You know who we are?" he said. "Who I am?"

"Fill it."

"You dumb bastard. You'll never live to spend it."

"Fill the sack. *Now.*"

Deighan's eyes, more than his gun, made up Mannlicher's mind for him. He picked up the sack, pushed around in his chair, began to savagely feed in the stacks of bills.

"The rest of you," Deighan said, "put your wallets, watches, jewelry on the table. Everything of value. Hurry it up."

The Texan said, "Listen heah—" and Deighan pointed the .38 at his head and said, "One more word, you're a dead man." The Texan made an effort to stare him down, but it was just to save face; after two or three seconds he lowered his gaze and began stripping the rings off his fingers.

The rest of them didn't make any fuss. Bellah was sweating; he kept swiping it out of his eyes, his hands moving in little jerks and twitches. Brandt's eyes were like dull knives, cutting away at Deighan's masked face. D'Allesandro showed no emotion of any kind. That was his trademark; he was your original iceman. They might have called him that, maybe, if he'd been like one of those old-timers who used an ice pick or a blade. As it was, with his preferences, the Shooter was the right name for him.

Mannlicher had the sack full now. The platinum ring on his left hand, with its circle of fat diamonds, made little gleams and glints in the shine from the low-hanging droplight. The idea of losing that bothered him even more than losing his money; he kept running the fingers of his other hand over the stones.

"The ring," Deighan said to him. "Take it off."

"Go to hell."

"Take it off or I'll put a third eye in the middle of your forehead. Your choice."

Mannlicher hesitated, tried to stare him down, didn't have any better luck at it than the Texan. There was a tense moment; then, because he didn't want to die over a piece of jewelry, he yanked the ring off, slammed it down hard in the middle of the table.

Deighan said, "Put it in the sack. The wallets and the rest of the stuff too."

This time Mannlicher didn't hesitate. He did as he'd been told.

"All right," Deighan said. "Now get up and go over by the bar. Lie down on the floor on your belly."

Mannlicher got up slowly, his jaw set and his teeth clenched as if to keep the violence from spewing out like vomit. He lay down on the floor. Deighan gestured at Brandt, said, "You next. Then the rest of you, one at a time."

When they were all on the floor he moved to the table, caught up the sack. "Stay where you are for ten minutes," he told them. "You move before that, or call

19

to the guy outside, I'll blow the place up. I got a grenade in my pocket, the fragmentation kind. Anybody doubt it?"

None of them said anything.

Deighan backed up into the spare bedroom, leaving the door open so he could watch them all the way to the window. He put his head out, saw no sign of the lookout. Still down by the lake somewhere. The whole thing had taken just a few minutes.

He swung out through the window, hurried away in the shadows—but in the opposite direction from the driveway and the road above. On the far side of the cabin there was a path that angled through the pine forest to the north; he found it, followed it at a trot. Enough moonlight penetrated through the branches overhead to let him see where he was going.

He was almost to the lakefront when the commotion started back there: voices, angry and pulsing in the night, Mannlicher's the loudest of them. They hadn't waited the full ten minutes, but then he hadn't expected them to. It didn't matter. The Shooter's cabin was invisible from here, cut off by a wooded finger of land a hundred yards wide. And they wouldn't be looking for him along the water, anyway. They'd be up on the road, combing that area; they'd figure automatically that his transportation was a car.

The hard yellow-and-black gleam of the lake was just ahead, the rushes and ferns where he'd tied up the rented Beachcraft inboard. He moved across the sandy strip of beach, waded out to his calves, dropped the loaded flour sack into the boat, then eased the craft free of the rushes before he lifted himself over the gunwale. The engine caught with a quiet rumble the first time he turned the key.

They were still making noise back at the cabin, blundering around like fools, as he eased away into the night.

2.

The motel was called the Whispering Pines. It was back off Highway 28 below Crystal Bay, a good half mile from the lake, tucked up in a grove of pines and Douglas fir. Deighan's cabin was the farthest from the office, detached from its nearest neighbor by thirty feet of open ground.

Inside he sat in darkness except for flickering light from the television. The set was an old one; the picture was riddled with snow and kept jumping every few seconds. But he didn't care; he wasn't watching it. Or listening to it: he had the sound turned off. It was on only because he didn't like waiting in the dark.

It had been after midnight when he came in—too late to make the ritual call to Fran, even though he'd felt a compulsion to do so. She went to bed at eleven-thirty; she didn't like the phone to ring after that. How could he blame her? When he was home and she was away at Sheila's or her sister's, he never wanted it to ring that late either.

It was one-ten now. He was tired, but not too tired.

The evening was still in his blood, warming him, like liquor or drugs that hadn't quite worn off yet. Mannlicher's face . . . that was an image he'd never forget. The Shooter's, too, and Brandt's, but especially Mannlicher's.

Outside, a car's headlamps made a sweep of light across the curtained window as it swung in through the motel courtyard. When it stopped nearby and the lights went out, Deighan thought: It's about time.

Footsteps made faint crunching sounds on gravel. Soft knock on the door. Soft voice following: "Prince? You in there?"

"Door's open."

A wedge of moonlight widened across the floor, not quite reaching to where Deighan sat in the lone chair with the .38 in his hand. The man who stood silhouetted in the opening made a perfect target—just a damned airhead, any way you looked at him.

"Prince?"

"I'm over here. Come on in, shut the door."

"Why don't you turn on a light?"

"There's a switch by the door."

The man entered, shut the door. There was a click and the ceiling globe came on. Deighan stayed where he was, but reached over with his left hand to turn off the TV.

Bellah stood blinking at him, running his palms along the sides of his expensive cashmere jacket. He said nervously, "For God's sake, put the gun away. What's the idea?"

"I'm the cautious type."

"Well, put it away. I don't like it."

Deighan got to his feet, slid the revolver into his belt holster. "How'd it go?"

"Hairy, damned hairy. Mannlicher was like a madman." Bellah took a handkerchief out of his pocket, wiped his forehead. His angular face was pale, shiny-damp. "I didn't think he'd take it this hard. Christ."

That's the trouble with people like you, Deighan thought. You never think. He pinched a cigarette out of his shirt pocket, lit it with the Zippo Fran had given him fifteen years ago. Fifteen years, and it still worked. Like their marriage, even with all the trouble. How long was it now? Twenty-two years in May? Twenty-three?

Bellah said, "He started screaming at D'Allesandro. I thought he was going to choke him."

"Who? Mannlicher?"

"Yeah. About the window in the spare bedroom."

"What'd D'Allesandro say?"

"He said he always keeps it locked, you must have jimmied it some way that didn't leave any traces. Mannlicher didn't believe him. He thinks D'Allesandro forgot to lock it."

"Nobody got the idea it was an inside job?"

"No."

"Okay then. Relax, Mr. Bellah. You're in the clear."

Bellah wiped his face again. "Where's the money?"

"Other side of the bed. On the floor."

"You count it?"

23

"No. I figured you'd want to do that."

Bellah went over there, picked up the flour sack, emptied it on the bed. His eyes were bright and hot as he looked at all the loose green. Then he frowned, gnawed at his lower lip, and poked at Mannlicher's diamond ring. "What'd you take this for? Mannlicher is more pissed about the ring than anything else. He said his mother gave it to him. It's worth ten thousand."

"That's why I took it," Deighan said. "Fifteen percent of the cash isn't a hell of a lot."

Bellah stiffened. "I set it all up, didn't I? Why shouldn't I get the lion's share?"

"I'm not arguing, Mr. Bellah. We agreed on a price; okay, that's the way it is. I'm only saying I got a right to a little something extra."

"All right, all right." Bellah was looking at the money again. "Must be at least two hundred thousand," he said. "That Texan, Donley, brought fifty grand alone."

"Plenty in his wallet too, then."

"Yeah."

Deighan smoked and watched Bellah count the loose bills and what was in the wallets and billfolds. There was an expression on the developer's face like a man has when he's fondling a naked woman. Greed, pure and simple. Greed was what drove Lawrence Bellah; money was his best friend, his lover, his god. He didn't have enough ready cash to buy the lakefront property down near Emerald Bay—property he stood

to make three to four million on, with a string of con-
dos—and he couldn't raise it fast enough any legitimate way; so he'd arranged to get it by knocking over
his own weekly poker game, even if it meant crossing
some hard people. He had balls, you had to give him
that. He was stupid as hell, and one of these days he
was liable to end up in pieces at the bottom of the lake,
but he did have balls.

He was also lucky, at least for the time being,
because the man he'd picked to do his strong-arm
work was Bob Prince. He had no idea the name was a
phony, no idea the whole package on Bob Prince was
the result of three years of careful manipulation. All he
knew was that Prince had a reputation as dependable,
easy to work with, not too smart or money-hungry, and
that he was willing to do any kind of muscle work.
Bellah didn't have an inkling of what he'd really done
by hiring Bob Prince. If he kept on being lucky, he
never would.

Bellah was sweating by the time he finished adding
up the take. "Two hundred and thirty-three thousand
and change," he said. "More than we figured on."

"My cut's thirty-five thousand," Deighan said.

"You divide fast." Bellah counted out two stacks,
hundreds and fifties, to one side of the flowered bed-
spread. Then he said, "Count it? Or do you trust me?"

Deighan grinned. He rubbed out his cigarette, went
to the bed, and took his time shuffling through the
stacks. "On the nose," he said when he was done.

Bellah stuffed the rest of the cash back into the flour

sack, leaving the watches and jewelry where they lay. He was still nervous, still sweating; he wasn't going to sleep much tonight, Deighan thought.

"That's it, then," Bellah said. "You going back to Chicago tomorrow?"

"Not right away. Thought I'd do a little gambling first."

"Around here? Christ, Prince . . ."

"No. Reno, maybe. I might even go down to Vegas."

"Just get away from Tahoe."

"Sure," Deighan said. "First thing in the morning."

Bellah went to the door. He paused there to tuck the flour sack under his jacket; it made him look as if he had a tumor on his left side. "Don't do anything with that jewelry in Nevada. Wait until you get back to Chicago."

"Whatever you say, Mr. Bellah."

"Maybe I'll need you again sometime," Bellah said. "You'll hear from me if I do."

"Anytime. Any old time."

When Bellah was gone, Deighan put five thousand dollars into his suitcase and the other thirty thousand into a knapsack he'd bought two days before at a South Shore sporting goods store. Mannlicher's diamond ring went into the knapsack, too, along with the better pieces among the rest of the jewelry. The watches and the other stuff were no good to him; he bundled those up in a hand towel from the bathroom, stuffed the bundle into the pocket of his down jacket. Then he had one more cigarette, set his portable alarm clock for six A.M., double-locked the door, and went to bed on the left side, with the revolver under the pillow near his right hand.

3.

In the dawn light the lake was like smoky blue glass, empty except for a few optimistic fishermen anchored close to the eastern shoreline. The morning was cold, autumn-crisp, but there was no wind. The sun was just beginning to rise, painting the sky and its scattered cloudstreaks in pinks and golds. There was old snow on the upper reaches of Mount Tallac, on some of the other Sierra peaks that ringed the lake.

Deighan took the Beachcraft out half a mile before he dropped the bundle of watches and worthless jewelry overboard. Then he cut off at a long diagonal to the north that brought him to within a few hundred yards of the Shooter's cabin. He had his fishing gear out by then, fiddling with the glass rod and tackle— just another angler looking for rainbow, Mackinaw, and cutthroat trout.

There wasn't anybody out and around at the Shooter's place. Deighan glided past at two knots, angled in to shore a couple of hundred yards beyond, where there were rushes and some heavy brush and trees overhanging the water. From there he had a pretty good view of the cabin, its front entrance, the Shooter's Caddy parked inside the carport.

It was eight o'clock, and the sun was all the way up,

when he switched off the engine and tied up at the bole of the collapsed pine. It was a few minutes past nine-thirty when D'Allesandro came out and walked around to the Caddy. He was alone. No chippies from the casino this morning, not after what had gone down last night. He might be going to the store for cigarettes, groceries, or to a café somewhere for breakfast. He might be going to see somebody, do some business. The important thing was, how long would he be gone?

Deighan watched him back his Caddy out of the carport, drive it away and out of sight on the road above. He stayed where he was, fishing, waiting. At the end of an hour, when the Shooter still hadn't come back, he started the boat's engine and took his time maneuvering around the wooden finger of land to the north and then into the cove where he'd anchored last night. He nosed the boat into the reeds and ferns, swung overboard, and pushed it farther in, out of sight. Then he caught up the knapsack and set off through the woods to the Shooter's cabin.

He made a slow half circle of the place, keeping to the trees. The carport was still empty. Nothing moved anywhere within the range of his vision. Finally he made his way down to the rear wall, around it and along the side until he reached the front door. He didn't like standing out here for even a little while because there was no cover; but this door was the only one into the house, except for sliding doors on the terrace and a porch on the other side, and you couldn't jimmy sliding doors easily and without leaving marks.

The same was true of windows. The Shooter would have made sure they were all secure anyway.

Deighan had one pocket of the knapsack open, the pick gun in his hand, when he reached the door. He'd got the pick gun from a housebreaker named Caldwell, an old-timer who was retired now; he'd also got some other tools and lessons in how to use them on the various kinds of locks. The lock on the Shooter's door was a flush-mounted, five-pin cylinder lock, with a steel lip on the door frame to protect the bolt and strike plate. That meant it was a lock you couldn't loid with a piece of plastic or a shim. It also meant that with a pick gun you could probably have it open in a couple of minutes.

Bending, squinting, he slid the gun into the lock. Set it, working the little knob on top to adjust the spring tension. Then he pulled the trigger—and all the pins bounced free at once and the door opened under his hand.

He slipped inside, nudged the door shut behind him, put the pick gun away inside the knapsack, and drew on a pair of thin plastic gloves. The place smelled of stale tobacco smoke and stale liquor. They hadn't been doing all that much drinking last night; maybe the Shooter had nibbled a few too many after the rest of them finally left. He didn't like losing money and valuables any more than Mannlicher did.

Deighan went through the front room. Somebody'd decorated the place for D'Allesandro: leather furniture, deer and antelope heads on the walls, Indian rugs on the floors, tasteful painting. Cocaine deals had paid for part of it; contract work, including two hits on greedy Oakland and San Francisco drug dealers, had paid for the rest. But the Shooter was still small-time. He wasn't bright enough to be anything else. Cards and dice and whores-in-training were all he really cared about.

The front room was no good; Deighan prowled quickly through the other rooms. D'Allesandro wasn't the kind to have an office or a den, but there was a big old-fashioned rolltop desk in a room with a TV set and one of those big movie-type screens. None of the desk drawers was locked. Deighan pulled out the biggest one, saw that it was loaded with Danish porn magazines, took the magazines out and set them on the floor. He opened the knapsack and transferred the thirty thousand dollars into the back of the drawer. He put Mannlicher's ring in there, too, along with the other rings and a couple of gold chains the Texan had been wearing. Then he stuffed the porn magazines in at the front and pushed the drawer shut.

On his way back to the front room he rolled the knapsack tight around the pick gun and stuffed them into his jacket pocket. He opened the door, stepped out. He'd just finished resetting the lock when he heard the car approaching on the road above.

He froze for a second, looking up there. He couldn't see the car because of a screen of trees; but then he heard its automatic transmission gear down as it slowed for the turn into the Shooter's driveway. He pulled the door shut and ran toward the lake, the only direction he could go. Fifty feet away the log-railed terrace began, raised up off the sloping ground on redwood pillars. Deighan caught one of the railings, hauled himself up, and half rolled through the gap between them. The sound of the oncoming car was loud in his ears as he landed, off balance, on the deck.

He went to one knee, came up again. The only way to tell if he'd been seen was to stop and look, but that was a fool's move. Instead he ran across the deck, climbed through the railing on the other side, dropped down, and tried to keep from making noise as he plunged into the woods. He stopped moving after thirty yards, where ferns and a deadfall formed a thick concealing wall. From behind it, with the .38 in his hand, he watched the house and the deck, catching his breath, waiting.

Nobody came up or out on the deck. Nobody showed himself anywhere. The car's engine had been shut off sometime during his flight; it was quiet now, except for birds and the faint hum of a powerboat out on the lake.

Deighan waited ten minutes. When there was still nothing to see or hear, he transcribed a slow curl through the trees to where he could see the front of the cabin. The Shooter's Caddy was back inside the carport, no sign of haste in the way it had been neatly slotted. The cabin door was shut. The whole area seemed deserted.

But he waited another ten minutes before he was

31

satisfied. Even then, he didn't holster his weapon until he'd made his way around to the cove where the Beachcraft was hidden. And he didn't relax until he was well out on the lake, headed back toward Crystal Bay.

4.

The Nevornia was one of South Shore's older clubs, but it had undergone some recent modernizing. Outside, it had been given a glass and gaudy-neon face-lift. Inside, they'd used more glass, some cut crystal, and a wine-red decor that included carpeting, upholstery, and gaming tables.

When Deighan walked in a few minutes before two, the banks of slots and the blackjack tables were getting moderately heavy play. That was because it was Friday; some of the small-time gamblers liked to get a jump on the weekend crowds. The craps and roulette layouts were quiet. The high rollers were like vampires: they couldn't stand the daylight, so they only came out after dark.

Deighan bought a roll of quarters at one of the change booths. There were a couple of dozen rows of slots in the main casino—flashy new ones, mostly, with a few of the old scrolled nickel-plated jobs mixed in for the sake of nostalgia. He stopped at one of the old quarter machines, fed in three dollars' worth. Lemons and oranges. He couldn't even line up two cherries for a three-coin drop. He smiled crookedly to himself, went away from the slots and into the long concourse that connected the main casino with the new, smaller addition at the rear.

There were telephone booths along one side of the concourse. Deighan shut himself inside one of them, put a quarter in the slot, pushed 0 and then the digits of his home number in San Francisco. When the operator came on he said it was a collect call; that was to save himself the trouble of having to feed in a handful of quarters. He let the circuit make exactly five burrs in his ear before he hung up. If Fran was home, she'd know now that he was all right. If she wasn't home, then she'd know it later when he made another five-ring call. He always tried to call at least twice a day, at different times, because sometimes she went out shopping or to a movie or to visit with Sheila and the kids.

It'd be easier if she just answered the phone, talked to him, but she never did when he was away. Never. Sheila or anybody else wanted to get hold of her, they had to call one of the neighbors or come over in person. She didn't want anything to do with him when he was away, didn't want to know what he was doing or even when he'd be back. "Suppose I picked up the phone and it wasn't you?" she'd said. "Suppose it was somebody telling me you were dead? I couldn't stand that." That part of it didn't make sense to him. If he were dead, somebody'd come by and tell it to her face; dead was dead, and what difference did it make how

33

she got the news? But he didn't argue with her. He didn't like to argue with her, and it didn't cost him anything to do it her way.

He slotted the quarter again and called the Shooter's number. Four rings, five, and D'Allesandro's voice said, "Yeah?"

"Mr. Carson?"

"Who?"

"Isn't this Paul Carson?"

"No. You got the wrong number."

"Oh, sorry," Deighan said, and rang off.

Another quarter in the slot. This time the number he punched out was the Nevornia's business line. A woman's voice answered, crisp and professional. He said, "Mr. Mannlicher. Tell him it's urgent."

"Whom shall I say is calling?"

"Never mind that. Just tell him it's about what happened last night."

"Sir, I'm afraid I can't—"

"Tell him last night's poker game, damn it. He'll talk to me."

There was a click and some canned music began to play in his ear. He lit a cigarette. He was on his fourth drag when the canned music quit and the fat man's voice said, "Frank Mannlicher. Who's this?"

"No names. Is it all right to talk on this line?"

"Go ahead, talk."

"I'm the guy who hit your game last night."

Silence for four or five seconds. Then Mannlicher said, "Is that so?" in a flat, wary voice.

"Ski mask, Smith & Wesson .38, grenade in my jacket pocket. The take was better than two hundred thousand. I got your ring—platinum with a circle of diamonds."

Another pause, shorter this time. "So why call me today?"

"How'd you like to get it all back—the money and the ring?"

"How?"

"Go pick it up. I'll tell you where."

"Yeah? Why should you do me a favor?"

"I didn't know who you were last night. I wasn't told. If I had been, I wouldn't of gone through with it. I don't mess with people like you, people with your connections."

"Somebody hired you, that it?"

"That's it."

"Who?"

"D'Allesandro."

"What?"

"The Shooter. D'Allesandro."

". . . Bullshit."

"You don't have to believe me. But I'm telling you—he's the one. He didn't tell me who'd be at the game, and now he's trying to screw me on the money. He says there was less than a hundred and fifty thousand in the sack; I know better."

"So now you want to screw him."

"That's right. Besides, I don't like the idea of you pushing to find out who I am, maybe sending somebody to pay me a visit someday. I figure if I give you the Shooter, you'll lose interest in me."

More silence. "Why'd he do it?" Mannlicher said in a different voice—harder, with the edge of violence it had held last night. "Hit the game like that?"

"He needs some big money, fast. He's into some kind of scam back east; he wouldn't say what it is."

"Where's the money and the rest of the stuff?"

"At his cabin. We had a drop arranged in the woods; I put the sack there last night, he picked it up this morning when nobody was around. The money's in his desk—the big rolltop. Your ring, too. That's where it was an hour ago, anyhow, when I walked out."

Mannlicher said, "In his desk," as if he were biting the words off something bitter.

"Go out there, see for yourself."

"If you're telling this straight, you got nothing to worry about from me. Maybe I'll fix you up with a reward or something. Where can I get in touch?"

"You can't," Deighan said. "I'm long gone as soon as I hang up this phone."

"I'll make it five thousand. Just tell me where you—"

Deighan broke the connection.

His cigarette had burned down to the filter; he dropped it on the floor, put his shoe on it before he left the booth. On his way out of the casino he paused long enough to push another quarter into the same slot machine he'd played before. More lemons and oranges. This time he didn't smile as he moved away.

Night Freight

5.

Narrow and twisty, hemmed in by trees, Old Lake Road branched off Highway 50 on the Nevada side and took two miles to get all the way to the lake. But it wasn't a dead end; another road picked it up at the lakefront and looped back out to the highway. There were several nice homes hidden away in the area—it was called Pine Acres—with plenty of space between them. The Shooter's cabin was a mile and a half from the highway, off an even narrower lane called Little Cove Road. The only other cabin within five hundred yards was a summer place that the owners had already closed up for the year.

Deighan drove past the intersection with Little Cove, went two-tenths of a mile, parked on the turnout at that point. There wasn't anybody else around when he got out, nothing to see except trees and little winks of blue that marked the nearness of the lake. If anybody came along, they wouldn't pay any attention to the car. For one thing, it was a '75 Ford Galaxy with nothing distinctive about it except the antenna for the GTE mobile phone. It was his—he'd driven it up from San Francisco—but the papers on it said it belonged to Bob Prince. For another thing, Old Lake Road was only a hundred yards or so from the water here, and there was a path through the trees to a strip of rocky beach. Local kids used it in the summer; he'd found that out from Bellah. Kids might have decided to stop here on a sunny autumn day as well. No reason for anybody to think otherwise.

He found the path, went along it a short way to where it crossed a little creek, dry now and so narrow it was nothing more than a natural drainage ditch. He followed the creek to the north, on a course he'd taken three days ago. It led him to a shelflike overhang topped by two chunks of granite outcrop that leaned against each other like a pair of old drunks. Below the shelf, the land fell away sharply to the Shooter's driveway some sixty yards distant. Off to the right, where the incline wasn't so steep and the trees grew in a pack, was the split-bole Douglas fir where he'd stood waiting last night. The trees were fewer and more widely spaced between here and the cabin, so that from behind the two outcrops you had a good look at the Shooter's property, Little Cove Road, the concrete pier, and the lake shimmering under the late-afternoon sun.

The Caddy Eldorado was still slotted inside the carport. It was the only car in sight. Deighan knelt behind where the outcrops came together to form a notch, rubbed tension out of his neck and shoulders while he waited.

He didn't have to wait long. Less than ten minutes had passed when the car appeared on Little Cove Road, slowed, turned down the Shooter's driveway. It wasn't Mannlicher's fancy limo; it was a two-year-old Chrysler—Brandt's, maybe. Brandt was driving it: Deighan had a clear view of him through the side window as the Chrysler pulled up and stopped near the cabin's front door. He could also see that the lone passenger was Mannlicher.

Brandt got out, opened the passenger door for the fat man, and the two of them went to the cabin. It look D'Allesandro ten seconds to answer Brandt's knock. There was some talk, not much; then Mannlicher and Brandt went in, and the door shut behind them.

All right, Deighan thought. He'd stacked the deck as well as he could; pretty soon he'd know how the hand—and the game—played out.

Nothing happened for maybe five minutes. Then he thought he heard some muffled sounds down there, loud voices that went on for a while, something that might have been a bang, but the distance was too great for him to be sure that he wasn't imagining them. Another four or five minutes went by. And then the door opened and Brandt came out alone, looked around, called something back inside that Deighan didn't understand. If there was an answer, it wasn't audible. Brandt shut the door, hurried down to the lake, went out onto the pier. The ChrisCraft was still tied up there. Brandt climbed on board, disappeared for thirty seconds or so, reappeared carrying a square of something gray and heavy. Tarpaulin, Deighan saw when Brandt came back up the driveway. Big piece of it—big enough for a shroud.

The Shooter's hand had been folded. That left three of them still in the game.

When Brandt had gone back inside with the tarp,

39

Deighan stood and half ran along the creek and through the trees to where he'd left the Ford. Old Lake Road was deserted. He yanked open the passenger door, leaned in, caught up the mobile phone, and punched out the emergency number for the county sheriff's office. An efficient-sounding male voice answered.

"Something's going on on Little Cove Road," Deighan said, making himself sound excited. "That's in Pine Acres, you know? It's the cabin at the end, down on the lake. I heard shots—people shooting at each other down there. It sounds like a war."

"What's the address?"

"I don't know the address, it's the cabin right on the lake. People *shooting* at each other. You better get right out there."

"Your name, sir?"

"I don't want to get involved. Just hurry, will you?"

Deighan put the receiver down, shut the car door, ran back along the path and along the creek to the shelf. Mannlicher and Brandt were still inside the cabin. He went to one knee again behind the outcrops, drew the .38, held it on his thigh.

It was another two minutes before the door opened down there. Brandt came out, looked around as he had before, went back inside—and then he and Mannlicher both appeared, one at each end of a big, tarp-wrapped bundle. They started to carry it down the driveway toward the lake. Going to put it on the boat, Deighan thought, take it out now or later on, when it's dark. Lake Tahoe was sixteen hundred feet deep in the middle. The bundle wouldn't have been the first somebody'd dumped out there.

He let them get clear of the Chrysler, partway down the drive, before he poked the gun into the notch, sighted, and fired twice. The shots went where he'd intended them to, wide by ten feet and into the roadbed so they kicked up gravel. Mannlicher and Brandt froze for an instant, confused. Deighan fired a third round, putting the slug closer this time, and that one panicked them: they let go of the bundle and began scrambling.

There was no cover anywhere close by; they both ran for the Chrysler. Brandt had a gun in his hand when he reached it, and he dropped down behind the rear deck, trying to locate Deighan's position. Mannlicher kept on scrambling around to the passenger door, pulled it open, pushed himself across the seat inside.

Deighan blew out the Chrysler's near front tire. Sighted, and blew out the rear tire. Brandt threw an answering shot his way, but it wasn't even close. The Chrysler was tilting in Deighan's direction as the tires flattened. Mannlicher pushed himself out of the car, tried to make a run for the cabin door with his arms flailing, his fat jiggling. Deighan put a bullet into the wall beside the door. Mannlicher reversed himself, fell in his frantic haste, crawled back behind the Chrysler.

Reloading the .38, Deighan could hear the sound of

cars coming up fast on Little Cove Road. No sirens, but revolving lights made faint blood-red flashes through the trees.

From behind the Chrysler Brandt fired again, wildly. Beyond him, on the driveway, one corner of the tarp-wrapped bundle had come loose and was flapping in the wind off the lake.

A county sheriff's cruiser, its roof light slashing the air, made the turn off Little Cove onto the driveway. Another one was right behind it. In his panic, Brandt straightened up when he saw them and fired once, blindly, at the first in line.

Deighan was on his feet by then, hurrying away from the outcrops, holstering his weapon. Behind him he heard brakes squeal, another shot, voices yelling, two more shots. All the sounds faded as he neared the turnout and the Ford. By the time he pulled out onto the deserted road, there was nothing to hear but the sound of his engine, the screeching of a jay somewhere nearby.

Brandt had thrown in his hand by now; so had Mannlicher.

This pot belonged to him.

6.

Fran was in the backyard, weeding her garden, when he got home late the following afternoon. He called to her from the doorway, and she glanced around and then got up, unsmiling, and came over to him. She was wearing jeans and one of his old shirts and a pair of gardening gloves, and her hair was tied in a long ponytail. Used to be a light, silky brown, her hair; now it was mostly gray. His fault. She was only forty-six. A woman of forty-six shouldn't be so gray.

She said, "So you're back." She didn't sound glad to see him, didn't kiss him or touch him at all. But her eyes were gentle on his face.

"I'm back."

"You all right? You look tired."

"Long drive. I'm fine; it was a good trip."

She didn't say anything. She didn't want to hear about it, not any of it. She just didn't want to know.

"How about you?" he asked. "Everything been okay?"

"Sheila's pregnant again."

"Christ. What's the matter with her? Why don't she get herself fixed? Or get Hank fixed?"

"She likes kids."

"I like kids too, but four's too many at her age. She's only twenty-seven."

"She wants eight."

"She's crazy," Deighan said. "What's she want to bring all those kids into a world like this for?"

There was an awkward moment. It was always awkward at first when he came back. Then Fran said, "You hungry?"

"You know me. I can always eat." Fact was, he was

43

starved. He hadn't eaten much up in Nevada, never did when he was away. And he hadn't had anything today except an English muffin and some coffee for breakfast in Truckee.

"Come into the kitchen," Fran said. "I'll fix you something."

They went inside. He got a beer out of the refrigerator; she waited and then took out some covered dishes, some vegetables. He wanted to say something to her, talk a little, but he couldn't think of anything. His mind was blank at times like this. He carried his beer into the living room.

The goddamn trophy case was the first thing he saw. He hated that trophy case; but Fran wouldn't get rid of it, no matter what he said. For her it was like some kind of shrine to the dead past. All the mementoes of his years on the force—twenty-two years, from beat patrolman in North Beach all the way up to inspector on the narcotics squad. The certificate he'd won in marksmanship competition at the police academy, the two citations from the mayor for bravery, other crap like that. Bones, that's all they were to him. Pieces of a rotting skeleton. What was the sense in keeping them around, reminding both of them of what he'd been, what he'd lost.

His fault he'd lost it, sure. But it was their fault too, goddamn them. The laws, the lawyers, the judges, the *system*. No convictions on half of all the arrests he'd ever made—half! Turning the ones like Mannlicher and Brandt and D'Allesandro loose, putting them right back on the street, letting them make their deals and their hits, letting them screw up innocent lives. Sheila's kids, his grandkids—lives like that. How could they blame him for being bitter? How could they blame him for taking too many drinks now and then?

He sat down on the couch, drank some of his beer, lit a cigarette. Ah Christ, he thought, it's not them. You know it wasn't them. It was *you*, you dumb bastard. They warned you twice about drinking on duty. And you kept on doing it, you were hog-drunk the night you plowed the departmental sedan into that vanload of teenagers. What if one of *those* kids had died? You were lucky, by God. You got off easy.

Sure, he thought. Sure. But he'd been a good cop, damn it, a cop inside and out; it was all he knew how to be. What was he supposed to do after they threw him off the force? Live on his half pension? Get a job as a part-time security guard? Forty-four years old, no skills, no friends outside the department—what the hell was he supposed to do?

He'd invented Bob Prince, that was what he'd done. He'd gone into business for himself.

Fran didn't understand. "You'll get killed one of these days," she'd said in the beginning. "It's vigilante justice," she'd said. "You think you're Rambo, is that it?" she'd said. She just didn't understand. To him it was the same job he'd always done, the only one he was any good at, only now *he* made up some of the

45

rules. He was no Rambo, one man up against thousands, a mindless killing machine; he hated that kind of phony flag-waving crap. It wasn't real. What he was doing, that was real. It meant something. But a hero? No. Hell, no. He was a sniper, that was all, picking off a weak or vulnerable enemy here and there, now and then. Snipers weren't heroes, for Christ's sake. Snipers were snipers, just like cops were cops.

He finished his beer and his cigarette, got up, went into Fran's sewing room. The five thousand he'd held out of the poker game take was in his pocket—money he felt he was entitled to because his expenses ran high sometimes, and they had to eat, they had to live. He put the roll into her sewing cabinet, where he always put whatever money he made as Bob Prince. She'd spend it when she had to, parcel it out, but she'd never mention it to him or anyone else. She'd told Sheila once that he had a sales job, he got paid in cash a lot, that was why he was away from home for such long periods of time.

When he walked back into the kitchen she was at the sink, peeling potatoes. He went over and touched her shoulder, kissed the top of her head. She didn't look at him; stood there stiffly until he moved away from her. But she'd be all right in a day or two. She'd be fine until the next time Bob Prince made the right kind of connection.

He wished it didn't have to be this way. He wished he could roll back the clock three years, do things differently, take the gray out of her hair and the pain out of her eyes. But he couldn't. It was just too late.

You had to play the cards you were dealt, no matter how lousy they were. The only thing that made it tolerable was that sometimes, on certain hands, you could find ways to stack the damned deck.

The central pharmacological ingredient in this story is completely factual, as is the once-upon-a-time use to which it is put here. When I first came across the information in a book on old-time druggists and their wares, I knew it would be perfect for a piece of fiction, but I couldn't seem to come up with the right format. I carried the notion around in the back of my mind for years, until I was asked to contribute to an anthology of medical horror stories, Diagnosis: Terminal, *edited by F. Paul Wilson. Then the creative juices finally began to bubble. Of all the tales in these pages, the dark parable of the "Angel of Mercy" ranks at or very near the top of my personal favorites.*

Angel of Mercy

Her name was Mercy.

Born with a second name, yes, like everyone else, but it had been so long since she'd used it she could scarce remember what it was. Scarce remember so many things about her youth, long faded now—except for Father, of course. It seemed, sometimes, that she had never had a youth at all. That she'd spent her whole life on the road, first with Caleb and then with Elias, jouncing from place to place in the big black traveling wagon, always moving, drifting, never settling anywhere. Birth to death, with her small deft hands working tirelessly and her eyes asquint in smoky lamplight and her head aswirl with medicines, mixtures, measurements, what was best for this ailment, what was the proper dosage for that one. . . .

Miss Mercy. Father had been the first to call her that, in his little apothecary shop in . . . what *was* the name of the town where she'd been born? Lester? No, Dexter. Dexter, Pennsylvania. "A druggist is an angel of mercy," he said to her when she was ten or eleven. "Your name comes from my belief in that, child. Mercy. Miss Mercy. And wouldn't *you* like to be an angel of mercy one day, too?"

"Oh yes, Father, yes! Will you show me how?"

And he had shown her, with great patience, because he had no sons and because he bore no prejudice against his daughter or the daughter of any man. He had shown her carefully and well for five or six or seven years, until Mr. President Lincoln declared war against the Confederate States of America and Father went away to bring his mercy to sick and wounded Union soldiers on far-off battlefields. But there was no mercy for him. On one of those battlefields, a place called Antietam, he was himself mortally wounded by cannon fire.

As soon as she received word of his death, she knew what she must do. She had no siblings, and Mother had died years before; Father's legacy was all that was left. And it seemed as though the next thing she knew, she was sitting on the high seat of the big black traveling wagon, alone in the beginning, then with Caleb and then Elias to drive the team of horses, bringing *her*

mercy to those in need. Death to birth, birth to death—
it was her true calling. Father would have been proud.
He would have understood and he would have been so
proud.

Miss Mercy. If it had been necessary to paint a name
on the side of the wagon, that was the name she would
have chosen. Just that and nothing more. It was what
Caleb had called her, too, from their very first meeting
in . . . Saint Louis, hadn't it been? Young and strong
and restless—there driving the wagon one day, gone
the next and never seen again. And Miss Mercy was
the only name Elias wrote on his pad of white paper
when the need arose, the name he would have spoken
aloud if he hadn't been born deaf and dumb. She had
chanced upon him down South somewhere. Georgia,
perhaps—he was an emancipated slave from the state
of Georgia. Chanced upon him, befriended him, and
they had been together ever since. Twenty years?
Thirty? Dear Elias. She couldn't have traveled so long
and so far, or done so much, if it were not for him.

In all the long years, how many miles had they traveled together? Countless number. North and east in the
spring and summer, south and west in the fall and winter. Ohio, Illinois, Minnesota, Iowa, Montana, Kansas,
Nebraska, Missouri, Oklahoma, Texas . . . maybe all
the states and territories there were. Civilization and
wilderness frontier. Ranches, farms, settlements.
Towns that had no druggist, towns that had druggists
with short supplies or too little understanding of their
craft. Cities, now and then, to replenish medicines that

could not be gotten elsewhere. Saint Louis and ...
Chicago? Yes, Chicago. Oh, she could scarce remember them all.

And everywhere they went, the people came. The
needy people with their aches and pains, ills and ailments, troubles and sorrows. First to marvel at her skill
with mortar and pestle and her vast pharmacopoeial
knowledge; at the cabinets and tight-fitted shelves
Elias had built to hold the myriad glass bottles filled
with liquids in all the colors of the rainbow, and below
the shelves the rows upon rows of drawers containing
ground and powdered drugs, herbs and barks, pastilles
and pills. And then to buy what they needed: cough
syrups, liniments, worm cures, liver medicines, stomach bitters, blood purifiers. And so much more: two-
grain quinine tablets, Bateman's drops, castor oil,
Epsom salts and Rochelle salts and Seidlitz powders,
paregorics and rheumatism tonics, bottles of Lydia E.
Pinkham's Vegetable Compound and Ford's Laxative
Compound and Dr. Williams's Pink Pills for Pale People. And, too, in private, with their hands and eyes
nervous and their voices low, embarrassed, sometimes
ashamed: potency elixirs and aphrodisiacs, emmena-
gogues and contraceptives, Apiol Compound for suppressed and painful menstruation, fluid extract of
kava-kava or emulsion of copaiba for gonorrhea, blue
ointment for crab lice.

Mostly they came during the daylight hours, but
now and then someone would come rapping on the

wagon's door after nightfall. And once in a long while, in the deep dark lonesome night—

"Oh, Miss Mercy, I need help. Can you find it in your heart to help me?"

"What is your trouble, my dear?"

"I've been a fool, such a fool. A man . . . I was too friendly with him and now I'm caught."

"You're certain you're with child?"

"Oh yes. There's no mistake."

"He won't marry you?"

"He can't. He's already married. Oh, I'm such a fool. Please, will you help me?"

"There, now, you mustn't cry. I'll help you."

"You'll give me something? Truly?"

"Truly."

"Apiol Compound? I've heard that it's rich enough in mucilage to bring on—"

"No, not that. Something more certain."

"Oh, Miss Mercy, you're true to your name. You're an angel of mercy."

And again, as always, she and Elias would be back on roads good and bad, empty and well traveled. Another town, another state—here, there, no pattern to their travels, going wherever the roads took them. Never lingering anywhere for more than a day or two, except when storm or flood or accident (and once, an Indian attack) stranded them. And as always the people would come, first to marvel and then to buy: morphine, digitalis, belladonna in carefully measured doses, Dover's powder, petroleum jelly, spirits of camphor and spirits of ammonia, bone liniment and witch hazel, citrate of magnesia, blackberry balsam, oil of sassafras, throat lozenges and eye demulcents, pile remedies and asthma cures, compounds for ailments of kidney and bladder and digestive tract.

And then again, in one of their stopping places, in the deep dark lonesome night—

"Miss Mercy, you don't know what your kindness means to me."

"I do know, child. I do."

"Such a burden, such an awful burden—"

"Yes, but yours will soon be lifted."

"Just one bottle of this liquid will see to that?"

"Just one. Then you'll have no more to fear."

"It smells so sweet. What does it contain?"

"Dried sclerotia of ergot, bark of slippery elm, apiol, and gum arabic."

"Will it taste bad?"

"No, my dear. I've mixed it with syrup."

"And I'm to take the whole bottle at once?"

"Yes. But only at the time of month I tell you. And then you must immediately dispose of the bottle where no one can ever find it. Will you promise?"

"Yes, Miss Mercy. Oh yes."

"And you must tell no one I helped you. Not even your dearest friend. Will you promise?"

"I promise. I'll never tell a soul, not a living soul."

And again, as always, she and Elias would be away at the break of dawn, when dew lay soft on the grasses and mist coated the land. And sitting beside him on the high seat, remembering the poor girl who had come in the night, she would ask herself once more, as she had so many times, what Father would have said if he'd known of the mixture of ergot and slippery elm, apiol and gum arabic. Would he still think of her as an angel of mercy? Or would he hate her for betraying a sacred trust? And the answer would be as it always was: No, he could never hate her; she must have no real doubt of that. He would understand that her only aim was to bring peace to those poor foolish girls. Peace and succor in their time of need. He *would* understand.

And she would stop fretting then, reassured of Father's absent pride, and soon that day would end and a new one would be born. And there would be new roads, new settlements and towns, new needs to serve—so many needs to serve.

And one day she saw that it was fall again, the leaves turning crimson and gold—time to turn south and west. But first there was another town, a little town with a name like many others, in a state that might have been Kansas or perhaps Nebraska. And late that night, as Miss Mercy sat weary but strong at her mixing table, her hands busy with mortar and pestle while the lamplight flickered bright, a rapping came soft and urgent on the wagon's door.

Her name was Verity.

Names and faces meant little to Miss Mercy; there were too many to remember even for a minute. But this girl was different somehow. The name lingered, and so she knew would the face. Thin, not pretty, pale hair peeking out from under her bonnet—older than most of the ones who came alone in the night. Older, sadder, but no wiser.

Miss Mercy invited her in, invited her to sit. Verity perched primly on the stool, hands together in her lap, mouth tight-pinched at the corners. She showed no nervousness, no fear or embarrassment. Determined was the word that came to Miss Mercy's mind.

Without preamble Verity said, "I understand you're willing to help girls in trouble."

"What sort of trouble, my dear?"

"The sort that comes to foolish and unmarried girls."

"You're with child?"

Verity nodded. "I come from Riverbrook, Iowa. Do you recall the town, Miss Mercy?"

"Riverbrook? Iowa? There are so many places . . ."

"You were there four months ago. In June. The second week of June."

"The second week of June. Well. If you say I was, my dear, then of course I was."

"A girl named Grace came to see you then. Grace Potter. Do you remember her?"

"So many come to me," Miss Mercy said. "My memory isn't what it once was. . . ."

"So many girls in trouble, you mean?"

"Sometimes. In the night, as you've come."

"And as Grace came."

"If you say so. As Grace came."

"You gave her something to abort her fetus. I'd like you to give me the same . . . medicine."

"If I do, will you promise to take it only at the time of month I tell you?"

"Yes."

"Will you promise to dispose of the bottle immediately after ingestion, where no one can ever find it?"

"Yes."

"And will you promise to tell no one that I helped you? Not even your dearest friend?"

"Yes."

"Then you shall have what you need."

Miss Mercy picked up her lamp, carried it to one of Elias's cabinets. When she handed the small brown unlabeled bottle to Verity, the girl removed its cork and sniffed the neck. Then Verity poured a drop onto her finger, touched her tongue to it.

"It tastes odd," she said.

"No odder than sweetened castor oil. I've mixed the compound with cherry syrup."

"Compound. What sort of compound?"

"Dried sclerotia of ergot, bark of slippery elm, apiol—"

"My God! All those blended together?"

"Yes, my dear. Why do you look so shocked?"

"Ergot contracts the womb, tightens it even more. So do dried slippery elm and apiol. All mixed together

57

and taken in a large dose at the wrong time of month . . . cramps, paralysis, death in agony. This liquid is pure poison to a pregnant woman!"

"No, you mustn't think that—"

"I do think it," Verity said, "because it's true." She had risen to her feet and was pointing a tremulous finger at Miss Mercy. "I've studied medicine. I work in Riverbrook as a nurse and midwife."

"Nurse? Midwife? But then—"

"Then I'm not with child? No, Miss Mercy, I'm not. The truth is, I have been three months searching for you, ever since I discovered a bottle exactly like this one that Grace Potter failed to dispose of. I thought you guilty of no more than deadly quackery before tonight, but now I know different. You deliberately murdered my sister."

"Murdered?" Now it was Miss Mercy who was shocked. "Oh no, my dear. No. I brought her mercy."

"You brought her death!"

"Mercy. Your sister, all of them—only mercy."

"All of them? How many others besides Grace?"

"Does the number truly matter?"

"Does it truly—! How many, Miss Mercy?"

"I can't say. So many miles, so many places . . ."

"How many?"

"Thirty? Forty? Fifty? I can scarce remember them all. . . ."

"Dear sweet Lord! You poisoned as many as *fifty* pregnant girls?"

"Unmarried girls. Poor foolish girls," Miss Mercy

said gently. "There are worse things than death, oh much worse."

"What could be worse than suffering the tortures of hell before the soul is finally released?"

"Enduring the tortures of hell for years, decades, a lifetime. Isn't a few hours of pain and then peace, eternal peace, preferable to lasting torment?"

"How can you believe that bearing a child out of wedlock is so wicked—?"

"No," Miss Mercy said, "the lasting torment is in knowing, seeing the child they've brought into the world. Bastard child, child of sin. Don't you see? God punishes the unwed mother. The wages of sin is death, but God's vengeance on the living is far more terrible. I saved your sister from that. I brought her and all the others mercy from *that*."

Again she picked up the lamp. With a key from around her neck she unlocked the small satin-lined cabinet Elias had made, lifted out its contents. This she set on the table, the flickering oil lamp close beside it.

Verity looked, and cried out, and tore her gaze away.

Lamplight shone on the glass jar and on the thick formaldehyde that filled it; made a glowing chimera of the tiny twisted thing floating there, with its face that did not seem quite human, with its appendage that might have been an arm and the other that might have been a leg, with its single blind staring eye.

"Now do you understand?" Miss Mercy said. "This is my son, mine and Caleb's. God's vengeance—my poor little bastard son."

And she lifted the jar in both hands and held it tight to her bosom, cradled it and began to rock it to and fro, crooning to the fetus inside—a sweet, sad lullaby that sent Verity fleeing from the wagon, away into the deep dark lonesome night.

"Night Freight," which originally saw print in Mike Shayne Mystery Magazine *in early 1967, was my second published story. (The first, "You Don't Know What It's Like," a shameless Hemingway pastiche, appeared in* Shell Scott Mystery Magazine *for November of 1966.) I revised it slightly several years ago for its publication in an anthology, but it still has a number of youthful flaws. I debated rewriting it for its inclusion here, finally decided against it. In a curious way the rough edges add to rather than detract from its nightmarish effect.*

Night Freight

He caught the freight in Phalene, down in the citrus belt, four days after they gave Joanie the divorce.

He waited in the yards. The northbound came along a few minutes past midnight. He hid in the shadows of the loading platform, watching the cars, and half the train had gone by before he saw the open box, the first one after a string of flats.

He trotted up alongside, hanging on to the big gray-and-white suitcase. There were heavy iron rungs running up the side of the box. He caught on with his right hand and got his left foot through the opening, then laid the suitcase inside and swung through behind it.

It smelled of dust in there, and just a bit of citrus, and he did not like the smell. It caught in his nose and in the back of his throat, and he coughed.

It was very dark, but he could see that the box was empty. He picked up the suitcase and went over and sat down against the far wall.

It was cold too. The wind came whistling in through the open door like a siren as the freight picked up speed. He wrapped his arms around his legs and sat there like that, hugging himself.

He thought about Joanie.

He knew he should not think about her. He knew that. It made things only that much worse when he thought about her. But every time he closed his eyes he could see her face.

He could see her smile, and the way her eyes, those soft brown eyes, would crinkle at the corners when she laughed. He could see the deep, silken brown of her hair, and the way it would turn almost gold when she stood in the sun, and the way that one little strand of hair kept falling straight down across the bridge of her nose, the funny little way it would do that, and how they had both laughed at it in the beginning.

No, he thought. No, I mustn't think about that.

He hugged his legs.

What had happened? he thought. Where did it go wrong?

But he knew what it was. They should never have moved to California.

Yes, that was it. If they had not moved to California, none of it would have happened.

Joanie hadn't wanted to go. She didn't like California.

But he had had that job offer. It was a good one, but it meant moving to California and that was what started it all; he was sure of that.

Joanie had tried, he knew that. She had tried hard at first. But she had wanted to go home. He'd promised her he would take her home, he'd promised her that, just as soon as he made some money.

But she had wanted to go right away. There were plenty of good jobs at home, she said. Why did he want to stay in California?

He'd been a fool. He should have taken her home right away, like she'd wanted, and to hell with the job. Then none of it would have happened. Everything would be all right, now.

But he hadn't done that. It had started a lot of fights between them, her wanting to go home and him wanting to stay there in California, and pretty soon they were fighting over a lot of things, just small things, and he had hated those times. He hated to fight with Joanie. It made him sick inside; it got him all mixed up and made his head pound.

He remembered the last fight they had. He remembered it very well. He remembered how he had broken the little china figurine of the palomino stallion. He hadn't wanted to break it. But he had.

Joanie hadn't said much to him after that fight. He'd tried to make it up to her, what he'd done, and had gone out and bought her another figurine and told her he was sorry. But she had gotten very cold and distant then. That was when he knew she didn't love him any more.

And then he'd come home from work that one night, and Joanie was gone, and there was just a note on the dining room table, three short sentences that said she was leaving him.

He didn't know what to do. He'd tried everywhere he could think of that she might have gone, the few friends they had made, hotels, but she had simply vanished. He thought at first she might have gome home, and made a long-distance call, but she was not there, and no, they didn't know where she was.

A week later her lawyer had come to see him.

He brought papers with him, a copy of the divorce statement, and told him when he was to appear in court. He had tried to make the lawyer tell her whereabouts, so he could see her and talk to her, but the lawyer had refused and said that if he tried to see her there would be a court order issued to restrain him.

He quit his job then, because he didn't care about the money anymore. All he cared about was Joanie. He could remember very little of what happened between then and the time the divorce came up.

He hadn't wanted to go to court. But he knew he had to go, if only just to see her again.

And when Joanie had come in, his heart had caught in his throat. He had stood up and called out her name, but she would not look at him.

Then her lawyer had gotten up and said how he had caused Joanie extreme mental anguish, and threatened her and caused her to fear for her life. And how he would go off his head and rant and rave like a wild man, and how he should be remanded by the court into psychiatric custody.

He had wanted to shout that it was all a lie, that he had never said anything to cause Joanie to fear for her life, never done any of the things they said, because he loved her, and how could he hurt the one person he truly loved?

But he had sat there and not said anything and listened to the judge grant Joanie the divorce. Then, sitting there, it had come to him why Joanie had left him, and told all those lies to her lawyer, and why she wanted a divorce and didn't love him anymore.

Another man.

It had come to him all of a sudden as he sat there that this was the answer, and he knew it was true. He did not know who the man could be, but he knew there was a man, knew it with a sudden and certain clarity.

He had turned and run out of the courtroom, and gone home and wept as only a man can in his grief.

The next day he had gone looking for her, through the entire city, block by block. For three days he had searched.

Then he had found her, living alone, in a flat near the river, and he had gone up there and tried to talk to her, to tell her he still loved her, no matter what, and to ask her about the other man. But she would not let him in, told him to go away and would not let him in. He had pounded on the door, pounded. . . .

His head had begun to pound now, thinking about it. His mind whirled and jumbled with the thoughts as he sat there in the empty box.

He lay down on the floor and pulled the suitcase to his body, holding on to it very tightly, and after a time, a long time, he slept.

He awoke to a thin patch of sunlight, shining in through the open door of the box car. He stood up and stretched, and his mind was clear now. He went over to the door and put his head outside.

The sun was rising in the sky, warm and bright. He looked around, trying to place where he was. The land was flat, and he could see brown foothills off in the distance, but it was nice and green in the meadows through which the freight was passing. He could smell alfalfa, and apple blooms, and he knew they had gotten up into northern California.

As he stood there, he could feel the train begin to slow. They came around a long bend. Up ahead he could see freight yards. The freight had begun to lose speed rapidly, now.

He could hear the hiss of air brakes and couplings banging together, and the train slid into the yards. There were two men standing in the shade of a shed out there, half-hidden behind it, dressed in khaki trousers and denim shirts, open down the front, and one of them had on a green baseball cap.

They just stood there, watching the freight as it slowed down.

He turned from the door and went over and sat down by the suitcase again. He was very thirsty, but he did not want to get off to go for a drink. He did not want anyone to see him.

He sat there for fifteen minutes; then he heard the whistle from the engine and the couplings banging together again, and the freight pulled out.

But just as it did, there was a scraping over by the door, and he saw two men, the same two who had been out by the shed, come scuttling in through the box door.

The freight picked up speed. The two men sat there, looking out. Then one of them stood and looked around, and saw him sitting there on the floor at the opposite end of the box.

"Well," this one said. He was the one in the green baseball cap. "Looks like we're going to have some company, Lon."

"Sure enough," Lon said, looking around.

They came over to where he was.

"You been riding long?" the one in the baseball cap said.

"Since Phalene," he said. He wished they had not come aboard. He wished they would go and leave him alone.

"Down in the citrus?"

"Yes."

"Where you headed for?"

"What?"

"You're going someplace, ain't you?"

"Yes," he said. "To Ridgemont."

"Where?"

"Ridgemont," he said again.

"Where's that?"

"In Idaho."

"You going all that way on the rails?"

67

"Yes."

"Well, that's a long pull. You want to watch yourself up there. They don't cotton much to fellows riding the freights."

"All right," he said.

They sat down. The one called Lon said, "Say, now, you wouldn't happen to have a smoke on you, would you, friend? I just been dying for a smoke."

"Yes," he said.

"Much obliged."

They both took one. They sat there, smoking, watching him. He could tell that they were thinking he did not look like a man who rode the rails. He was not like them. The one in the baseball cap kept looking at his suitcase.

It was very hot in the box car, now. The two men gave off a kind of sour odor of dirt and sweat. This, mingled with the heat, made his stomach crawl.

He stood and went over to the door to get some air. He was conscious of their eyes on his back. It made him feel uneasy to have them watching him like that.

The freight moved on at considerable speed. They rode in silence most of the day, but the two men continued to watch him. They talked between themselves at brief intervals, but never to him, except when one of them would ask him for another cigarette.

As the afternoon turned into night, it began to cool down. Very suddenly there was a chill in the air. He could smell the salt then, sharp and fresh.

The one in the baseball cap buttoned his shirt up to his throat. "Getting cool," he said.

"We're running up the coast," the one called Lon said. "Be damned cold tonight."

They kept looking at him, then over at his suitcase. "You know, it sure would be nice if we had something to keep us warm on a cold night like it's going to be," the one in the baseball cap said.

"Sure would," Lon said.

"Say, friend," the one in the baseball cap said. "You wouldn't want to let us have anything in that bag there, would you?"

"What do you mean?" he said.

"Well, it's sure going to be chilly tonight. Be real fine if you was to have something in there to keep us warm."

"Like what?"

"Maybe a blanket. Or a coat. Like that."

"No."

"You sure, now?"

"There's nothing in there like that."

"You wouldn't want to be holding out on a couple of fellows, now would you?"

"No."

"Then suppose you just open up that case and let us have a look inside," Lon said.

He put his hand on the case.

"You got no right," he said.

"Well, I say we do," the one in the baseball cap said. "I say we got plenty of right."

"Sure we do," Lon said.

69

They stood up.

"Come on, friend," the one in the baseball cap said. "Open up that case."

He stood up too.

"No," he said. "Stay away. I'm warning you."

"He's warning us," the one in the baseball cap said. "You get that, Lon?"

"Sure," Lon said. "He's warning us."

They stood there, the two men staring at him. He clutched the suitcase tightly in his right hand. Then, as they stood there, the freight began to slow. They were coming into a siding.

Outside it had begun to get dark. There were long shadows inside the box car.

The men watched each other, warily, and then, suddenly, Lon made a grab for the suitcase, and the one in the baseball cap pushed him back up against the wall of the box, and Lon tore the suitcase from his fingers.

He backed up against the wall. He was breathing hard. They shouldn't have done that, he thought. I told them. They shouldn't have done that.

He took out the knife.

Lon stopped pawing at the catch on the suitcase. They were both staring at him.

"Hey!" Lon said. "Hey, now."

"All right," he said to them. "I told you."

"Take it easy," the one in the baseball cap said, staring at the knife.

"Put the suitcase down," he said to Lon.

"Sure," Lon said. "You just take it easy."

"It was just a joke, friend," the one in the baseball cap said. "You know. A couple of fellows having a little game."

"That's it," Lon said. "Just a joke."

"We wasn't going to take nothing," the one in the baseball cap said.

He held the knife straight out in front of him. The blade was flat and wide and very sharp.

"Put it down," he said again.

"Sure," Lon said. He leaned down, never taking his eyes off the knife, and let go of the suitcase. The catch had been loosened in the struggle, and from Lon's pawing, and when it hit the floor of the box, it came open.

He said, "You get off this train. Right now. You just get off this train." He moved the knife in a wide circle and took a step toward them.

The one in the baseball cap said, "Oh, my God!" He took a step backward, and his face was the color of chalk. The freight was at a standstill, now.

"Get off," he said again. His head had begun to hurt.

The one in the baseball cap backed to the door, watching the knife, and caught on to the jamb and then turned and stepped off. Lon ran to the door and jumped off after him.

He put the knife away. He stood there for a time, and his mind whirled, and for a moment, just a moment, he remembered what had happened last night with Joanie—how he had forced his way into her flat,

71

raging with anger, and told her he knew about the other man, and how she had denied it and said she was going to call the police, and how, then, he had hit her, and hit her again, and then he had seen the knife, the knife there on the table in the kitchen, the flat, sharp knife, and then it went black for him again and he could not remember anything.

The freight had begun to pull out of the siding. It was picking up speed. The whistle sounded in the night.

He turned and walked to where the suitcase lay, open on the floor of the box. He knelt down and began to cry.

He said, "It's all right now. We're going home. Going home to Ridgemont. Just like I promised you, Joanie. We're going home for good."

Joanie's head stared up at him from the open suitcase.

"Liar's Dice" was the basis for a 1995 USA-Cable TV movie called (over my screams of protest) Tails You Live, Heads You're Dead. *The film essentially begins where the story ends, supplying a ready answer to the question the narrator—and the reader—is left to contemplate. This is the problem with the movie, which has nowhere to go other than into the realm of the cat-and-mouse, serial-killer subgenre, with routine results. The story's enigmatic ending is far more terrifying, to my mind, than the film's resolution, or any that I might have tacked on myself. You may not agree, of course. Your call.*

Liar's Dice

"Excuse me. Do you play liar's dice?"

I looked over at the man two stools to my right. He was about my age, early forties: average height, average weight, brown hair, medium complexion—really a pretty nondescript sort except for a pleasant and disarming smile. Expensively dressed in an Armani suit and a silk jacquard tie. Drinking white wine. I had never seen him before. Or had I? There was something familiar about him, as if our paths *had* crossed somewhere or other, once or twice.

Not here in Tony's, though. Tony's is a suburban-mall bar that caters to the shopping trade from the big department and grocery stores surrounding it. I stopped in no more than a couple of times a month, usually when Connie asked me to pick up something at Safeway on my way home from San Francisco, occasionally when I had a Saturday errand to run. I knew the few regulars by sight, and it was never very crowded anyway. There were only four patrons at the moment: the nondescript gent and myself on stools, and a young couple in a booth at the rear.

"I do play, as a matter of fact," I said to the fellow. Fairly well too, though I wasn't about to admit that. Liar's dice and I were old acquaintances.

"Would you care to shake for a drink?"

"Well, my usual limit is one . . ."

"For a chit for your next visit, then."

"All right, why not? I feel lucky tonight."

"Do you? Good. I should warn you, I'm very good at the game."

"I'm not so bad myself."

"No, I mean I'm *very* good. I seldom lose."

It was the kind of remark that would have nettled me if it had been said with even a modicum of conceit. But he wasn't bragging; he was merely stating a fact, mentioning a special skill of which he felt justifiably proud. So instead of annoying me, his comment made me eager to test him.

We introduced ourselves; his name was Jones. Then I called to Tony for the dice cups. He brought them down, winked at me, said, "No gambling now," and went back to the other end of the bar. Strictly speaking, shaking dice for drinks and/or money is illegal in

California. But nobody pays much attention to nuisance laws like that, and most bar owners keep dice cups on hand for their customers. The game stimulates business. I know because I've been involved in some spirited liar's dice tournaments in my time.

Like all good games, liar's dice is fairly simple—at least in its rules. Each player has a cup containing five dice, which he shakes out but keeps covered so only he can see what is showing face up. Then each makes a declaration or "call" in turn: one of a kind, two of a kind, three of a kind, and so on. Each call has to be higher than the previous one, and is based on what the player *knows* is in his hand and what he *thinks* is in the other fellow's—the combined total of the ten dice. He can lie or tell the truth, whichever suits him; but the better liar he is, the better his chances of winning. When one player decides the other is either lying or has simply exceeded the laws of probability, he says, "Come up," and then both reveal their hands. If he's right, he wins.

In addition to being a clever liar, you also need a good grasp of mathematical odds and the ability to "read" your opponent's facial expressions, the inflection in his voice, his body language. The same skills an experienced poker player has to have, which is one reason the game is also called liar's poker.

Jones and I each rolled one die to determine who would go first; mine was the highest. Then we shook all five dice in our cups, banged them down on the bar. What I had showing was four treys and a deuce.

"Your call, Mr. Quint."

"One five," I said.

"One six."

"Two deuces."

"Two fives."

"Three treys."

"Three sixes."

I considered calling him up, since I had no sixes and he would need three showing to win. But I didn't know his methods and I couldn't read him at all. I decided to keep playing.

"Four treys."

"Five treys."

"Six treys."

Jones smiled and said, "Come up." And he had just one trey (and no sixes). I'd called six treys and there were only five in our combined hands; he was the winner.

"So much for feeling lucky," I said, and signaled Tony to bring another white wine for Mr. Jones. On impulse I decided a second Manhattan wouldn't hurt me and ordered that too.

Jones said, "Shall we play again?"

"Two drinks is definitely my limit."

"For dimes, then? Nickels or pennies, if you prefer."

"Oh, I don't know . . ."

"You're a good player, Mr. Quint, and I don't often find someone who can challenge me. Besides, I have a passion as well as an affinity for liar's dice. Won't you indulge me?"

I didn't see any harm in it. If he'd wanted to play for larger stakes, even a dollar a hand, I might have taken him for a hustler despite his Armani suit and silk tie. But how much could you win or lose playing for a nickel or a dime a hand? So I said, "Your call first this time," and picked up my dice cup.

We played for better than half an hour. And Jones wasn't just good; he was uncanny. Out of nearly twenty-five hands, I won two—*two*. You could chalk up some of the disparity to luck, but not enough to change the fact that his skill was remarkable. Certainly he was the best I'd ever locked horns with. I would have backed him in a tournament anywhere, anytime.

He was a good winner, too: no gloating or chiding. And a good listener, the sort who seems genuinely (if superficially) interested in other people. I'm not often gregarious, especially with strangers, but I found myself opening up to Jones—and this in spite of him beating the pants off me the whole time.

I told him about Connie, how we met and the second honeymoon trip we'd taken to Lake Louise three years ago and what we were planning for our twentieth wedding anniversary in August. I told him about Lisa, who was eighteen and a freshman studying film at UCLA. I told him about Kevin, sixteen now and captain of his high school baseball team, and the five-hit, two–home run game he'd had last week. I told him what it was like working as a design engineer for one of the largest engineering firms in the country, the nagging dissatisfaction and the desire to be my own boss

77

someday, when I had enough money saved so I could afford to take the risk. I told him about remodeling our home, the boat I was thinking of buying, the fact that I'd always wanted to try hang gliding but never had the courage.

Lord knows what else I might have told him if I hadn't noticed the polite but faintly bored expression on his face, as if I were imparting facts he already knew. It made me realize just how much I'd been nattering on, and embarrassed me a bit. I've never liked people who talk incessantly about themselves, as though they're the focal point of the entire universe. I can be a good listener myself; and for all I knew, Jones was a lot more interesting than bland Jeff Quint.

I said, "Well, that's more than enough about me. It's your turn, Jones. Tell me about yourself."

"If you like, Mr. Quint." Still very formal. I'd told him a couple of times to call me Jeff but he wouldn't do it. Now that I thought about it, he hadn't mentioned his own first name.

"What is it you do?"

He laid his dice cup to one side. I was relieved to see that; I'd had enough of losing but I hadn't wanted to be the one to quit. And it was getting late—dark outside already—and Connie would be wondering where I was. A few minutes of listening to the story of his life, I thought, just to be polite, and then—

"To begin with," Jones was saying, "I travel."

"Sales job?"

"No. I travel because I enjoy traveling. And because I can afford it. I have independent means."

"Lucky you. In more ways than one."

"Yes."

"Europe, the South Pacific—all the exotic places?"

"Actually, no. I prefer the U.S."

"Any particular part?"

"Wherever my fancy leads me."

"Hard to imagine anyone's fancy leading him to Bayport," I said. "You have friends or relatives here?"

"No, I have business in Bayport."

"Business? I thought you said you didn't need to work. . . ."

"Independent means, Mr. Quint. That doesn't preclude a purpose, a direction in one's life."

"You do have a profession, then?"

"You might say that. A profession and a hobby combined."

"Lucky you," I said again. "What is it?"

"I kill people," he said.

I thought I'd misheard him. "You . . . what?"

"I kill people."

"Good God. Is that supposed to be a joke?"

"Not at all. I'm quite serious."

"What do you mean, you *kill* people?"

"Just what I said."

"Are you trying to tell me you're . . . some kind of paid assassin?"

"Not at all. I've never killed anyone for money."

79

"Then why . . . ?"

"Can't you guess?"

"No, I can't guess. I don't want to guess."

"Call it personal satisfaction," he said.

"What people? Who?"

"No one in particular," Jones said. "My selection process is completely random. I'm very good at it too. I've been killing people for . . . let's see, nine and a half years now. Eighteen victims in thirteen states. And, oh yes, Puerto Rico—one in Puerto Rico. I don't mind saying that I've never even come close to being caught."

I stared at him. My mouth was open; I knew it but I couldn't seem to unlock my jaw. I felt as if reality had suddenly slipped away from me, as if Tony had dropped some sort of mind-altering drug into my second Manhattan and it was just now taking effect. Jones and I were still sitting companionably, on adjacent stools now, he smiling and speaking in the same low, friendly voice. At the other end of the bar Tony was slicing lemons and limes into wedges. Three of the booths were occupied now, with people laughing and enjoying themselves. Everything was just as it had been two minutes ago, except that instead of me telling Jones about being a dissatisfied design engineer, he was calmly telling me he was a serial murderer.

I got my mouth shut finally, just long enough to swallow into a dry throat. Then I said, "You're crazy, Jones. You must be insane."

"Hardly, Mr. Quint. I'm as sane as you are."

"I don't believe you killed eighteen people."

"Nineteen," he said. "Soon to be twenty."

"Twenty? You mean . . . someone in Bayport?"

"Right here in Bayport."

"You expect me to believe you intend to pick somebody at random and just . . . murder him in cold blood?"

"Oh no, there's more to it than that. Much more."

"More?" I said blankly.

"I choose a person at random, yes, but carefully. Very carefully. I study my target, follow him as he goes about his daily business, learn everything I can about him, down to the minutest detail. Then the cat and mouse begins. I don't murder him right away; that wouldn't give sufficient, ah, satisfaction. I wait . . . observe . . . plan. Perhaps, for added spice, I reveal myself to him. I might even be so bold as to tell him to his face that he's my next victim."

My scalp began to crawl.

"Days, weeks . . . then, when the victim least expects it, a gunshot, a push out of nowhere in front of an oncoming car, a hypodermic filled with digitalin and jabbed into the body on a crowded street, simulating heart failure. There are many ways to kill a man. Did you ever stop to consider just how many different ways there are?"

"You . . . you're not saying—"

"What, Mr. Quint? That I've chosen *you?*"

81

"Jones, for God's sake!"

"But I have," he said. "You are to be number twenty."

One of my hands jerked upward, struck his arm. Involuntary spasm; I'm not a violent man. He didn't even flinch. I pulled my hand back, saw that it was shaking, and clutched the fingers tight around the beveled edge of the bar.

Jones took a sip of wine. Then he smiled—and winked at me.

"Or then again," he said, "I might be lying."

". . . What?"

"Everything I've just told you might be a lie. I might not have killed nineteen people over the past nine and a half years; I might not have killed anyone, ever."

"I don't . . . I don't know what you—"

"Or I might have told you part of the truth . . . that's another possibility, isn't it? Part fact, part fiction. But in that case, which is which? And to what degree? Am I a deadly threat to you, or am I nothing more than a man in a bar playing a game?"

"Game? What kind of sick—"

"The same one we've been playing all along. Liar's dice."

"Liar's. . . ?"

"My own special version," he said, "developed and refined through years of practice. The perfect form of the game, if I do say so myself—exciting, unpredictable, filled with intrigue and mortal danger for myself as well as my opponent."

I shook my head. My mind was a seething muddle; I couldn't seem to fully grasp what he was saying.

"I don't know any more than you do at this moment how you'll play your part of the hand, Mr. Quint. That's where the excitement and the danger lies. Will you treat what I've said as you would a bluff? Can you afford to take that risk? Or will you act on the assumption that I've told the monstrous truth, or at least part of it?"

"Damn you . . ." Weak and ineffectual words, even in my own ears.

"And if you do believe me," he said, "what course of action will you take? Attack me before I can harm you, attempt to kill me . . . here and now in this public place, perhaps, in front of witnesses who will swear the attack was unprovoked? Try to follow me when I leave, attack me elsewhere? I might be armed, and an excellent shot with a handgun. Go to the police . . . with a wild-sounding and unsubstantiated story that they surely wouldn't believe? Hire a detective to track me down? Attempt to track me down yourself? Jones isn't my real name, of course, and I've taken precautions against anyone finding out my true identity. Arm yourself and remain on guard until, if and when, I make a move against you? How long could you live under such intense pressure without making a fatal mistake?"

He paused dramatically. "Or—and this is the most exciting prospect of all, the one I hope you choose—will you mount a clever counterattack, lies and deceptions of your own devising? Can you actually hope to beat me at my own game? Do you dare to try?"

He adjusted the knot in his tie with quick, deft movements, smiling at me in the back-bar mirror—not the same pleasant smile as before. This one had shark's teeth in it. "Whatever you do, I'll know about it soon afterward. I'll be waiting . . . watching . . . and I'll know. And then it will be my turn again."

He slid off his stool, stood poised behind me. I just sat there; it was as if I were paralyzed.

"Your call, Mr. Quint," he said. And he was gone into the night.

Most of my horror fiction, as the entries in this collection demonstrate, is of the character-driven, generally unbloody variety; I gladly leave the slice-and-dice type to those who enjoy reading it and are adept at perpetrating it. "Out Behind the Shed" is probably the subtlest and most ambiguous of all that I've written— a story to make you ponder as well as shudder, after the fashion of William Fryer Harvey's classic "August Heat."

Out Behind the Shed

There was a dead guy behind the parts shed.

I went out there to get a Ford oil pan for Barney and I saw him lying on his back in the weedy grass. He didn't have a face. There was blood and bone and pulp and black scorch marks where his face used to be. I couldn't even guess if he was anybody I knew.

I stood there shivering. It was cold . . . Jesus, it was cold for late March. The sky was all glary, like the sun coming off a sheet-metal roof. Only there wasn't any sun. Just a shiny silver overcast, so cold-hot bright it hurt your eyes to look at it. The wind was big and gusty, the kind that burns right through clothing and puts a rash like frostbite on your skin. No matter what I'd done all day I couldn't seem to get warm.

I'd known right off, as soon as I got out of bed, that it was going to be a bad day. The cold and the funny bright sky was one thing. Another was Madge. She'd started in on me about money again even before she made the coffee. How we were barely making ends meet and couldn't even afford to get the TV fixed, and why couldn't I find a better-paying job or let her go to work part-time or at least take a second job myself, nights, to bring in a little extra. The same old song and dance. The only old tune she hadn't played was the one about how much she ached for another kid before she got too old, as if two wasn't enough. Then I came in here to work and Barney was in a grumpy mood on account of a head cold and the fact that we hadn't had three new repair jobs in a week. Maybe he'd have to do some retrenching if things didn't pick up pretty soon, he said. That was the word he used, retrenching. Laying me off was what he meant. I'd been working for him five years, steady, never missed a day sick, never screwed up on a single job, and he was thinking about firing me. What would I do then? Thirty-six years old, wife and two kids, house mortgaged to the hilt, no skills except auto mechanic and nobody hiring mechanics right now. What the hell would I do?

Oh, it was a bad day, all right. I hadn't thought it could get much worse, but now I knew that it could.

Now there was this dead guy out here behind the shed.

I ran back inside the shop. Barney was still banging away under old Mrs. Cassell's Ford, with his legs sticking out over the end of the roller cart. I yelled at him to slide out. He did and I said, "Barney . . . Barney, there's a dead guy out by the parts shed."

He said, "You trying to be funny?"

"No," I said. "No kidding and no lie. He's out there in the grass behind the shed."

"Another of them derelicts come in on the freights, I suppose. You sure he's dead? Maybe he's just passed out."

"*Dead*, Barney. I know a dead guy when I see one."

He hauled up on his feet. He was a big Swede, five inches and fifty pounds bigger than me, and he had a way of looming over you that made you feel even smaller. He looked down into my face and then scowled and said in a different voice, "Froze to death?"

"No," I said. "He hasn't got a face anymore. His face is all blown away."

"Jesus. Somebody killed him, you mean?"

"Somebody must of. Who'd do a thing like that, Barney? Out behind our shed?"

He shook his head and cracked one of his big gnarly knuckles. The sound echoed like a gunshot in the cold garage. Then, without saying anything else, he swung around and fast-walked out through the rear door.

I didn't go with him. I went over and stood in front of the wall heater. But I still couldn't get warm. My shoulders kept hunching up and down inside my overalls and I couldn't feel my nose or ears or the tips of my fingers, as if they weren't there anymore. When I looked at my hands, they were all red and chapped, like Madge's hands after she's been washing clothes or dishes. They twitched a little, too; the tendons were like worms wiggling under a handkerchief.

Pretty soon Barney came back. He had a funny look on his moon face but it wasn't the same kind he'd had when he went out. He said, "What the hell, Joe? I got no time for games and neither do you."

"Games?"

"There's nobody behind the shed," he said.

I stared at him. Then I said, "In the grass, not ten feet past the far corner."

"I looked in the grass," Barney said. His nose was running from the cold. He wiped it off on the sleeve of his overalls. "I looked all over. There's no dead guy. There's nobody."

"But I saw him. I swear to God."

"Well, he's not there now."

"Somebody must of come and dragged him off, then."

"Who'd do that?"

"Same one who killed him."

"There's no blood or nothing," Barney said. He was back to being grumpy. His voice had that hard edge and his eyes had a squeezed look. "None of the grass is even flattened down. You been seeing things, Joe."

"I tell you, it was the real thing."

"And I tell *you*, it wasn't. Go out and take another look, see for yourself. Then get that oil pan out of the shed and your ass back to work. I promised old lady Cassell we'd have her car ready by five-thirty."

I went outside again. The wind had picked up a couple of notches, turned even colder; it was like fire against my bare skin. The hills east of town were all shimmery with haze, like in one of those desert mirages. There was a tree smell in the air but it wasn't the usual good pine-and-spruce kind. It was a eucalyptus smell, even though there weren't any eucalyptus trees within two miles of here. It made me think of cat piss.

I put my head down and walked slow over to the parts shed. And stopped just as I reached it to draw in a long breath. And then went on to where I could see past the far corner.

The dead guy was there in the grass. Lying right where I'd seen him before, laid out on his back with one leg drawn up and his face blown away.

The wind gusted just then, and when it did it made sounds like howls and moans. I wanted to cover my ears. Cover my eyes, too, to keep from seeing what was in the grass. But I didn't do either one. All I did was stand there shivering with my eyes wide open, trying to blink away some of the shimmery haze that seemed to have crawled in behind them. Nothing much was clear now, inside or out—nothing except the dead guy.

"Joe!"

Barney, somewhere behind me. I didn't turn around but I did back up a couple of steps. Then I backed up some more, until I was past the corner and couldn't see the dead guy anymore. Then I swung around and ran to where Barney was in the shop doorway.

"He's there, Barney, he's there, he's there—"

He gave me a hard crack on the shoulder. It didn't hurt; only the cold hurt where it touched my face and hands. He said, "Get hold of yourself, man."

"I *swear* it," I said, "right where I saw him before."

"All right, take it easy."

"I don't know how you missed seeing him," I said. I pulled at his arm. "I'll show you, come on."

I kept tugging on him and finally he came along, grumbling. I led the way out behind the shed. The dead guy was still there, all right. I blew out the breath I'd been holding and said, "Didn't I tell you? Didn't I?"

Barney stared down at the dead guy. Then he stared at me with his mouth open a little and his nose dripping snot. He said, "I don't see anything."

"You don't . . . what?"

"Grass, just grass."

"What's the matter with you? You're looking right at him!"

"The hell I am. The only two people out here are you and me."

I blinked and blinked and shook my head and blinked some more but the dead guy didn't go away.

He was *there*. I started to bend over and touch him, to make absolutely sure, but I couldn't do it. He'd be cold, as cold as the wind—colder. I couldn't stand to touch anything that cold and dead.

"I've had enough of this," Barney said.

I made myself look at him instead of the dead guy. The cat piss smell had gotten so strong I felt like gagging.

"He's there," I said, pleading. "Oh God, Barney, can't you see him?"

"There's nobody there. How many times do I have to say it? You better go on inside, Joe. Both of us better. It's freezing out here." He put a hand on my arm but I shook it off. That made him mad. "All right," he said, "if that's the way you want it. How about if I call Madge? Or maybe Doc Kiley?"

"No," I said.

"Then quit acting like a damn fool. Get a grip on yourself, get back to work. I mean it, Joe. Any more of this crap and you'll regret it."

"No," I said again. "You're lying to me. That's it, isn't it? You're lying to me."

"Why would I lie to you?"

"I don't know, but that's what you're doing. Why don't you want me to believe he's there?"

"Goddamn it, *there's nobody there!*"

Things just kept happening today—bad things one right after another, things that made no sense. The cold, Madge, Barney, the dead guy, the haze, the cat

91

piss smell, Barney again—and now a cold wind chilling me inside as well as out, as if icy gusts had blown right in through my flesh and were howling and prowling around my heart. I'd never felt like this before. I'd never been this cold or this scared or this frantic.

I pulled away from Barney and ran back into the shop and into the office and unlocked the closet and took out the duck gun he lets me keep in there because Madge don't like guns in the house. When I got back to the shed, Barney was just coming out with a Ford oil pan in his gnarly hands. His mouth pinched up tight and his eyes got squinty when he saw me.

He said, "What the hell's the idea bringing that shotgun out here?"

"Something's going on," I said, "something crazy. You see that dead guy there or don't you?"

"You're the one who's crazy, Joe. Give me that thing before somebody gets hurt."

He took a step toward me. I backed up and leveled the duck gun at him. "Tell me the truth," I said, desperate now, "tell me you see him lying there!"

He didn't tell me. Instead he gave a sudden lunge and got one hand on the barrel and tried to yank the gun away and oh Jesus him pulling on it like that made me jerk the trigger. The load of birdshot hit him full on and he screamed and the wind screamed with him and then he stopped but the wind didn't. Inside and out, the wind kept right on screaming.

I stood looking down at him lying in the grass with one leg drawn up and his face blown away. I could see him clear, even through that shimmery haze. Just him down there. Nobody else.

Just Barney.

My series character, the "Nameless Detective," has been around almost as long as I have; he was "born" more than thirty years ago in the pages of Alfred Hitchcock's Mystery Magazine, *and since then has appeared in some twenty-six novels and two collections. "Souls Burning" is the only "Nameless" story in these pages, included for two reasons: it's much more a psychological horror story than a detective story, and it's by far the darkest of any of his cases—as shadow-haunted, in fact, as any story in* Night Freight. *Maxim Jakubowski, who first bought it for* New Crimes 3, *stated in his acceptance note, "You must care deeply about what this story has to say." Perceptive fellow, Maxim.*

Souls Burning

Hotel Majestic, Sixth Street, downtown San Francisco. A hell of an address—a hell of a place for an ex-con not long out of Folsom to set up housekeeping. Sixth Street, south of Market—South of the Slot, it used to be called—is the heart of the city's Skid Road and has been for more than half a century.

Eddie Quinlan. A name and a voice out of the past, neither of which I'd recognized when he called that morning. Close to seven years since I had seen or spoken to him, six years since I'd even thought of him. Eddie Quinlan. Edgewalker, shadow-man with no real

95

substance or purpose, drifting along the narrow cat-walk that separates conventional society from the underworld. Information-seller, gofer, small-time bag-man, doer of any insignificant job, legitimate or other-wise, that would help keep him in food and shelter, liquor and cigarettes. The kind of man you looked at but never really saw: a modern-day Yehudi, the little man who wasn't there. Eddie Quinlan. Nobody, loser—fall guy. Drug bust in the Tenderloin one night six and a half years ago; one dealer setting up another, and Eddie Quinlan, small-time bagman, caught in the middle; hard-assed judge, five years in Folsom, good-bye Eddie Quinlan. And the drug dealers? They walked, of course. Both of them.

And now Eddie was out, had been out for six months. And after six months of freedom, he'd called me. Would I come to his room at the Hotel Majestic tonight around eight? He'd tell me why when he saw me. It was real important—would I come? All right, Eddie. But I couldn't figure it. I had bought informa-tion from him in the old days, bits and pieces for five or ten dollars; maybe he had something to sell now. Only I wasn't looking for anything and I hadn't put the word out, so why pick me to call?

If you're smart, you don't park your car on the street at night South of the Slot. I put mine in the Fifth and Mission Garage at seven forty-five and walked over to Sixth. It had rained most of the day and the streets were still wet, but now the sky was cold and clear. The kind of night that is as hard as black glass, so that light seems to bounce off the dark instead of shining through it; lights and their colors so bright and sharp-reflecting off the night and the wet surfaces that the glare is like splinters against your eyes.

Friday night, and Sixth Street was teeming. Side-walks jammed—old men, young men, bag ladies, painted ladies, blacks, whites, Asians, addicts, push-ers, muttering mental cases, drunks leaning against walls in tight little clusters while they shared paper-bagged bottles of sweet wine and cans of malt liquor; men and women in filthy rags, in smart new outfits topped off with sunglasses, carrying ghetto blasters and red-and-white canes, some of the canes in the hands of individuals who could see as well as I could, carrying a hidden array of guns and knives and other lethal instruments. Cheap hotels, greasy spoons, seedy taverns, and liquor stores complete with barred windows and cynical proprietors that stayed open well past midnight. Laughter, shouts, curses, threats; bick-ering and dickering. The stenches of urine and vomit and unwashed bodies and rotgut liquor, and over those like an umbrella, the subtle effluvium of despair. Predators and prey, half-hidden in shadow, half-revealed in the bright, sharp dazzle of fluorescent lights and bloody neon.

It was a mean street, Sixth, one of the meanest, and I walked it warily. I may be fifty-eight, but I'm a big man and I walk hard too; and I look like what I am.

97

Two winos tried to panhandle me and a fat hooker in an orange wig tried to sell me a piece of her tired body, but no one gave me any trouble.

The Majestic was five stories of old wood and plaster and dirty brick, just off Howard Street. In front of its narrow entrance, a crack dealer and one of his customers were haggling over the price of a baggie of rock cocaine; neither of them paid any attention to me as I moved past them. Drug deals go down in the open here, day and night. It's not that the cops don't care, or that they don't patrol Sixth regularly; it's just that the dealers outnumber them ten to one. On Skid Road any crime less severe than aggravated assault is strictly low priority.

Small, barren lobby: no furniture of any kind. The smell of ammonia hung in the air like swamp gas. Behind the cubbyhole desk was an old man with dead eyes that would never see anything they didn't want to see. I said, "Eddie Quinlan," and he said, "Two-oh-two" without moving his lips. There was an elevator but it had an out of order sign on it; dust speckled the sign. I went up the adjacent stairs.

The disinfectant smell permeated the second floor hallway as well. Room 202 was just off the stairs, fronting on Sixth; one of the metal 2s on the door had lost a screw and was hanging upside down. I used my knuckles just below it. Scraping noise inside, and a voice said, "Yeah?" I identified myself. A lock clicked, a chain rattled, the door wobbled open, and for the first time in nearly seven years I was looking at Eddie Quinlan.

He hadn't changed much. Little guy, about five-eight, and past forty now. Thin, nondescript features, pale eyes, hair the color of sand. The hair was thinner and the lines in his face were longer and deeper, almost like incisions where they bracketed his nose. Otherwise he was the same Eddie Quinlan.

"Hey," he said, "thanks for coming. I mean it, thanks."

"Sure, Eddie."

"Come on in."

The room made me think of a box—the inside of a huge rotting packing crate. Four bare walls with the scaly remnants of paper on them like psoriatic skin, bare uncarpeted floor, unshaded bulb hanging from the center of a bare ceiling. The bulb was dark; what light there was came from a low-wattage reading lamp and a wash of red-and-green neon from the hotel's sign that spilled in through a single window. Old iron-framed bed, unpainted nightstand, scarred dresser, straight-backed chair next to the bed and in front of the window, alcove with a sink and toilet and no door, closet that wouldn't be much larger than a coffin.

"Not much, is it," Eddie said.

I didn't say anything.

He shut the hall door, locked it. "Only place to sit is that chair there. Unless you want to sit on the bed? Sheets are clean. I try to keep things clean as I can."

"Chair's fine."

I went across to it; Eddie put himself on the bed. A room with a view, he'd said on the phone. Some view. Sitting here you could look down past Howard and up across Mission—almost two full blocks of the worst street in the city. It was so close you could hear the beat of its pulse, the ugly sounds of its living and its dying.

"So why did you ask me here, Eddie? If it's information for sale, I'm not buying right now."

"No, no, nothing like that. I ain't in the business anymore."

"Is that right?"

"Prison taught me a lesson. I got rehabilitated." There was no sarcasm or irony in the words; he said them matter-of-factly.

"I'm glad to hear it."

"I been a good citizen ever since I got out. No lie. I haven't had a drink, ain't even been in a bar."

"What are you doing for money?"

"I got a job," he said. "Shipping department at a wholesale sporting goods outfit on Brannan. It don't pay much, but it's honest work."

I nodded. "What is it you want, Eddie?"

"Somebody I can talk to, somebody who'll understand—that's all I want. You always treated me decent. Most of 'em, no matter who they were, they treated me like I wasn't even human. Like I was a turd or something."

"Understand what?"

"About what's happening down there."

"Where? Sixth Street?"

"Look at it," he said. He reached over and tapped the window; stared through it. "Look at the people . . . there, you see that guy in the wheelchair and the one pushing him? Across the street there?"

I leaned closer to the glass. The man in the wheelchair wore a military camouflage jacket, had a heavy wool blanket across his lap; the black man manipulating him along the crowded sidewalk was thick-bodied, with a shiny bald head. "I see them."

"White guy's name is Baxter," Eddie said. "Grenade blew up under him in 'Nam and now he's a paraplegic. Lives right here in the Majestic, on this floor down at the end. Deals crack and smack out of his room. Elroy, the black dude, is his bodyguard and roommate. Mean, both of 'em. Couple of months ago, Elroy killed a guy over on Minna that tried to stiff them. Busted his head with a brick. You believe it?"

"I believe it."

"And they ain't the worst on the street. Not the worst."

"I believe that too."

"Before I went to prison I lived and worked with people like that and I never saw what they were. I mean I just never saw it. Now I do, I see it clear— every day walking back and forth to work, every night from up here. It makes you sick after a while, the things you see when you see 'em clear."

"Why don't you move?"

"Where to? I can't afford no place better than this."

"No better room, maybe, but why not another neighborhood? You don't have to live on Sixth Street."

"Wouldn't be much better, any other neighborhood I could buy into. They're all over the city now, the ones like Baxter and Elroy. Used to be it was just Skid Road and the Tenderloin and the ghettos. Now they're everywhere, more and more every day. You know?"

"I know."

"Why? It don't have to be this way, does it?"

Hard times, bad times: alienation, poverty, corruption, too much government, not enough government, lack of social services, lack of caring, drugs like a cancer destroying society. Simplistic explanations that were no explanations at all and as dehumanizing as the ills they described. I was tired of hearing them and I didn't want to repeat them, to Eddie Quinlan or anybody else. So I said nothing.

He shook his head. "Souls burning everywhere you go," he said, and it was as if the words hurt his mouth coming out.

Souls burning. "You find religion at Folsom, Eddie?"

"Religion? I don't know, maybe a little. Chaplain we had there, I talked to him sometimes. He used to say that about the hardtimers, that their souls were burning and there wasn't nothing he could do to put out the fire. They were doomed, he said, and they'd doom others to burn with 'em."

I had nothing to say to that either. In the small

102

silence a voice from outside said distinctly, "Dirty bastard, what you doin' with my pipe?" It was cold in there, with the hard bright night pressing against the window. Next to the door was a rusty steam radiator but it was cold too; the heat would not be on more than a few hours a day, even in the dead of winter, in the Hotel Majestic.

"That's the way it is in the city," Eddie said. "Souls burning. All day long, all night long, souls on fire."

"Don't let it get to you."

"Don't it get to *you*?"

". . . Yes. Sometimes."

He bobbed his head up and down. "You want to do something, you know? You want to try to fix it somehow, put out the fires. There has to be a way."

"I can't tell you what it is," I said.

He said, "If we all just did *something*. It ain't too late. You don't think it's too late?"

"No."

"Me neither. There's still hope."

"Hope, faith, blind optimism—sure."

"You got to believe," he said, nodding. "That's all, you just got to believe."

Angry voices rose suddenly from outside; a woman screamed, thin and brittle. Eddie came off the bed, hauled up the window sash. Chill damp air and street noises came pouring in: shouts, cries, horns honking, cars whispering on the wet pavement, a Muni bus clattering along Mission; more shrieks. He leaned out, peering downward.

103

"Look," he said, "look."

I stretched forward and looked. On the sidewalk below, a hooker in a leopard-skin coat was running wildly toward Howard; she was the one doing the yelling. Chasing behind her, tight black skirt hiked up over the tops of net stockings and hairy thighs, was a hideously rouged transvestite waving a pocket knife. A group of winos began laughing and chanting "Rape! Rape!" as the hooker and the transvestite ran zigzagging out of sight on Howard.

Eddie pulled his head back in. The flickery neon wash made his face seem surreal, like a hallucinogenic vision. "That's the way it is," he said sadly. "Night after night, day after day."

With the window open, the cold was intense; it penetrated my clothing and crawled on my skin. I'd had enough of it, and of this room and Eddie Quinlan and Sixth Street.

"Eddie, just what is it you want from me?"

"I already told you. Talk to somebody who understands how it is down there."

"Is that the only reason you asked me here?"

"Ain't it enough?"

"For you, maybe." I got to my feet. "I'll be going now."

He didn't argue. "Sure, you go ahead."

"Nothing else you want to say?"

"Nothing else." He walked to the door with me, unlocked it, and then put out his hand. "Thanks for coming. I appreciate it, I really do."

"Yeah. Good luck, Eddie."

"You too," he said. "Keep the faith."

I went out into the hall, and the door shut gently and the lock clicked behind me.

Downstairs, out of the Majestic, along the mean street and back to the garage where I'd left my car. And all the way I kept thinking: There's something else, something more he wanted from me . . . and I gave it to him by going there and listening to him. But what? What did he really want?

I found out later that night. It was all over the TV—special bulletins and then the eleven o'clock news.

Twenty minutes after I left him, Eddie Quinlan stood at the window of his room-with-a-view, and in less than a minute, using a high-powered semiautomatic rifle he'd taken from the sporting goods outfit where he worked, he shot down fourteen people on the street below. Nine dead, five wounded, one of the wounded in critical condition and not expected to live. Six of the victims were known drug dealers; all of the others also had arrest records, for crimes ranging from prostitution to burglary. Two of the dead were Baxter, the paraplegic Vietnam vet, and his bodyguard, Elroy.

By the time the cops showed up, Sixth Street was empty except for the dead and the dying. No more targets. And up in his room, Eddie Quinlan had sat on the bed and put the rifle's muzzle in his mouth and used his big toe to pull the trigger.

My first reaction was to blame myself. But how

could I have known, or even guessed? Eddie Quinlan. Nobody, loser, shadow-man without substance or purpose. How could anyone have figured him for a thing like that?

Somebody I can talk to, somebody who'll understand—that's all I want.

No. What he'd wanted was somebody to help him justify to himself what he was about to do. Somebody to record his verbal suicide note. Somebody he could trust to pass it on afterward, tell it right and true to the world.

You want to do something, you know? You want to try to fix it somehow, put out the fires. There has to be a way.

Nine dead, five wounded, one of the wounded in critical condition and not expected to live. Not that way.

Souls burning. All day long, all night long, souls on fire.

The soul that had burned tonight was Eddie Quinlan's.

There is a tale behind this tale. It was nominated for an Edgar for best short story of 1978 by the Mystery Writers of America, and didn't win for one major reason: I didn't vote for it. It so happened that in 1979 I was chairman of the five-person MWA committee whose task it was to select five nominees and a winner from among the previous year's short story crop. "Strangers in the Fog" was nominated by one of the other committee members, received two first-place votes, and would have won on points if I'd put it at the top of my own list. Instead, suffering from a crisis of conscience, I cast my ballot for the story with the other two first-place votes, even though I wasn't convinced—still am not convinced after a recent rereading—that it was any better than mine. I've never won an Edgar, despite five other nominations in various categories, and chances are I never will. So . . . did I do the right thing, the wise thing? What would you have done?

Strangers in the Fog

Hannigan had just finished digging the grave, down in the tule marsh where the little saltwater creek flowed toward the Pacific, when the dark shape of a man came out of the fog.

Startled, Hannigan brought the shovel up and cocked it weaponlike at his shoulder. The other man had materialized less than twenty yards away, from the direction of the beach, and had stopped the moment he saw Hannigan. The diffused light from Hannigan's lantern did not quite reach the man; he was a black silhouette against the swirling billows of mist. Beyond him the breakers lashed at the shore in a steady pulse.

Hannigan said, "Who the hell are you?"

The man stood staring down at the roll of canvas near Hannigan's feet, at the hole scooped out of the sandy earth. He seemed to poise himself on the balls of his feet, body turned slightly, as though he might bolt at any second. "I'll ask you the same question," he said, and his voice was tense, low-pitched.

"I happen to live here." Hannigan made a gesture to his left with the shovel, where a suggestion of shimmery light shone high up through the fog. "This is a private beach."

"Private graveyard, too?"

"My dog died earlier this evening. I didn't want to leave him lying around the house."

"Must have been a pretty big dog."

"He was a Great Dane," Hannigan said. He wiped moisture from his face with his free hand. "You want something, or do you just like to take strolls in the fog?"

The man came forward a few steps, warily. Hannigan could see him more clearly then in the pale lantern glow: big, heavy-shouldered, damp hair flattened across his forehead, wearing a plaid lumberman's jacket, brown slacks, and loafers.

"You got a telephone I can use?"

"That would depend on why you need to use it."

"I could give you a story about my car breaking down," the big man said, "but then you'd just wonder what I'm doing down here instead of up on the Coast Highway."

"I'm wondering that anyway."

"It's safe down here, the way I figured it."

"I don't follow," Hannigan said.

"Don't you listen to your radio or TV?"

"Not if I can avoid it."

"So you don't know about the lunatic who escaped from the state asylum at Tescadero."

The back of Hannigan's neck prickled. "No," he said.

"Happened late this afternoon," the big man said. "He killed an attendant at the hospital—stabbed him with a kitchen knife. He was in there for the same kind of thing. Killed three people with a kitchen knife."

Hannigan did not say anything.

The big man said, "They think he may have headed north, because he came from a town up near the Oregon border. But they're not sure. He may have come south instead—and Tescadero is only twelve miles from here."

Hannigan gripped the handle of the shovel more tightly. "You still haven't said what *you're* doing down here in the fog."

"I came up from San Francisco with a girl for the weekend," the big man said. "Her husband was supposed to be in Los Angeles, on business, only I guess he decided to come home early. When he found her gone he must have figured she'd come up to this summer place they've got and so he drove up without calling first. We had just enough warning for her to throw me out."

"You let this woman throw you out?"

"That's right. Her husband is worth a million or so, and he's generous. You understand?"

"Maybe," Hannigan said. "What's the woman's name?"

"That's my business."

"Then how do I know you're telling me the truth?"

"Why wouldn't I be?"

"You might have reasons for lying."

"Like if I was the escaped lunatic, maybe?"

"Like that."

"If I was, would I have told you about him?"

Again Hannigan was silent.

"For all I know," the big man said, "*you* could be the lunatic. Hell, you're out here digging a grave in the middle of the night—"

"I told you, my dog died. Besides, would a lunatic dig a grave for somebody he killed? Did he dig one for that attendant you said he stabbed?"

"Okay, neither one of us is the lunatic." The big man paused and ran his hands along the side of his coat. "Look, I've had enough of this damned fog; it's starting to get to me. Can I use your phone or not?"

"Just who is it you want to call?"

"Friend of mine in San Francisco who owes me a favor. He'll drive up and get me. That is, if you wouldn't mind my hanging around your place until he shows up."

Hannigan thought things over and made up his mind. "All right. You stand over there while I finish putting Nick away. Then we'll go up."

The big man nodded and stood without moving. Hannigan knelt, still grasping the shovel, and rolled the canvas-wrapped body carefully into the grave. Then he straightened, began to scoop in sandy earth from the pile to one side. He did all of that without taking his eyes off the other man.

When he was finished he picked up the lantern, then gestured with the shovel, and the big man came around the grave. They went up along the edge of the creek, Hannigan four or five steps to the left. The big man kept his hands up and in close to his chest, and he walked with the tense springy stride of an animal prepared to attack or flee at any sudden movement. His gaze hung on Hannigan's face; Hannigan made it reciprocal.

"You have a name?" Hannigan asked him.

"Doesn't everybody?"

"Very funny. I'm asking your name."

"Art Vickery, if it matters."

"It doesn't, except that I like to know who I'm letting inside my house."

"I like to know whose house I'm going into," Vickery said.

111

Hannigan told him. After that neither of them had anything more to say.

The creek wound away to the right after fifty yards, into a tangle of scrub brush, sage, and tule grass; to the left and straight ahead were low rolling sand dunes, and behind them the earth became hard-packed and rose sharply into the bluff on which the house had been built. Hannigan took Vickery onto the worn path between two of the dunes. Fog massed around them in wet gray swirls, shredding as they passed through it, reknitting again at their backs. Even with the lantern, visibility was less than thirty yards in any direction, although as they neared the bluff the house lights threw a progressively brighter illumination against the screen of mist.

They were halfway up the winding path before the house itself loomed into view—a huge redwood-and-glass structure with a balcony facing the sea. The path ended at a terraced patio, and there were wooden steps at the far end that led up alongside the house.

When they reached the steps Hannigan gestured for Vickery to go up first. The big man did not argue; but he ascended sideways, looking back down at Hannigan, neither of his hands touching the railing. Hannigan followed by four of the wood runners.

At the top, in front of the house, was a parking area and a small garden. The access road that came in from the Coast Highway and the highway itself were invisible in the misty darkness. The light over the door burned dully, and as Vickery moved toward it Hannigan shut off the lantern and put it and the shovel down against the wall. Then he started after the big man.

He was about to tell Vickery that the door was unlocked and to go on in when another man came out of the fog.

Hannigan saw him immediately, over on the access road, and stopped with the back of his neck prickling again. This newcomer was about the same size as Vickery, and Hannigan himself; thick through the body, dressed in a rumpled suit but without a tie. He had wildly unkempt hair and an air of either agitation or harried intent. He hesitated when he saw Hannigan and Vickery, then he came toward them holding his right hand against his hip at a spot covered by his suit jacket.

Vickery had seen him by this time and he was up on the balls of his feet again, nervously watchful. The third man halted opposite the door and looked back and forth between Hannigan and Vickery. He said, "One of you the owner of this house?"

"I am," Hannigan said. He gave his name. "Who are you?"

"Lieutenant McLain, Highway Patrol. You been here all evening, Mr. Hannigan?"

"Yes."

"No trouble of any kind?"

"No. Why?"

"We're looking for a man who escaped from the

hospital at Tescadero this afternoon," McLain said. "Maybe you've heard about that?"

Hannigan nodded.

"Well, I don't want to alarm you, but we've had word that he may be in this vicinity."

Hannigan wet his lips and glanced at Vickery.

"If you're with the Highway Patrol," Vickery said to McLain, "how come you're not in uniform?"

"I'm in Investigation. Plainclothes."

"Why would you be on foot? And alone? I thought the police always traveled in pairs."

McLain frowned and studied Vickery for a long moment, penetratingly. His eyes were wide and dark and did not blink much. At length he said, "I'm alone because we've had to spread ourselves thin in order to cover this whole area, and I'm on foot because my damned car came up with a broken fanbelt. I radioed for assistance, and then I came down here because I didn't see any sense in sitting around waiting and doing nothing."

Hannigan remembered Vickery's words on the beach: *I could give you a story about my car breaking down*. He wiped again at the dampness on his face.

Vickery said, "You mind if we see some identification?"

McLain took his hand away from his hip and produced a leather folder from his inside jacket pocket. He held it out so Hannigan and Vickery could read it. "That satisfy you?"

The folder corroborated what McLain had told them

about himself; but it did not contain a picture of him. Vickery said nothing.

Hannigan asked, "Have you got a·photo of this lunatic?"

"None that will do us any good. He destroyed his file before he escaped from the asylum, and he's been in there sixteen years. The only pictures we could dig up are so old, and he's apparently changed so much, the people at Tescadero tell us there's almost no likeness anymore."

"What about a description?"

"Big, dark-haired, regular features, no deformities or identifying marks. That could fit any one of a hundred thousand men or more in Northern California."

"It could fit any of the three of us," Vickery said.

McLain studied him again. "That's right, it could."

"Is there anything else about him?" Hannigan asked. "I mean, could he pretend to be sane and get away with it?"

"The people at the hospital say yes."

"That makes it even worse, doesn't it?"

"You bet it does," McLain said. He rubbed his hands together briskly. "Look, why don't we talk inside? It's pretty cold out here."

Hannigan hesitated. He wondered if McLain had some other reason for wanting to go inside, and when he looked at Vickery it seemed to him the other man was wondering the same thing. But he could see no way to refuse without making trouble.

He said, "I guess so. The door's open."

For a moment all three of them stood motionless, McLain still watching Vickery intently. Vickery had begun to fidget under the scrutiny. Finally, since he was closest to the door, he jerked his head away, opened it, and went in sideways, the same way he had climbed the steps from the patio. McLain kept on waiting, which left Hannigan no choice except to follow Vickery. When they were both inside, McLain entered and shut the door.

The three of them went down the short hallway into the big beam-ceilinged family room. McLain glanced around at the fieldstone fireplace, the good reproductions on the walls, the tasteful modern furnishings. "Nice place," he said. "You live here alone, Mr. Hannigan?"

"No, with my wife."

"Is she here now?"

"She's in Vegas. She likes to gamble and I don't."

"I see."

"Can I get you something? A drink?"

"Thanks, no. Nothing while I'm on duty."

"I wouldn't mind having one," Vickery said. He was still fidgeting because McLain was still watching him and had been the entire time he was talking to Hannigan.

Near the picture window that took up the entire wall facing the ocean was a leather-topped standing bar; Hannigan crossed to it. The drapes were open and wisps of the gray fog outside pressed against the glass like skeletal fingers. He put his back to the window and lifted a bottle of bourbon from one of the shelves inside the bar.

"I didn't get your name," McLain said to Vickery.

"Art Vickery. Look, why do you keep staring at me?"

McLain ignored that. "You a friend of Mr. Hannigan's?"

"No," Hannigan said from the bar. "I just met him tonight, a few minutes ago. He wanted to use my phone."

McLain's eyes glittered. "Is that right?" he said. "Then you don't live around here, Mr. Vickery?"

"No, I don't live around here."

"Your car happened to break down too, is that it?"

"Not exactly."

"What then—exactly?"

"I was with a woman, a married woman, and her husband showed up unexpectedly." There was sweat on Vickery's face now. "You know how that is."

"No," McLain said, "I don't. Who is this woman?"

"Listen, if you're with the Highway Patrol as you say, I don't want to give you a name."

"What do you mean, *if* I'm with the Highway Patrol as I say? I told you I was, didn't I? I showed you my identification, didn't I?"

"Just because you're carrying it doesn't make it yours."

McLain's lips thinned and his eyes did not blink at all now. "You trying to get at something, mister? If so, maybe you'd better just spit it out."

117

"I'm not trying to get at anything," Vickery said. "There's an unidentified lunatic running around loose in this damned fog."

"So you're not even trustful of a law officer."

"I'm just being careful."

"That's a good way to be," McLain said. "I'm that way myself. Where do you live, Vickery?"

"In San Francisco."

"How were you planning to get home tonight?"

"I'm going to call a friend to come pick me up."

"Another lady friend?"

"No."

"All right. Tell you what. You come with me up to where my car is, and when the tow truck shows up with a new fanbelt I'll drive you down to Bodega. You can make your call from the patrol station there."

A muscle throbbed in Vickery's temple. He tried to match McLain's stare, but it was only seconds before he averted his eyes.

"What's the matter?" McLain said. "Something you don't like about my suggestion?"

"I can make my call from right here."

"Sure, but then you'd be inconveniencing Mr. Hannigan. You wouldn't want to do that to a total stranger, would you?"

"*You're* a total stranger," Vickery said. "I'm not going out in that fog with you, not alone and on foot."

"I think maybe you are."

"No. I don't like those eyes of yours, the way you keep staring at me."

"And I don't like the way you're acting, or your story, or the way *you* look," McLain said. His voice had got very soft, but there was a hardness underneath that made Hannigan—standing immobile now at the bar—feel ripples of cold along his back. "We'll just be going, Vickery. Right now."

Vickery took a step toward him, and Hannigan could not tell if it was involuntary or menacing. Immediately McLain swept the tail of his suit jacket back and slid a gun out of a holster on his hip, centered it on Vickery's chest. The coldness on Hannigan's back deepened; he found himself holding his breath.

"Outside, mister," McLain said.

Vickery had gone pale and the sweat had begun to run on his face. He shook his head and kept on shaking it as McLain advanced on him, as he himself started to back away. "Don't let him do it," Vickery said desperately. He was talking to Hannigan but looking at the gun. "Don't let him take me out of here!"

Hannigan spread his hands. "There's nothing I can do."

"That's right, Mr. Hannigan," McLain said, "you just let me handle things. Either way it goes with this one, I'll be in touch."

A little dazedly, Hannigan watched McLain prod Vickery into the hall, to the door; heard Vickery shout something. Then they were gone and the door slammed shut behind them.

Hannigan got a handkerchief out of his pocket and mopped his forehead. He poured himself a drink, swallowed it, poured and drank a second. Then he went to the door.

Outside, the night was silent except for the rhythmic hammering of the breakers in the distance. There was no sign of Vickery or McLain. Hannigan picked up the shovel and the lantern from where he had put them at the house wall and made his way down the steps to the patio, down the fogbound path toward the tule marsh.

He thought about the two men as he went. Was Vickery the lunatic? Or could it be McLain? Well, it didn't really matter; all that mattered now was that Vickery might say something to somebody about the grave. Which meant that Hannigan had to dig up the body and bury it again in some other place.

He hadn't intended the marsh to be a permanent burial spot anyway; he would find a better means of disposal later on. Once that task was taken care of, he could relax and make a few definite plans for the future. Money was made to be spent, particularly if you had a lot of it. It was too bad he had never been able to convince Karen of that.

At the gravesite Hannigan set the lantern down and began to unearth the strangled body of his wife.

And that was when the third man, a stranger carrying a long sharp kitchen knife, crept stealthily out of the fog. . . .

Probably my best-known horror story, "Peekaboo" was written for a Charles Grant–edited anthology called Nightmares. *Written backward, in a sense, because the plot evolved from the last line, which magically appeared one morning in my overheated brain, rather than devolved to it as is usually the case. It's one of those exercises in cauld grue that depends for its effects not so much on the author's imagination as on the reader's. The real horror here lies in what happens* after *the last line—and I'll bet that in nine out of ten cases, the reader's version is nastier and more terrifying than my own would be. . . .*

Peekaboo

Roper came awake with the feeling that he wasn't alone in the house.

He sat up in bed, tense and wary, a crawling sensation on the back of his scalp. The night was dark, moonless; warm clotted black surrounded him. He rubbed sleep mucus from his eyes, blinking, until he could make out the vague grayish outlines of the open window in one wall, the curtains fluttering in the hot summer breeze.

Ears straining, he listened. But there wasn't anything to hear. The house seemed almost graveyard-still, void of even the faintest of night sounds.

What was it that had woken him up? A noise of

some kind? An intuition of danger? It might only have been a bad dream, except that he couldn't remember dreaming. And it might only have been imagination, except that the feeling of not being alone was strong, urgent.

There's somebody in the house, he thought.

Or some *thing* in the house?

In spite of himself Roper remembered the story the nervous real estate agent in Whitehall had told him about this place. It had been built in the early 1900s by a local family, and when the last of them died off a generation later it was sold to a man named Lavolle who had lived in it for forty years. Lavolle had been a recluse whom the locals considered strange and probably evil; they hadn't had anything to do with him. But then he'd died five years ago, of natural causes, and evidence had been found by county officials that he'd been "some kind of devil worshiper" who had "practiced all sorts of dark rites." That was all the real estate agent would say about it.

Word had got out about that and a lot of people seemed to believe the house was haunted or cursed or something. For that reason, and because it was isolated and in ramshackle condition, it had stayed empty until a couple of years ago. Then a man called Garber, who was an amateur parapsychologist, leased the place and lived here for ten days. At the end of that time somebody came out from Whitehall to deliver groceries and found Garber dead. Murdered. The real estate agent wouldn't talk about how he'd been killed; nobody else would talk about it either.

Some people thought it was ghosts or demons that had murdered Garber. Others figured it was a lunatic—maybe the same one who'd killed half a dozen people in this part of New England over the past couple of years. Roper didn't believe in ghosts or demons or things that went bump in the night; that kind of supernatural stuff was for rural types like the ones in Whitehall. He believed in psychotic killers, all right, but he wasn't afraid of them; he wasn't afraid of anybody or anything. He'd made his living with a gun too long for that. And the way things were for him now, since the bank job in Boston had gone sour two weeks ago, an isolated backcountry place like this was just what he needed for a few months.

So he'd leased the house under a fake name, claiming to be a writer, and he'd been here for eight days. Nothing had happened in that time: no ghosts, no demons, no strange lights or wailings or rattling chains—and no lunatics or burglars or visitors of any kind. Nothing at all.

Until now.

Well, if he *wasn't* alone in the house, it was because somebody human had come in. And he sure as hell knew how to deal with a human intruder. He pushed the blankets aside, swung his feet out of bed, and eased open the nightstand drawer. His fingers groped inside, found his .38 revolver and the flashlight he kept in there with it; he took them out. Then he stood, made his way carefully across to the bedroom door, opened it a crack, and listened again.

The same heavy silence.

Roper pulled the door wide, switched on the flash, and probed the hallway with its beam. No one there. He stepped out, moving on the balls of his bare feet. There were four other doors along the hallway: two more bedrooms, a bathroom, and an upstairs sitting room. He opened each of the doors in turn, swept the rooms with the flash, then put on the overhead lights.

Empty, all of them.

He came back to the stairs. Shadows clung to them, filled the wide foyer below. He threw the light down there from the landing. Bare mahogany walls, the lumpish shapes of furniture, more shadows crouching inside the arched entrances to the parlor and the library. But that was all: no sign of anybody, still no sounds anywhere in the warm dark.

He went down the stairs, swinging the light from side to side. At the bottom he stopped next to the newel post and used the beam to slice into the blackness in the center hall. Deserted. He arced it around into the parlor, followed it with his body turned sideways to within a pace of the archway. More furniture, the big fieldstone fireplace at the far wall, the parlor windows reflecting glints of light from the flash. He glanced back at the heavy darkness inside the library, didn't see or hear any movement over that way, and reached out with his gun hand to flick the switch on the wall inside the parlor.

Nothing happened when the electric bulbs in the old-fashioned chandelier came on; there wasn't anybody lurking in there.

Roper turned and crossed to the library arch and scanned the interior with the flash. Empty bookshelves, empty furniture. He put on the chandelier. Empty room.

He swung the cone of light past the staircase, into the center hall—and then brought it back to the stairs and held it there. The area beneath them had been walled on both sides, as it was in a lot of these old houses, to form a coat or storage closet; he'd found that out when he first moved in and opened the small door that was set into the staircase on this side. But it was just an empty space now, full of dust—

The back of his scalp tingled again. And a phrase from when he was a kid playing hide-and-seek games popped into his mind.

Peekaboo, I see you. Hiding under the stair.

His finger tightened around the butt of the .38. He padded forward cautiously, stopped in front of the door. And reached out with the hand holding the flash, turned the knob, jerked the door open, and aimed the light and the gun inside.

Nothing.

Roper let out a breath, backed away to where he could look down the hall again. The house was still graveyard-quiet; he couldn't even hear the faint grumblings its old wooden joints usually made in the night. It was as if the whole place was wrapped in a breathless waiting hush. As if there was some kind of unnatural presence at work here—

Screw that, he told himself angrily. No such things as ghosts and demons. There seemed to be presence here, all right—he could feel it just as strongly as before—but it was a human presence. Maybe a burglar, maybe a tramp, maybe even a goddamn lunatic. But *human*.

He snapped on the hall lights and went along there to the archway that led into the downstairs sitting room. First the flash and then the electric wall lamps told him it was deserted. The dining room off the parlor next. And the kitchen. And the rear porch.

Still nothing.

Where was he, damn it? Where was he hiding?

The cellar? Roper thought.

It didn't make sense that whoever it was would have gone down there. The cellar was a huge room, walled and floored in stone, that ran under most of the house; there wasn't anything in it except spiderwebs and stains on the floor that he didn't like to think about, not after the real estate agent's story about Lavolle and his dark rites. But it was the only place left that he hadn't searched.

In the kitchen again, Roper crossed to the cellar door. The knob turned soundlessly under his hand. With the door open a crack, he peered into the thick darkness below and listened. Still the same heavy silence.

He started to reach inside for the light switch. But then he remembered that there wasn't any bulb in the socket above the stairs; he'd explored the cellar by flashlight before, and he hadn't bothered to buy a bulb. He widened the opening and aimed the flash downward, fanning it slowly from left to right and up and down over the stone walls and floor. Shadowy shapes appeared and disappeared in the bobbing light: furnace, storage shelves, a wooden wine rack, the blackish gleaming stains at the far end, spiderwebs like tattered curtains hanging from the ceiling beams.

Roper hesitated. Nobody down there either, he thought. Nobody in the house after all? The feeling that he wasn't alone kept nagging at him—but it *could* be nothing more than imagination. All that business about devil-worshiping and ghosts and demons and Garber being murdered and psychotic killers on the loose might have affected him more than he'd figured. Might have jumbled together in his subconscious all week and finally come out tonight, making him imagine menace where there wasn't any. Sure, maybe that was it.

But he had to make certain. He couldn't see all of the cellar from up here; he had to go down and give it a full search before he'd be satisfied that he really was alone. Otherwise he'd never be able to get back to sleep tonight.

Playing the light again, he descended the stairs in

the same wary movements as before. The beam showed him nothing. Except for the faint whisper of his breathing, the creak of the risers when he put his weight on them, the stillness remained unbroken. The odors of dust and decaying wood and subterranean dampness dilated his nostrils; he began to breathe through his mouth.

When he came off the last of the steps he took a half dozen strides into the middle of the cellar. The stones were cold and clammy against the soles of his bare feet. He turned to his right, then let the beam and his body transcribe a slow circle until he was facing the stairs.

Nothing to see, nothing to hear.

But with the light on the staircase, he realized that part of the wide, dusty area beneath them was invisible from where he stood—a mass of clotted shadow. The vertical boards between the risers kept the beam from reaching all the way under there.

The phrase from when he was a kid repeated itself in his mind: *Peekaboo, I see you. Hiding under the stair.*

With the gun and the flash extended at arm's length, he went diagonally to his right. The light cut away some of the thick gloom under the staircase, letting him see naked stone draped with more gray webs. He moved closer to the stairs, ducked under them, and put the beam full on the far joining of the walls.

Empty.

For the first time Roper began to relax. Imagination,

no doubt about it now. No ghosts or demons, no burglars or lunatics hiding under the stair. A thin smile
curved the corners of his mouth. Hell, the only one
hiding under the stair was himself—

"Peekaboo," a voice behind him said.

"Thirst" is a variation on one of the classic themes of fantasy/horror fiction. I like to flatter myself that it has a gritty Twilight Zone *feel—two men wandering on foot in a trackless, unnamed desert waste, faced with the most basic of all human instincts: survival. As Flake and March plod on beneath the merciless sun, I can imagine Rod Serling stepping out from behind a reddish outcrop and delivering one of his lyrical post-teaser introductions. Any reader who has that same imaginative flash will be paying me the highest of compliments.*

Thirst

March said, "We're going to die out here, Flake."

"Don't talk like that."

"I don't want to die this way."

"You're not going to die."

"I don't want to die of thirst, Flake!"

"There are worse ways."

"No, no, there's no worse way."

"Quit thinking about it."

"How much water is left?"

"A couple of swallows apiece, that's all."

"Let me have my share. My throat's on fire!"

Flake stopped slogging forward and squinted at March for a few seconds. He took the last of the canteens from his shoulder, unscrewed the cap, and drank two mouthfuls to make sure he got them. Then he handed the canteen to March.

March took it with nerveless fingers. He sank to his knees in the reddish desert sand, his throat working spasmodically as he drank. When he had licked away the last drop, he cradled the canteen to his chest and knelt there rocking with it.

Flake watched him dispassionately. "Come on, get up."

"What's the use? There's no more water. We're going to die of thirst."

"I told you to shut up about that."

March looked up at him with eyes like a wounded animal's. "You think he made it, Flake?"

"Who, Brennan?"

"Yes, Brennan."

"What do you want to think about him for?"

"He didn't take all the gasoline for the Jeep."

"He had enough."

March whimpered, "Why, Flake? Why'd he do it?"

"Why the hell you think he did it?"

"Those deposits we found are rich, the ore samples proved that—sure. But there's more than enough for all of us."

"Brennan's got the fever. He wants it all."

"But he was our friend, our partner!"

"Forget about him," Flake said. "We'll worry about Brennan when we get out of this desert."

March began to laugh. "That's a good one, by God. That's rich."

"What's the matter with you?"

"When we get out of this desert, you said. *When.* Oh, that's a funny one—"

Flake slapped him. March grew silent, his dusty fingers moving like reddish spiders on the surface of the canteen. "You're around my neck like a goddamn albatross," Flake said. "You haven't let up for three days now. I don't know why I don't leave you and go on alone."

"No, Flake, please . . ."

"Get up, then."

"I can't. I can't move."

Flake caught March by the shoulders and lifted him to his feet. March stood there swaying. Flake began shuffling forward again, pulling March along by one arm. The reddish sand burned beneath their booted feet. Stillness, heat, nothing moving, hidden eyes watching them, waiting. Time passed, but they were in a state of timelessness.

"Flake."

"What is it now?"

"Can't we rest?"

Flake shaded his eyes to look skyward. The sun was falling now, shot through with blood-colored streaks; it had the look of a maniac's eye.

"It'll be dark in a few hours," he said. "We'll rest then."

To ease the pressure of its weight against his spine, Flake adjusted the canvas knapsack of dry foodstuffs. March seemed to want to cry, watching him, but there was no moisture left in him for tears. He stumbled after Flake.

They had covered another quarter of a mile when Flake came to a sudden standstill. "There's something out there," he said.

"I don't see anything."

"There," Flake said, pointing.

"What is it?"

"I don't know. We're too far away."

They moved closer, eyes straining against swollen, peeling lids. "Flake!" March cried. "Oh Jesus, Flake, it's the Jeep!"

Flake began to run, stumbling, falling once in his haste. The Jeep lay on its side near a shallow dry wash choked with mesquite and smoke trees. Three of its tires had blown out, the windshield was shattered, and its body dented and scored in a dozen places.

Flake staggered up to it and looked inside, looked around it and down into the dry wash. There was no sign of Brennan, no sign of the four canteens Brennan had taken from their camp in the Red Hills.

March came lurching up. "Brennan?"

"Gone."

"On foot, like us?"

"Yeah."

"What happened? How'd he wreck the Jeep?"

"Blowout, probably. He lost control and rolled it over."

"Can we fix it? Make it run?"

Night Freight

"No."

"Why not? Christ, Flake!"

"Radiator's busted, three tires blown, engine and steering probably bunged up too. How far you think we'd get if we could get it started?"

"Radiator," March said. "Flake, the *radiator* . . ."

"I already checked. If there was any water left after the smashup, Brennan got it."

March made another whimpering sound. He sank to his knees, hugging himself, and began the rocking motion again.

"Get up," Flake said.

"It's no good, we're going to die of thirst—"

"You son of a bitch, get up! Brennan's out there somewhere with the canteens. Maybe we can find him."

"How? He could be anywhere . . ."

"Maybe he was bunged up in the crash, too. If he's hurt he couldn't have got far. We might still catch him."

"He's had three days on us, Flake. This must have happened the first day out."

Flake said nothing. He turned away from the Jeep and followed the rim of the dry wash to the west. March remained kneeling on the ground, watching him, until Flake was almost out of sight; then he got to his feet and began to lurch spindle-legged after him.

It was almost dusk when Flake found the first canteen.

He had been following a trail that had become visible not far from the wrecked Jeep. At that point there had been broken clumps of mesquite, other signs to indicate Brennan was hurt and crawling more than he was walking. The trail led through the arroyo, where it hooked sharply to the south, then continued into the sun-baked wastes due west—toward the town of Sandoval, the starting point of their mining expedition two months earlier.

The canteen lay in the shadow of a clump of rabbitbrush. Flake picked it up, shook it. Empty. He glanced over his shoulder, saw March a hundred yards away shambling like a drunk, and then struck out again at a quickened pace.

Five minutes later he found the second canteen, empty, and his urgency grew and soared. He summoned reserves of strength and plunged onward in a loose trot.

He had gone less than a hundred and fifty yards when he saw the third canteen—and then, some distance beyond it, the vulture. The bird had glided down through the graying sky, was about to settle near something in the shade of a natural stone bridge. Flake ran faster, waving his arms, shouting hoarsely in his burning throat. The vulture slapped the air with its heavy wings and lifted off again. But it stayed nearby, circling slowly, as Flake reached the motionless figure beneath the bridge and dropped down beside it.

Brennan was still alive, but by the look of him and

by the faint irregularity of his pulse, he wouldn't be alive for long. His right leg was twisted at a grotesque angle. As badly hurt as he was, he had managed to crawl the better part of a mile in three days.

The fourth canteen was gripped in Brennan's fingers. Flake pried it loose, upended it over his mouth. Empty. He cast it away and shook Brennan savagely by the shoulders, but the bastard had already gone into a coma. Flake released him, worked the straps on the knapsack on Brennan's back. Inside were the ore samples and nothing else.

Flake struggled to his feet when he heard March approaching, but he didn't turn. He kept staring down at Brennan from between the blistered slits of his eyes.

"Flake! You found Brennan!"

"Yeah, I found him."

"Is he dead?"

"Almost."

"What about water? Is there—?"

"No. Not a drop."

"Oh, God, Flake!"

"Shut up and let me think."

"That's it, we're finished, there's no hope now . . ."

"Goddamn you, quit your whining."

"We're going to end up like him," March said. "We're going to die, Flake, die of thirst—"

Flake backhanded him viciously, knocked him to his knees. "No, we're not," he said. "Do you hear me? We're not."

"We are, we are, we are . . ."

"We're *not* going to die," Flake said.

They came out of the desert four days later—burnt, shriveled, caked head to foot with red dust like human figures molded from soft stone.

Their appearance and the subsequent story of their ordeal caused considerable excitement in Sandoval, much more so than the rich ore samples in Flake's knapsack. They received the best of care. They were celebrities as well as rich men; they had survived the plains of hell, and that set them apart, in the eyes of the people of Sandoval, from ordinary mortals.

It took more than a week before their burns and infirmities had healed enough so that they could resume normal activity. In all that time March was strangely uncommunicative. At first the doctors had been afraid that he might have to be committed to an asylum; his eyes glittered in an unnatural way and he made sounds deep in his throat that were not human sounds. But then he began to get better, even if he still didn't have much to say. Flake thought that March would be his old self again in time. When you were a rich man, all your problems were solved in time.

Flake spent his first full day out of bed in renting them a fancy hacienda and organizing mining operations on their claim in the Red Hills. That night, when he returned to their temporary quarters, he found March sitting in the darkened kitchen. He told him all about the arrangements, but March didn't seem to be interested. Shrugging, Flake got down a bottle of tequila and poured himself a drink.

Behind him March said, "I've been thinking, Flake."

"Good for you. What about?"

"About Brennan."

Flake licked the back of his hand, salted it, licked off the salt, and drank the shot of tequila. "You'd better forget about Brennan," he said.

"I can't forget about him," March said. His eyes were bright. "What do you suppose people would say if we told them the whole story? Everything that happened out there in the desert."

"Don't be a damned fool."

March smiled. "We were thirsty, weren't we? So thirsty."

"That's right. And we did what we had to do to survive."

"Yes," March said. "We did what we had to do."

He stood up slowly and lifted a folded square of linen from the table. Under it was a long, thin carving knife. March picked up the knife and held it in his hand. Sweat shone on his skin; his eyes glittered now like bits of phosphorous. He took a step toward Flake.

Flake felt sudden fear. He opened his mouth to tell March to put the knife down, to ask him what the hell he thought he was doing. But the words caught in his throat.

"You know what we are, Flake? You know what

we—what *I*—became out there the night we cut Brennan open and drained his blood into those four big canteens?"

Flake knew, then, and he tried desperately to run—too late. March tripped him and knocked him down and straddled him, the knife held high.

"I'm still thirsty," March said.

Ah, marriage. Some people consider it a perfectly natural state, one of contentment if not actual bliss. It's also called an institution, others note, and who wants to be locked up in an institution? More than a few find it so unbearable, after a while, that they yearn desperately to be free of their spouses. But if divorce isn't a viable option, then what? One of the darker forms of "Wishful Thinking," perhaps . . .

Wishful Thinking

When I got home from work, a little after six as usual, Jerry Macklin was sitting slumped on his front porch. Head down, long arms hanging loose between his knees. Uh-oh, I thought. I put the car in the garage and walked back down the driveway and across the lawn strip onto the Macklins' property.

"Hi there, Jerry."

He looked up. "Oh, hello, Frank."

"Hot enough for you?"

"Hot," he said. "Yes, it's hot."

"Only June and already in the nineties every day. Looks like we're in for another blistering summer."

"I guess we are."

"How about coming over for a beer before supper?"

He waggled his head. He's long and loose, Jerry, with about twice as much neck as anybody else. When he shakes his big head, it's like watching a bulbous flower bob at the end of a stalk. As always these days, his expression was morose. He used to smile a lot, but not much since his accident. About a year ago he fell off a roof while on his job as a building inspector, damaged some nerves and vertebrae in his back, and was now on permanent disability.

"I killed Verna a little while ago," he said.

"Is that right?"

"She's in the kitchen. Dead on the kitchen floor."

"Uh-huh," I said.

"We had another big fight and I went and got my old service pistol out of the attic. She didn't even notice when I came back down with it, just started in ragging on me again. I shot her right after she called me a useless bum for about the thousandth time."

"Well," I said. Then I said, "A gun's a good way to do it, I guess."

"The best way," Jerry said. "All the other ways, they're too uncertain or too bloody. A pistol really is the best."

"Well, I ought to be getting on home."

"I wonder if I should call the police."

"I wouldn't do that if I were you, Jerry."

"No?"

"Wouldn't be a good idea."

"Hot day like this, maybe I—"

"Jerry!" Verna's voice, from inside the house. Loud and demanding, but with a whiny note underneath. "How many times do I have to ask you to come in here and help me with supper? The potatoes need peeling."

"Damn," Jerry said.

Sweat had begun to run on me; I mopped my face with my handkerchief. "If you feel like it," I said, "we can have that beer later on."

"Sure, okay."

"I'll be in the yard after supper. Come over anytime."

His head wobbled again, up and down this time. Then he stood, wincing on account of his back, and shuffled into his house, and I walked back across and into mine. Mary Ellen was in the kitchen, cutting up something small and green by the sink. Cilantro, from the smell of it.

"I saw you through the window," she said. "What were you talking to Jerry about?"

"Three guesses."

"Oh, Lord. I suppose he killed Verna again."

"Yep."

"Where and how this time?"

"In the kitchen. With his service pistol."

"That man. Three times now, or is it four?"

"Four."

"Other people have nice normal neighbors. We have to have a crazy person living next door."

"Jerry's harmless, you know that. He was as normal as anybody before he fell off that roof."

"Harmless," Mary Ellen said. "Famous last words."

I went over and kissed her neck. Damp, but it still tasted pretty good. "What're you making there?"

"Ceviche."

143

Bill Pronzini

"What's ceviche?"

"Cold fish soup. Mexican style."

"Sounds awful."

"It isn't. You've had it before."

"Did I like it?"

"You loved it."

"Sounds wonderful, then. I'm going to have a beer. You want one?"

"I don't think so." Pretty soon she said, "He really ought to see somebody."

"Who?"

"Jerry."

"See who? You mean a head doctor?"

"Yes. Before he really does do something to Verna."

"Come on, honey. Jerry can't even bring himself to step on a bug. And Verna's enough to drive any man a little crazy. Either she's mired in one of her funks or on a rampage about something or other. And she's always telling him how worthless and lazy she thinks he is."

"She has a point," Mary Ellen said. "All he does all day is sit around drinking beer and staring at the tube."

"Well, with his back the way it is—"

"His back doesn't seem to bother him when he decides to work in his garden."

"Hey, I thought you liked Jerry."

"I do like Jerry. It's just that I can see Verna's side, the woman's side. He was no ball of fire before the accident, and he's never let her have children—"

"That's her story. He says he's sterile."

144

"Well, whatever. I still say she has some justification for being moody and short-tempered, especially in this heat."

"I suppose."

"Anyhow," Mary Ellen said, "her moods don't give Jerry the right to keep pretending he's killed her. And I don't care how harmless he seems to be, he could snap someday. People who have violent fantasies often do. Every day you read about something like that in the papers or see it on the TV news."

" 'Violent fantasies' is too strong a term in Jerry's case."

"What else would you call them?"

"He doesn't sit around all day thinking about killing Verna. I got that much out of him after he scared hell out of me the first time. They have a fight and he goes out on the porch and sulks and that's when he imagines her dead. And only once in a while. It's more like . . . wishful thinking."

"Even so, it's not healthy and it's potentially dangerous. I wonder if Verna knows."

"Probably not, or she'd be making his life even more miserable. We can hear most of what she yells at him all the way over here as it is."

"Somebody ought to tell her."

"You're not thinking of doing it? You don't even like the woman." Which was true. Jerry and I were friendly enough, to the point of going fishing together a few times, but the four of us had never done couples things. Verna wasn't interested. Didn't seem to want much to do with Mary Ellen or me. Or anyone else, for that matter, except a couple of old women friends.

"I might go over and talk to her," Mary Ellen said. "Express concern about Jerry's behavior, if nothing more."

"I think it'd be a mistake."

"Do you? Well, you're probably right."

"So you're going to do it anyway."

"Not necessarily. I'll have to think about it."

Mary Ellen went over to talk to Verna two days later. It was a Saturday and Jerry'd gone off somewhere in their car. I was on the front porch fixing a loose shutter when she left, and still there and still fixing when she came back less than ten minutes later.

"That was fast," I said.

"She didn't want to talk to me." Mary Ellen looked and sounded miffed. "She was barely even civil."

"Did you tell her about Jerry's wishful thinking?"

"No. I didn't have a chance."

"What did you say to her?"

"Hardly anything except that we were concerned about Jerry."

"We," I said. "As in me too."

"Yes, we. She shut me off right there. As much as told me to mind my own business."

"Well?" I said gently.

"Oh, all right, maybe we should. It's her life, after

all. And it'll be as much her fault as Jerry's if he suddenly decides to make his wish come true."

Jerry killed Verna three more times in July. Kitchen again, their bedroom, the backyard. Tenderizing mallet, clock radio, manual strangulation—so I guess he'd decided a gun wasn't the best way after all. He seemed to grow more and more morose as the summer wore on, while Verna grew more and more sullen and contentious. The heat wave we were suffering through didn't help matters any. The temperatures were up around a hundred degrees half the days that month and everybody was bothered in one way or another.

Jerry came over one evening in early August while Mary Ellen and I were having fruit salad under the big elm in our yard. He had a six-pack under one arm and a look on his face that was half-hunted, half-depressed.

"Verna's on another rampage," he said. "I had to get out of there. Okay if I sit with you folks for a while?"

"Pull up a chair," I said. At least he wasn't going to tell us he'd killed her again.

Mary Ellen asked him if he'd like some fruit salad, and he said no, he guessed fruit and yogurt wouldn't mix with beer. He opened a can and drank half of it at a gulp. It wasn't his first of the day by any means.

"I don't know how much more of that woman I can take," he said.

"That bad, huh?"

"That bad. Morning, noon, and night—she never gives me a minute's peace anymore."

Mary Ellen said, "Well, there's a simple solution, Jerry."

"Divorce? She won't give me one. Says she'll fight it if I file, take me for everything she can if it goes through."

"Some women hate the idea of living alone."

Jerry's head waggled on its neck-stalk. "It isn't that," he said. "Verna doesn't believe in divorce. Never has, never will. Till death do us part—that's what she believes in."

"So what're you going to do?" I asked him.

"Man, I just don't know. I'm at my wits' end." He drank the rest of his beer in broody silence. Then he unfolded, wincing, to his feet. "Think I'll go back home now. Have a look in the attic."

"The attic?"

"See if I can find my old service pistol. A gun really is the best way to do it, you know."

After he was gone Mary Ellen said, "I don't like this, Frank. He's getting crazier all the time."

"Oh, come on."

"He'll go through with it one of these days. You mark my words."

"If that's the way you feel," I said, "why don't you try talking to Verna again? Warn her."

"I would if I thought she'd listen. But I know she won't."

"What else is there to do, then?"

148

"You could try talking to Jerry. Try to convince him to see a doctor."

"It wouldn't do any good. He doesn't think he needs help, any more than Verna does."

"At least try. Please, Frank."

"All right, I'll try. Tomorrow night, after work."

When I came home the next sweltering evening, one of the Macklins was sitting slumped on the front porch. But it wasn't Jerry, it was Verna. Head down, hands hanging between her knees. It surprised me so much I nearly swerved the car off onto our lawn. Verna almost never sat out on their front porch, alone or otherwise. She preferred the glassed-in back porch because it was air-conditioned.

The day had been another hundred-plus scorcher, and I was tired and soggy and I wanted a shower and a beer in the worst way. But I'd promised Mary Ellen I'd talk to Jerry—and it puzzled me about Verna sitting on the porch that way. So I went straight over there from the garage.

Verna looked up when I said hello. Her round, plain face was red with prickly heat and her colorless hair hung limp and sweat-plastered to her skin. There was a funny look in her eyes and around her mouth, a look that made me feel uneasy.

"Frank," she said. "Lord, it's hot, isn't it?"

"And no relief in sight. Where's Jerry?"

"In the house."

"Busy? I'd like to talk to him."

"You can't."

"No? How come?"

"He's dead."

"What?"

"Dead," she said. "I killed him."

I wasn't hot anymore; it was as if I'd been doused with ice water. "Killed him? Jesus, Verna—"

"We had a fight and I went and got his service pistol and shot him in the back of the head while he was watching TV."

"When?" It was all I could think of to say.

"Little while ago."

"The police . . . have you called the police?"

"No."

"Then I'd better—"

The screen door popped open with a sudden creaking sound. I jerked my gaze that way, and Jerry was standing there big as life. "Hey, Frank," he said.

I gaped at him with my mouth hanging open.

"Look like you could use a cold one. You too, Verna."

Neither of us said anything.

Jerry said, "I'll get one for each of us," and the screen door banged shut.

I looked at Verna again. She was still sitting in the same posture, head down, staring at the steps with that funny look on her face.

"I know about him killing me all the time," she said. "Did you think I didn't know, didn't hear him saying it?"

There were no words in my head. I closed my mouth.

"I wanted to see how it felt to kill him the same way," Verna said. "And you know what? It felt good."

I backed down the steps, started to turn away. But I was still looking at her and I saw her head come up, I saw the odd little smile that changed the shape of her mouth.

"Good," she said, "but not good enough."

I went home. Mary Ellen was upstairs, taking a shower. When she came out I told her what had just happened.

"My God, Frank. The heat's made her as crazy as he is. They're two of a kind."

"No," I said, "they're not. They're not the same at all."

"What do you mean?"

I didn't tell her what I meant. I didn't have to, because just then in the hot, dead stillness we both heard the crack of the pistol shot from next door.

I've always been fascinated by the werewolf legend. In the late seventies I edited an anthology of quality stories built around the theme, Werewolf!, *but it wasn't until 1991 that I was able to work up a satisfactory plot for a lycanthropic tale of my own. The impetus was an invitation to contribute to an anthology called* The Ultimate Werewolf, *edited by Byron Preiss; "Ancient Evil" was the result of that and a considerable amount of head-scratching and brain-cudgeling.*

Ancient Evil

Listen to me. You'd better listen.

You fools, you think you know so much. Space flight, computer technology, genetic engineering . . . you take them all for granted now. But once your kind scoffed at them, refused to believe in the possibility of their existence. You were proven wrong.

You no longer believe in Us. We will prove you wrong.

We exist. We have existed as long as you. We are not superstition, We are not folklore, We are not an imaginary terror. We are the real terror, the true terror. We are all your nightmares come true.

Believe it. Believe me. I am the proof.

We look like men, We walk and talk like men, in your

153

presence We act like men. But We are not men. Believe
that too.

  We are the ancient evil. . . .

They might never have found him if Hixon hadn't
gone off to take a leak.

For three days they'd been searching the wooded
mountain country above the valley where their sheep
grazed. Tramping through heavy timber and muggy
late-summer heat laden with stinging flies and mosqui-
toes; following the few man-made and animal trails,
cutting new trails of their own. They'd flushed several
deer, come across the rotting carcass of a young elk,
spotted a brown bear and followed its spoor until they
lost it at one of the network of streams. But that was
all. No wolf or mountain lion sign. Hixon and DeVries
kept saying it had to be a wolf or a mountain cat that
had been killing the sheep; Larrabee wasn't so sure.
And yet, what the hell else could it be?

Then, on the morning of the fourth day, while they
were climbing among deadfall pine along the shoulder
of a ridge, Hixon went to take his leak. And came back
after a few minutes all red-faced and excited, with his
fly still half-unzipped.

"I seen something back in there," he said. "God-
damnedest thing, down a ravine."

"What'd you see?" Larrabee asked him. He'd made
himself the leader; he had lost the most sheep and he
was the angriest.

"Well, I think it was a man."

"You think?"

"He was gone before I could use the glasses."

"Hunter, maybe," DeVries said.

Hixon wagged his head. "Wasn't no hunter. No ordinary man, either."

"The hell you say. What was he then?"

"I don't know," Hixon said. "I never seen the like."

"Dressed how?"

"Wasn't dressed, not in clothes. I swear he was wearing some kind of animal skins. And he had hair all over his head and face, long shaggy hair."

"Bigfoot," DeVries said and laughed.

"Damn it, Hank, I ain't kidding. He was your size, mine."

"Sun and shadows playing tricks."

"No, by God. I know what I saw."

Larrabee asked impatiently, "Where'd he go?"

"Down the ravine. There's a creek down there."

"He see or hear you?"

"Don't think so. I was quiet."

DeVries laughed again. "Quiet pisser, that's you."

Larrabee adjusted the pack that rode his shoulders; ran one hand back and forth along the stock of his .300 Savage rifle. His mouth was set tight. "All right," he said, "we'll go have a look."

"Hell, Ben," DeVries said, "you don't reckon it's some *man* been killing our sheep?"

"Possible, isn't it? I never did agree with you and

155

Charley. No wolf or cat takes sheep down that way, tears them apart. And don't leave any sign coming or going."

"No man does either."

"No ordinary man. No sane man."

"Jesus, Ben . . ."

"Come on," Larrabee said. "We're wasting time."

. . . How many of Us are there? Not many. A few hundred . . . We have never been more than a few hundred. Scattered across continents. In cities and small towns, in wildernesses. Hot climes and cold. Moving, always moving, never too long in one place. Hiding among you, the bold and clever ones. Hiding alone, the ones like me.

This is our legacy:

Hiding.

Hunting.

Hungering.

You think you've been hungry but you haven't. You don't know what it means to be hungry all the time, to have the blood-taste in your mouth and the blood-craving in your brain and the blood-heat in your loins.

But some of you will find out. Many of you, someday. Unless you listen and believe.

Each new generation of Us is bolder than the last. And hungrier . . .

The ravine was several hundred yards long, narrow, crowded with trees and brush. The stream was little more than a trickle among sparkly mica rocks. They

followed it without cutting any sign of the man Hixon
had seen, if a man was what he'd seen; without hearing
anything except for the incessant hum of insects, the
yammering cries of jays and magpies.

The banks of the ravine shortened, sloped gradually upward into level ground: a small ragged
meadow ringed by pine and spruce, strewn with
brush and clumps of summer-browned ferns. They
stopped there to rest, to wipe sweat-slick off their
faces.

"No damned sign," Hixon said. "How could he
come through there without leaving any sign?"

DeVries said, "He doesn't exist, that's how."

"I tell you I saw him. I know what I saw."

Larrabee paid no attention to them. He had been
scanning with his naked eye; now he lifted the binoculars that hung around his neck and scanned with those.
He saw nothing anywhere. Not even a breeze stirred
the branches of the trees.

"Which way now?" Hixon asked him.

Larrabee pointed to the west, where the terrain rose
to a bare knob. "Up there. High ground."

"You ask me," DeVries said, "we're on a snipe
hunt."

"You got any better suggestions?"

"No. But even if there is somebody around here,
even if we find him . . . I still don't believe it's a man
we're after. All those sheep with their throats ripped
out, hunks of the carcasses torn off and carried
away . . . a man wouldn't do that."

"Not even a lunatic?"

". . . What kind of lunatic butchers sheep?"

"Psycho," Hixon said. "Blown out on drugs, maybe."

Larrabee nodded. He'd been thinking about it as they tracked. "Or a Vietnam vet, or one of those back-to-nature dropouts. They come into wild country like this, alone, and it gets to this one or that one and they go off their heads."

DeVries didn't want to believe it. "I still say it's an animal, a wolf or a cat."

"Man goes crazy in the wilderness," Larrabee said, "that's just what he turns into—an animal, a damned wolf on the prowl."

He wiped his hands on his trousers, took a drier grip on the Savage, and led the way toward higher ground.

. . . We are not all the same. Your stupid folklore says We are but We're not. Over the centuries We have undergone genetic changes, just as you have; We have evolved. You are children of your time. So are We.

My hunger is for animal flesh, animal blood. Sheep. Cattle. Dogs. Smaller creatures with fur and pulsing heart. They are my prey. One here, two there, ten in this county, fifty or a hundred in that state. You think it is one animal killing another—natural selection, survival of the fittest. You are right but you are also wrong.

Believe it.

We are not all the same. Others of Us have different

hungers. Human flesh, human blood—yes. But that isn't all. We have evolved; our tastes have altered, grown discriminating. Male flesh and male blood. Female. Child. And not always do We desire the soft flesh of the throat, the bright sweet blood from the jugular. And not always do We use our teeth to open our victims. And not always do We feed in a frenzy.

I am one of the old breed—not the most fearsome of Us. And sickened by the things I'm compelled to do; that is why I'm warning you. The new breed . . . it is with the new breed that the ultimate terror lies.

We are not all the same. . . .

Larrabee stood on the bare knob, staring through his binoculars, trying to sharpen the focus. Below, across a hollow choked with brush and deadfall, a grassy, rock-littered slope lifted toward timber. The sun was full on the slope and the hot noon-glare struck fiery glints from some of the rocks, created thick shadows around some of the others, making it hard for him to pick out details. Nothing moved over there except the sun-dazzle. It was just a barren slope—and yet there was something about it. . . .

Up near the top, where the timber started: rocks thickly bunched in tall grass, the way the brush was drawn in around that one massive outcrop. Natural or not? He just couldn't tell for sure from this distance.

Beside him Hixon asked, "What is it, Ben? You see something over there?"

"Maybe." Larrabee gave him the glasses, told him

159

where to look. Pretty soon he said, "Seem to you somebody might've pulled that brush in around the base of the outcrop?"

"Could be, yeah. That damned sun . . ."

"Let me see," DeVries said, but he couldn't tell either.

They went down into the hollow, Larrabee moving ahead of the other two. The deadfall tangle was like a bonepile, close-packed, full of jutting points and splintered edges; it took him ten minutes to find a way across to the slope. He'd been carrying his rifle at port arms, but as he started upslope he extended the muzzle in front of him, slid his finger inside the trigger guard.

The climb was easy enough. They went up three abreast, not fast, not slow. A magpie came swooping down at them, screaming; DeVries cursed and slashed at it with his rifle. Larrabee didn't turn his head. His eyes, unblinking, were in a lock-stare on the rocks and brush near the timber above.

They were within fifty yards of the outcrop when a little breeze kicked up, blew downhill. As soon as it touched them they stopped, all three at once.

"Jesus," Hixon said, "you smell that?"

"Wolf smell," DeVries said.

"Worse than that. Something dead up there . . ."

Larrabee said, "Shut up, both of you." His finger was on the Savage's trigger now. He drew a breath and began to climb again, more warily than before.

The breeze had died, but after another thirty yards the smell was in his nostrils without it. Hixon had been right: death smell. It seemed to mingle with the heat, to form a miasma that made his eyes burn. Behind him he heard DeVries gag, mutter something, spit.

Somewhere nearby the magpie was still screeching at them. But no longer flying around where they were—as if it were afraid to get too close to that outcrop.

Larrabee climbed to within twenty feet of it. That was close enough for him to see that the brush had been dragged in around its base, all right. Some of the smaller rocks looked to have been carried here, too, and set down as part of the camouflage arrangement.

Hixon and DeVries had stopped a few paces below him. In a half whisper DeVries asked, "You see anything, Ben?"

Larrabee didn't answer. He was working saliva through a dry mouth, staring hard at the dark foul-smelling opening of a cave.

. . . Haven't you ever wondered why there have been so many unexplained disappearances in the past few decades? Why so many children are kidnapped? Why there is so seldom any trace of the missing ones?

Haven't you ever wondered about all the random murders, so many more of them now than in the past, and why the bloody remains of certain victims are left behind?

You fools, you blind fools, who do you think the serial killers really are? . . .

* * *

They were all staring at the cave now, standing side by side with rifles trained on the opening, breathing thinly through their mouths. The death-stink seemed to radiate out of the hole, so that it was an almost tangible part of the day's heat.

Larrabee broke his silence. He called out, "If you're in there you better come out. We're armed."

Nothing. Stillness.

"Now what?" DeVries asked.

"We take a look inside."

"Not me. I ain't going in there."

"We don't have to go in. We'll shine a light inside."

"That's still too close for me."

"Do it myself then," Larrabee said angrily. "Charley, get the flashlight out of my pack."

Hixon went around behind him and opened the pack and found the six-cell flash he carried; tested it against his hand to make sure the batteries were still good. "What the hell," he said, "I'll work the light. You're a better shot than me, Ben."

Larrabee tied his handkerchief over his nose and mouth; it helped a little against the stench. Hixon did the same. "All right, let's get it done. Hank, you keep your rifle up and your eyes open."

"Count on it," DeVries said.

They had to prod brush out of the way to reach the cave mouth. It was larger than it had seemed from a distance, four feet high and three feet wide—large enough so that a man didn't have to get down on all

162

fours and crawl inside. The sun-glare made the blackness within a solid wall.

Larrabee stood off a little ways, butted the Savage against his shoulder, took a bead on the opening. "Okay," he said to Hixon, "put the light in there."

Hixon switched on, sent the six-cell's beam probing inside the cave.

Almost instantly the light impaled a crouching shape—big, hairy, wild-eyed. The thing snarled, a sound that was only half-human, and came hurtling out at them with teeth bared and hands hooked like claws. Hixon yelled, dropped the flashlight, tried to dodge out of the way. Larrabee triggered his rifle, but the suddenness of the attack threw his aim off, made him miss. The man-beast slammed into Hixon, threw him down; slashed at him, opened a bloody gash along his neck and shoulder; swung snarling toward Larrabee and launched himself like an animal as Larrabee, fighting panic, jacked another shell into firing position.

He wouldn't have had time to get off a second shot if DeVries hadn't held his ground below, if DeVries hadn't fired twice while the man-beast was in midlunge.

The first bullet knocked him aside, brought a keening cry out of him and put him down in the brush; the second missed high, whanged off rock. By then Larrabee had set himself, taken aim again. He shot the bugger at point-blank range—blew the left side of his head off. Even so, his rage was such that he jacked another shell into the chamber and without thinking shot him again, in the chest this time, exploding the heart.

The last of the echoes died away, leaving a stillness that was painful in Larrabee's ears—like a shattering noise just beyond the range of his hearing. He got his breathing under control and went in loose-legged strides to where Hixon lay writhing on the ground, clutching at his bloody neck. DeVries was there too, his face pale and sweat-studded; he kept saying, "Jesus God," over and over, as if he were praying.

Hixon's wound wasn't as bad as it first seemed: a lot of blood but no arteries severed. DeVries had a first aid kit in his pack; Larrabee got it out and swabbed anti-septic on the gash, wrapped some gauze around it. Hixon was still glazed with shock, so they moved him over against one of the rocks, in the shade. Then they went to look at what they'd killed.

It was a man, all right. Six feet, two hundred pounds, black beard and hair so thick and matted that it all but hid his features. Fingernails as long and sharp as talons. The one eye that was left was a muddy brown, the white of it so veined it looked bloody. Skins from different animals, roughly sewn together, draped part of the thick-muscled body; the skins and the man's bare flesh were encrusted with filth, months or years of it. The stench that came off the corpse made Larrabee want to puke.

DeVries said hoarsely, "You ever in your life see anything like that?"

"I never want to see anything like it again."

"Crazy—he must've been crazy as hell. The way he come out of that cave . . ."

"Yeah," Larrabee said.

"He'd have killed you if I hadn't shot him. You and Charley and then me, all three of us. It was in his eyes . . . a goddamn madman."

Larrabee didn't respond to that. After a few seconds he turned and started away.

"Where you going?" DeVries said behind him.

"Find out what's inside that cave."

. . . I am one of the old breed—not the most fearsome of Us. And sickened by the things I'm compelled to do; that is why I'm warning you. The new breed . . . it is with the new breed that the ultimate terror lies.

We are not all the same. . . .

DeVries wouldn't go into the cave, wouldn't even go near the mouth, so Larrabee went in alone. He took the Savage as well as the flashlight, and he went in slow and wary. He didn't want any more surprises.

He had to walk hunched over for the first few feet. Then the cave opened up into a chamber nearly six feet high and not much larger than a prison cell. He put the light on the walls, on the floor: more animal skins, heaps of flesh-rotted bones, splatters and streaks of dried blood everywhere. Things had been killed as well as eaten in here, Christ knew what things.

The stink was so bad that he couldn't stand it for more than a few seconds. When he turned to get out of there, the flash beam illuminated a kind of natural shelf in the wall. There were some things on the shelf—the stub of a candle stuck in a clot of its own grease, what appeared to be a ragged pocket notebook, other things he didn't want to examine too closely. On impulse he caught up the notebook by one edge, brought it out with him into the hot clean air.

Hixon was up on his feet, standing with DeVries twenty feet from the entrance; he was still a little shaky but the glazed look was gone from his eyes. He said, "Bad in there?"

"As bad as it gets."

"What'd you find?" DeVries asked. He was looking at what Larrabee held between his left thumb and forefinger.

Larrabee squinted at it, holding it away from his face because of the smell. Kid's spiral-bound notebook, the covers torn and stained, the ruled paper inside almost black with filth and dried blood. But on half a dozen pages there was writing, old writing done with a pencil pressed hard and angry so that the words were still legible. Larrabee put his back to the sun so he could read it better.

. . . Believe it. Believe me. I am the proof.
We look like men, We walk and talk like men, in your

*presence We act like men. But We are not men. Believe
that too.*

We are the ancient evil. . . .

Wordlessly Larrabee handed the notebook to DeVries,
who made a faint disgusted sound when he touched it.
But he read what was written inside. So did Hixon.

"Man oh man," Hixon said when he was done, with
a kind of awe in his voice. "Ben, you don't think . . . ?"

"It's bullshit," Larrabee said. "Ravings of a lunatic."

"Sure. Sure. Only . . ."

"Only what?"

"I don't know, it . . . I don't know."

"Come on, Charley," DeVries said. "You don't buy
any of that crap, do you? Some kind of monster—a
werewolf, for Christ's sake?"

"No. It's just . . . maybe we ought to take this back
with us, give it to the sheriff."

Larrabee gave him a hard look. "The body too, I
suppose? Lug it twenty miles in this heat, smelling the
way it does, leaking blood?"

"Not that, no. But we got to report it, don't we? Tell
the law what happened?"

"Hell we do. How's it going to look? He's got three
bullets in him, two of mine and one of Hank's. He
jumped us out of a cave, three of us with rifles and him
without a weapon, and we blew him away—how's that
going to sound?"

"But it was self-defense. The sheriff'll believe
that. . . ."

"Will he? I'm not going to take the chance."

"Ben's right," DeVries said. "Neither am I."

"What do we do then?"

"Bury him," Larrabee said. "Forget any of this ever happened."

"Bury the notebook too?"

"What notebook?" Larrabee said.

. . . You fools, you blind fools . . .

They dug the grave for the crazy sheep-killing man and his crazy legacy in the grass above the outcrop. Deep, six feet deep, so the predators couldn't get at him.

Writers are forever being asked where they get their ideas. We chafe at the question because it is really unanswerable. Ideas come from everywhere and nowhere. Some develop slowly, requiring a good deal of thought and reshaping. Others seem to fall out of the blue and smack the muse's head like the apple allegedly struck Isaac Newton's. Take this story, for instance. One day I was browsing through some old mystery magazines, and halfway through a wholly different and not very good tale of a menaced family, "The Monster" suddenly appeared. Full-born and nasty, first sentence to last, title included. I wrote it in an hour, virtually as you'll read it here—and I seldom consider any piece of writing finished without extensive revisions. Ideas? Hey, don't ask me where they come from.

The Monster

He was after the children.

Meg knew it, all at once, as soon as he was inside the house. She couldn't have said exactly how she knew. He was pleasant enough on the surface, smiling, friendly. Big and shaggy-haired in his uniform, hairy all over like a bear. But behind his smile and underneath his fur there was menace, evil. She felt it, intuited it—a mother's instinct for danger. He was after

Kate and Bobby. One of those monsters who preyed on little children, hurt them, did unspeakable things to them—

"Downstairs or upstairs?" he said.

". . . What?"

"The stopped-up drain. Downstairs here or upstairs?"

A feeling of desperation was growing in her, spreading toward panic. She didn't know what to do. "I think you'd better leave." The words were out before she realized what she was saying.

"Huh? I just got here, Mrs. Thompson. Your husband said you got a stopped-up drain—that's right, isn't it?"

Why did I let him in? she thought. Just because he said Philip sent him, that doesn't make it so. And even if Philip did send him . . . Oh God, why him, of all the plumbers in this city?

"No," she said. "No, it . . . it's all right now. It's working again, there's nothing wrong with it."

He wasn't smiling anymore. "You kidding me?"

"Why would I do that?"

"Yeah, why? Over at the door you said you been expecting me, come on in and fix the drain."

"I didn't—"

"You did, lady. Look, I haven't got time to play games. And it's gonna cost you sixty-five bucks whether I do any work or not, so you might as well let me take a look."

"It's all right now, I tell you."

"Okay, maybe it is. But if it was stopped-up once today, it could happen again. You never know with the pipes in these old houses. So where is it, up or down?"

"Please . . ."

"Upstairs, right? Yeah, now I think of it, your husband said it was in the upstairs bathroom."

No! The word was like a scream in her mind. The upstairs bathroom was between their room, hers and Philip's, and the nursery. Baby Kate in her crib, not even a year old, and Bobby, just two, napping in his bed . . . so innocent and helpless . . . and this man, this beast—

He moved past her to the stairs, hefting his tool kit in one huge, scab-knuckled hand. "You want to show me where it is?"

"No!" She cried it aloud this time.

"Hey," he said, "you don't have to bust my eardrums." He shook his head the way Philip did sometimes when he was vexed with her. "Well, I can find it myself. Can't hide a bathroom from an old hand like me."

He started up the stairs.

She stood paralyzed, staring in horror as he climbed. She tried to shriek at him to stop, go away, don't hurt the babies, but her voice had frozen in her throat. If any harm came to Kate and Bobby, she could never forgive herself—she would shrivel up and die. So many childless years, all the doctors who'd told her and Philip that she could never conceive, and then the sudden miracle of her first pregnancy and Bobby's

171

birth, the second miracle that was Kate. . . . If she let either of them be hurt she would be as much of a monster as the one climbing the stairs—

Stop him!

The paralysis left her as abruptly as it had come on; her legs pumped, carried her headlong into the kitchen. A knife, the big butcher knife . . . She grabbed it out of the rack, raced back to the stairs.

He was already on the second floor. She couldn't see him, but she could hear his heavy menacing tread in the hallway, going down the hallway.

Toward the nursery.

Toward Kate and Bobby.

She rushed upstairs, clutching the knife, her terror so immense now it felt as though her head would burst. She ran into the hallway, saw him again—and her heart skipped a beat, the fear ripped inside her like an animal trying to claw its way out of a cage.

He was standing in the nursery doorway, looking in at the children.

She lunged at him with the knife upraised. He turned just before she reached him, and his mouth shaped startled words. But the only sound he made was an explosive grunt when she plunged the knife into his chest.

His mouth flew open; his eyes bulged so wide she thought for an instant they would pop out like seeds from a squeezed orange. One scarred hand plucked at the knife handle. The other groped in her direction, as if to catch and crush her. She leapt back against the far wall, stood huddled against it as he staggered away, still grunting and plucking at the knife handle.

She saw him fall once, lurch upright again, finally reach the top of the stairs; then the grunting ended in a long heaving sigh and he sagged and toppled forward. The sounds he made rolling and bouncing down the stairs were as loud and terrible as the thunder that had terrified her as a child, that still frightened her sometimes on storm-heavy nights.

The noises stopped at last and there was silence.

Meg pushed away from the wall, hurried into the nursery. Bobby, incredibly, was still asleep; he had the face of a golden-haired angel, lying pooched on his side with his tiny arms outstretched. Kate was awake and fussing. Meg picked her up, held her tight, soothed and rocked and murmured to her until the fussing stopped and her tears dried. When the baby was tucked up asleep in her crib, Meg steeled herself and then made her way slowly out to the stairs and down.

The evil one lay crumpled and smeared with red at the bottom. His eyes still bulged, wide open and staring. Dead.

And that was good, it was *good*, because it meant that the children were safe again.

She stepped over him, shuddering, and went to the phone in the kitchen. She called the police first, then Philip at his office to ask him to please come home right away.

173

* * *

A detective sergeant and two uniformed officers arrived first. Meg explained to the detective what had happened, and he seemed very sympathetic. But he was still asking questions when Philip came.

Philip put his strong arms around her, held her; she leaned close to him as always, because he was the only person since her daddy died who had ever made her feel safe. He didn't ask her any questions. He made her sit down in the living room, went with the detective to look at what lay under the sheet at the foot of the stairs.

". . . don't understand it," Philip was saying. "He was highly recommended to me by a friend. Reliable, honest, trustworthy—the best plumber in town."

"Then you did send him over to fix a stopped-up drain."

"Yes. I told my wife I was going to. I just don't understand. Did he try to attack her? Is that why she stabbed him?"

"Not her, no. She said he was after your children. Upstairs in the nursery where they're asleep."

"Oh my God," Philip said.

He must have sensed her standing there because he turned to look at her. I had to do it, Philip, she told him with her eyes. He was a monster and I had to protect the children. Our wonderful son Bobby, sweet baby Kate . . . I'm their mother, I couldn't let them be hurt, could I?

But he didn't believe her. She saw the disbelief in his face before he turned away again, and then she heard him lie to the detective. He lied, he lied, Philip lied—

"We don't have any children," he said.

I couldn't sell this story when I wrote it. One editor bounced it as being "too biblical for our readers," which is my nomination as the single most asinine reason on record for rejecting a writer's work. "Dear Contributors: Thank you for submitting your book, The Holy Bible, which has merit but is too mystical for our readers. Do try us again with something more down-to-earth." Is it any wonder writers go crazy?

His Name was Legion

His name was Legion.

No, sir, I mean that literal—Jimmy Legion, that was his name. He knew about the biblical connection, though. Used to say, "My name is Legion," like he was Christ Himself quoting Scripture.

Religious man? No, sir! Furthest thing from it. Jimmy Legion was a liar, a blasphemer, a thief, a fornicator, and just about anything else you can name. A pure hellion—a devil's son if ever there was one. Some folks in Wayville said that after he ran off with Amanda Sykes that September of 1931, he sure must have crossed afoul of the law and come to a violent end. But nobody rightly knew for sure. Not about him, nor about Amanda Sykes either.

He came to Wayville in early summer of that year, 1931. Came in out of nowhere in a fancy new Ford car, seemed to have plenty of money in his pockets;

claimed he was a magazine writer. Wayville wasn't much in those days—just a small farm town with a population of around five hundred. Hardly the kind of place you'd expect a man like Legion to gravitate to. Unless he was hiding out from the law right then, which is the way some folks figured it—but only after he was gone. While he lived in Wayville he was a charmer.

First day I laid eyes on him, I was riding out from town with saddlebags and a pack all loaded up with small hardware—

Yes, that's right—saddlebags. I was only nineteen that summer, and my family was too poor to afford an automobile. But my father gave me a horse of my own when I was sixteen—a fine light-colored gelding that I called Silverboy—and after I was graduated from high school I went to work for Mr. Hazlitt at Wayville Hardware.

Depression had hit everybody pretty hard in our area, and not many small farmers could afford the gasoline for truck trips into town every time they needed something. Small merchants like Mr. Hazlitt couldn't afford it either. So what I did for him, I used Silverboy to deliver small things like farm tools and plumbing supplies and carpentry items. Rode him most of the time, hitched him to a wagon once in a while when the load was too large to carry on horseback. Mr. Hazlitt called me Ben Boone the Pony Express Deliveryman, and I liked that fine. I was full of spirit and adventure back then.

*Experience the Ultimate in Fear
Every Other Month...
From Leisure Books!*

As a member of the Leisure Horror Book Club,
you'll enjoy the best new horror by the best writers
in the genre, writers who know how to chill your
blood. Upcoming book club releases include
First-Time-in-Paperback novels by such acclaimed
authors as:

*Douglas Clegg   Ed Gorman
John Shirley   Elizabeth Massie
J.N. Williamson   Richard Laymon
Graham Masterton   Bill Pronzini
Mary Ann Mitchell   Tom Piccirilli
Barry Hoffman*

SAVE BETWEEN $3.72 AND $6.72
EACH TIME YOU BUY.
THAT'S A SAVINGS OF UP TO NEARLY 40%!

Every other month Leisure Horror Book Club brings
you three terrifying titles from Leisure Books,
America's leading publisher of horror fiction.
EACH PACKAGE SAVES YOU MONEY.
And you'll never miss a new title.

Here's how it works:

Each package will carry a FREE 10-DAY EXAMINATION
privilege. At the end of that time, if you decide
to keep your books, simply pay the low invoice price
of $11.25, no shipping or handling charges added.
HOME DELIVERY IS ALWAYS FREE!
There's no minimum number of books to buy,
and you may cancel at any time.

AND AS A CHARTER MEMBER,
YOUR FIRST THREE-BOOK
SHIPMENT IS TOTALLY FREE!
IT'S A BARGAIN YOU CAN'T BEAT!

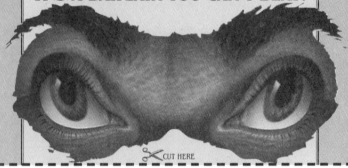

✂ CUT HERE

Mail to: Leisure Horror Book Club,
P.O. Box 6613, Edison, NJ 08818-6613

YES! I want to subscribe to the Leisure Horror Book Club. Please send
my 3 FREE BOOKS. Then, every other month I'll receive the three newest
Leisure Horror Selections to preview FREE for 10 days. If I decide to
keep them, I will pay the Special Members Only discounted price of just
$3.75 each, a total of $11.25. This saves me between $3.72 and $6.72
off the bookstore price. There are no shipping, handling or other charges.
There is no minimum number of books I must buy and I may cancel the
program at any time. In any case, the 3 FREE BOOKS are mine to keep—
at a value of between $14.97 and $17.97. Offer valid only in the USA.

NAME:_____

ADDRESS:_____

   CITY:_____ STATE:_____

   ZIP:_____ PHONE:_____

▙ **LEISURE BOOKS,** A Division of Dorchester Publishing Co., Inc.

Anyhow, this afternoon I'm talking about I was riding Silverboy out to the Baker farm when I heard a roar on the road behind me. Then a car shot by so fast and so close that Silverboy spooked and spilled both of us down a ten-foot embankment.

Wasn't either of us hurt, but we could have been—we could have been killed. I only got a glimpse of the car, but it was enough for me to identify it when I got back to Wayville. I went hunting for the owner and found him straightaway inside Chancellor's Cafe.

First thing he said to me was, "*My* name is Legion."

Well, we had words. Or rather, I had the words; he just stood there and grinned at me, all wise and superior, like a professor talking to a bumpkin. Handsome brute he was, few years older than me, with slicked-down hair and big brown eyes and teeth so white they glistened like mica rocks in the sun.

He shamed me, is what he did, in front of a dozen of my friends and neighbors. Said what happened on the road was my fault, and why didn't I go somewhere and curry my horse, *he* had better things to do than argue road right-of-ways.

Every time I saw him after that he'd make some remark to me. Polite, but with brimstone in it—I guess you know what I mean. I tried to fight him once, but he wouldn't fight. Just stood grinning at me like the first time, hands down at his sides, daring me. I couldn't hit him that way, when he wouldn't defend himself. I wanted to, but I was raised better than that.

If me and some of the other young fellows disliked

him, most of the girls took to him like flies to honey. All they saw were his smile and his big brown eyes and his city charm. And his lies about being a magazine writer.

Just about every day I'd see him with a different girl, some I'd dated myself on occasion, such as Bobbie Jones and Dulcea Wade. Oh, he was smooth and evil, all right. He ruined more than one of those girls, no doubt of that. Got Dulcea Wade pregnant, for one, although none of us found out about it until after he ran off with Amanda Sykes.

Falsehoods and fornication were only two of his sins. Like I said before, he was guilty of much more than that. Including plain thievery.

He wasn't in town more than a month before folks started missing things. Small amounts of cash money, valuables of one kind or another. Mrs. Cooley, who owned the boardinghouse where Legion took a room, lost a solid gold ring her late husband gave her. But she never suspected Legion, and hardly anybody else did either until it was too late.

All this went on for close to three months—the lying and the fornicating and the stealing. It couldn't have lasted much longer than that without the truth coming out, and I guess Legion knew that best of all. It was a Friday in late September that he and Amanda Sykes disappeared together. And when folks did learn the truth about him, all they could say was good riddance to him and her both—the Sykeses among them, because they were decent God-fearing people.

Night Freight

I reckon I was one of the last to see either of them. Fact is, in a way I was responsible for them leaving as sudden as they did.

At about two o'clock that Friday afternoon I left Mr. Hazlitt's store with a scythe and some other tools George Pickett needed on his farm, and rode out the north road. It was a burning hot day, no wind at all—I remember that clear. When I was two miles outside Wayville, and about two more from the Pickett farm, I took Silverboy over to a stream that meandered through a stand of cottonwoods. He was blowing pretty hard because of the heat, and I wanted to give him a cool drink. Give myself a cool drink too.

But no sooner did I rein him up to the stream than I spied two people lying together in the tall grass. And I mean "lying together" in the biblical sense—no need to explain further. It was Legion and Amanda Sykes.

Well, they were so involved in their sinning that they didn't notice me until I was right up to them. Before I could turn Silverboy and set him running, Legion jumped up and grabbed hold of me and dragged me down to the ground. He cursed me like a crazy man; I never saw anybody that wild and possessed before or since.

"I'll teach you to spy on me, Ben Boone!" he shouted, and he hit me a full right-hand wallop on the face. Knocked me down in the grass and bloodied my nose, bloodied it so bad I couldn't stop the flow until a long while later.

Then he jumped on me and pounded me two more

181

blows until I was half-senseless. And after that he reached in my pocket and took my wallet— stole my wallet and all the money I had.

Amanda Sykes just sat there covering herself with her dress and watching. She never said a word the whole time.

It wasn't a minute later they were gone. I saw them get into this Ford that was hidden in the cottonwoods nearby and roar away. I couldn't have stopped them with a rifle, weak as I was.

When my strength finally came back I washed the blood off me as best I could, and rode Silverboy straight back to Wayville to report to the local constable. He called in the state police and they put out a warrant for the arrest of Legion and Amanda Sykes, but nothing came of it. Police didn't find them; nobody ever heard of them again.

Yes, sir, I know the story doesn't seem to have much point right now. But it will in just a minute. I wanted you to hear it first the way I told it back in 1931—the way I been telling it over and over in my own mind ever since then so I could keep on living with myself.

A good part of it's lies, you see. Lies worse than Jimmy Legion's.

That's why I asked you to come, Reverend. Doctors here at the hospital tell me my heart's about ready to give out. They don't figure I'll last the week. I can't die with sin on my soul. Time's long past due for me to make peace with myself and with God.

The lies? Mostly what happened on that last afternoon, after I came riding up to the stream on my way to the Pickett farm. About Legion attacking me and bloodying me and stealing my wallet. About him and Amanda Sykes running off together. About not telling of the sinkhole near the stream that was big enough and deep enough to swallow anything smaller than a house.

Those things, and the names of two of the three of us that were there.

No, I didn't mean *him.* Everything I told you about him is the truth as far as I know it, including his name.

His name was Legion.

But Amanda's name wasn't Sykes. Not anymore it wasn't, not for five months prior to that day.

Her name was Amanda Boone.

Yes, Reverend, that's right—she was my wife. I'd dated those other girls, but I'd long *courted* Amanda; we eloped over the state line before Legion arrived and got married by a justice of the peace. We did it that way because her folks and mine were dead-set against either of us marrying so young—not that they knew we were at such a stage. We kept that part of our relationship a secret too, I guess because it was an adventure for the both of us, at least in the beginning.

My name? Yes, it's really Ben Boone. Yet it *wasn't* on that afternoon. The one who chanced on Legion and Amanda out there by the stream, who caught them sinning and listened to them laugh all shameless and say they were running off together . . . he wasn't Ben Boone at all.

His name, Reverend, that one who sat grim on his pale horse with Farmer Pickett's long, new-honed scythe in one hand . . .

His name was Death.

The genesis of this story was a vacation trip to the somewhat remote Caribbean island of Anguilla. Put a writer on an empty beach made eerie by moonlight and shadow, let him watch huge stormclouds gathering on the horizon, then let him see what may or may not be a night swimmer emerge from the sea too far away for easy recognition, and voila! *Dark suspense with a dark and rhythmic Caribbean beat. . . .*

Out of the Depths

He came tumbling out of the sea, dark and misshapen, like a being that was not human. A creature from the depths; or a jumbee, the evil spirit of West Indian superstition. Fanciful thoughts, and Shea was not a fanciful woman. But on this strange, wild night nothing seemed real or explicable.

At first, with the moon hidden behind the running scud of clouds, she'd seen him as a blob of flotsam on a breaking wave. The squall earlier had left the sea rough and the swells out toward the reef were high, their crests stripped of spume by the wind. The angry surf threw him onto the strip of beach, dragged him back again; another wave flung him up a little farther. The moon reappeared then, bathing sea and beach and rocks in the kind of frost-white shine you found only in the Caribbean. Not flotsam—something alive. She saw his arms extend, splayed fingers dig into the sand to hold himself against the backward pull of the sea. Saw him raise a smallish head above a massive, deformed torso, then squirm weakly toward the nearest jut of rock. Another wave shoved him the last few feet. He clung to the rock, lying motionless with the surf foaming around him.

Out of the depths, she thought.

The irony made her shiver, draw the collar of her coat more tightly around her neck. She lifted her gaze again to the rocky peninsula farther south. Windflaw Point, where the undertow off its tiny beach was the most treacherous on the island. It had taken her almost an hour to marshal her courage to the point where she was ready—almost ready—to walk out there and into the ocean. *Into* the depths. Now . . .

Massive clouds sealed off the moon again. In the heavy darkness Shea could just make him out, still lying motionless on the fine coral sand. Unconscious? Dead? I ought to go down there, she thought. But she could not seem to lift herself out of the chair.

After several minutes he moved again: dark shape rising to hands and knees, then trying to stand. Three tries before he was able to keep his legs from collapsing under him. He stood swaying, as if gathering strength; finally staggered onto the path that led up through rocks and sea grape. Toward the house. Toward her.

On another night she would have felt any number of emotions by this time: surprise, bewilderment, curiosity, concern. But not on this night. There was a numbness in her mind, like the numbness in her body from the cold wind. It was as if she were dreaming, sitting there on the open terrace—as if she'd fallen asleep hours ago, before the clouds began to pile up at sunset and the sky turned the color of a blood bruise.

A new storm was making up. Hammering northern this time, from the look of the sky. The wind had shifted, coming out of the northeast now; the clouds were bloated and simmering in that direction and the air had a charged quality. Unless the wind shifted again soon, the rest of the night would be even wilder.

Briefly the clouds released the moon. In its white glare she saw him plodding closer, limping, almost dragging his left leg. A man, of course—just a man. And not deformed: what had made him seen that way was the life jacket fastened around his upper body. She remembered the lights of a freighter or tanker she had seen passing on the horizon just after nightfall, ahead of the squall. Had he gone overboard from that somehow?

He had reached the garden, was making his way past the flamboyant trees and the thick clusters of frangipani. Heading toward the garden door and the kitchen; she'd left the lights on in there and the jalousies open. It was the lights that had drawn him here, like a beacon that could be seen a long distance out to sea.

A good thing she'd left them on or not? She didn't want him here, a cast up stranger, hurt and needing attention—not on this night, not when she'd been so close to making the walk to Windflaw Point. But neither could she refuse him access or help. John would have, if he'd been drunk and in the wrong mood. Not her. It was not in her nature to be cruel to anyone, except perhaps herself.

Abruptly Shea pushed herself out of the chair. He hadn't seen her sitting in the restless shadows, and he didn't see her now as she moved back across the terrace to the sliding glass doors to her bedroom. Or at least if he did see her, he didn't stop or call out to her. She hurried through the darkened bedroom, down the hall, and into the kitchen. She was halfway to the garden door when he began pounding on it.

She unlocked and opened the door without hesitation. He was propped against the stucco wall, arms hanging and body slumped with exhaustion. Big and youngish, that was her first impression. She couldn't see his face clearly.

"Need some help," he said in a thick, strained voice. "Been in the water . . . washed up on your beach . . ."

"I know, I saw you from the terrace. Come inside."

"Better get a towel first. Coral ripped a gash in my foot . . . blood all over your floor."

"All right. I'll have to close the door. The wind. . . ."

"Go ahead."

She shut the door and went to fetch a towel, a blanket, and the first aid kit. On the way back to the kitchen she turned the heat up several degrees. When she opened up to him again she saw that he'd shed the life jacket. His clothing was minimal: plaid wool shirt, denim trousers, canvas shoes, all nicked and torn by coral. Around his waist was a pouch-type waterproof belt, like a workman's utility belt. One of the pouches bulged slightly.

She gave him the towel, and when he had it wrapped around his left foot he hobbled inside. She took his arm, let him lean on her as she guided him to the kitchen table. His flesh was cold, sea-puckered; the touch of it made her feel a tremor of revulsion. It was like touching the skin of a dead man.

When he sank heavily onto one of the chairs, she dragged another chair over and lifted his injured leg onto it. He stripped off what was left of his shirt, swaddled himself in the blanket. His teeth were chattering.

The coffeemaker drew her; she poured two of the big mugs full. There was always hot coffee ready and waiting, no matter what the hour—she made sure of that. She drank too much coffee, much too much, but it was better than drinking what John usually drank. If she—

"You mind sweetening that?"

She half turned. "Sugar?"

"Liquor. Rum, if you have it."

"Jamaican rum." That was what John drank.

"Best there is. Fine."

She took down an open bottle, carried it and the mugs to the table, and watched while he spiked the coffee, drank, then poured more rum and drank again. Color came back into his stubbled cheeks. He used part of the blanket to rough-dry his hair.

189

He was a little older than she, early thirties, and in good physical condition: broad chest and shoulders, muscle-knotted arms. Sandy hair cropped short, thick sandy brows, a long-chinned face burned dark from exposure to the sun. The face was all right, might have been attractive except for the eyes. They were a bright off-blue color, shielded by lids that seemed perpetually lowered like flags at half-mast, and they didn't blink much. When the eyes lifted to meet and hold hers something in them made her look away.

"I'll see what I can do for your foot."

"Thanks. Hurts like hell."

The towel was already soaking through. Shea unwrapped it carefully, revealing a deep gash across the instep just above the tongue of his shoe. She got the shoe and sock off. More blood welled out of the cut.

"It doesn't look good. You may need a doctor—"

"No," he said, "no doctor."

"It'll take stitches to close properly."

"Just clean and bandage it, okay?"

She spilled iodine onto a gauze pad, swabbed at the gash as gently as she could. The sharp sting made him suck in his breath, but he didn't flinch or utter another sound. She laid a second piece of iodined gauze over the wound and began to wind tape tightly around his foot to hold the skin flaps together.

He said, "My name's Tanner. Harry Tanner."

"Shea Clifford."

"Shea. That short for something?"

"It's a family name."

"Pretty."

"Thank you."

"So are you," he said. "Real pretty with your hair all windblown like that."

She glanced up at him. He was smiling at her. Not a leer, just a weary smile, but it wasn't a good kind of smile. It had a predatory look, like the teeth-baring stretch of a wolf's jowls.

"No offense," he said.

"None taken." She lowered her gaze, watched her hands wind and tear tape. Her mind still felt numb. "What happened to you? Why were you in the water?"

"That damned squall a few hours ago. Came up so fast I didn't have time to get my genoa down. Wave as big as a house knocked poor little *Wanderer* into a full broach. I got thrown clear when she went over or I'd have sunk with her."

"Were you sailing alone?"

"All alone."

"Single-hander? Or just on a weekend lark?"

"Single-hander. You know boats, I see."

"Yes. Fairly well."

"Well, I'm a sea tramp," Tanner said. "Ten years of island-hopping and this is the first time I ever got caught unprepared."

"It happens. What kind of craft was *Wanderer*?"

"Bugeye ketch. Thirty-nine feet."

"Shame to lose a boat like that."

He shrugged. "She was insured."

191

"How far out were you?"

"Five or six miles. Hell of a long swim in a choppy sea."

"You're lucky the squall passed as quickly as it did."

"Lucky I was wearing my life jacket, too," Tanner said. "And lucky you stay up late with your lights on. If it weren't for the lights I probably wouldn't have made shore at all."

Shea nodded. She tore off the last piece of tape and then began putting the first aid supplies away in the kit.

Tanner said, "I didn't see any other lights. This house the only one out here?"

"The only one on this side of the bay, yes."

"No close neighbors?"

"Three houses on the east shore, not far away."

"You live here alone?"

"With my husband."

"But he's not here now."

"Not now. He'll be home soon."

"That so? Where is he?"

"In Merrywing, the town on the far side of the island. He went out to dinner with friends."

"While you stayed home."

"I wasn't feeling well earlier."

"Merrywing. Salt Cay?"

"That's right."

"British-owned, isn't it?"

"Yes. You've never been here before?"

"Not my kind of place. Too small, too quiet, too

rich. I prefer the livelier islands—St. Thomas, Nassau, Jamaica."

"St. Thomas isn't far from here," Shea said. "Is that where you were heading?"

"More or less. This husband of yours—how big is he?"

". . . Big?"

"Big enough so his clothes would fit me?"

"Oh," she said, "yes. About your size."

"Think he'd mind if you let me have a pair of his pants and a shirt and some underwear? Wet things of mine are giving me a chill."

"No, of course not. I'll get them from his room."

She went to John's bedroom. The smells of his cologne and pipe tobacco were strong in there; they made her faintly nauseous. In haste she dragged a pair of white linen trousers and a pullover off hangers in his closet, turned toward the dresser as she came out. And stopped in midstride.

Tanner stood in the open doorway, leaning against the jamb, his half-lidded eyes fixed on her.

"*His* room," he said. "Right."

"Why did you follow me?"

"Felt like it. So you don't sleep with him."

"Why should that concern you?"

"I'm naturally curious. How come? I mean, how come you and your husband don't share a bed?"

"Our sleeping arrangements are none of your business."

"Probably not. Your idea or his?"

193

"What?"

"Separate bedrooms. Your idea or his?"

"Mine, if you must know."

"Maybe he snores, huh?"

She didn't say anything.

"How long since you kicked him out of your bed?"

"I didn't kick him out. It wasn't like that."

"Sure it was. I can see it in your face."

"My private affairs—"

"—are none of my business. I know. But I also know the signs of a bad marriage when I see them. A bad marriage and an unhappy woman. Can't tell me you're not unhappy."

"All right," she said.

"So why don't you divorce him? Money?"

"Money has nothing to do with it."

"Money has something to do with everything."

"It isn't money."

"He have something on you?"

"No."

"Then why not just dump him?"

You're not going to divorce me, Shea. Not you, not like the others. I'll see you dead first. I mean it, Shea. You're mine and you'll stay mine until I decide I don't want you anymore. . . .

She said flatly, "I'm not going to talk about my marriage to you. I don't know you."

"We can fix that. I'm an easy guy to know."

She moved ahead to the dresser, found underwear and socks, put them on the bed with the trousers and pullover. "You can change in here," she said, and started for the doorway.

Tanner didn't move.

"I said—"

"I heard you, Shea."

"Mrs. Clifford."

"Clifford," he said. Then he smiled, the same wolfish lip-stretch he'd shown her in the kitchen. "Sure—Clifford. Your husband's name wouldn't be John, would it? John Clifford?"

She was silent.

"I'll bet it is. John Clifford, Clifford Yacht Designs. One of the best marine architects in Miami. Fancy motor sailers and racing yawls."

She still said nothing.

"House in Miami Beach, another on Salt Cay—this house. And you're his latest wife. Which is it, number three or number four?"

Between her teeth she said, "Three."

"He must be what, fifty now? And worth millions. Don't tell me money's not why you married him."

"I won't tell you anything."

But his wealth wasn't why she'd married him. He had been kind and attentive to her at first. And she'd been lonely after the bitter breakup with Neal. John had opened up a whole new, exciting world to her: travel to exotic places, sailing, the company of interesting and famous people. She hadn't loved him, but she had been fond of him; and she'd convinced herself she would learn to love him in time. Instead, when he revealed his dark side to her, she had learned to hate him.

Tanner said, "Didn't one of his other wives divorce him for knocking her around when he was drunk? Seems I remember reading something like that in the Miami papers a few years back. That why you're unhappy, Shea? He knock *you* around when he's drinking?"

Without answering, Shea pushed past him into the hallway. He didn't try to stop her. In the kitchen again, she poured yet another cup of coffee and sat down with it. Even with her coat on and the furnace turned up, she was still cold. The heat from the mug failed to warm her hands.

She knew she ought to be afraid of Harry Tanner. But all she felt inside was a deep weariness. An image of Windflaw Point, the tiny beach with its treacherous undertow, flashed across the screen of her mind—and was gone again just as swiftly. Her courage, or maybe her cowardice, was gone too. She was no longer capable of walking out to the point, letting the sea have her. Not tonight and probably not ever again.

She sat listening to the wind clamor outside. It moaned in the twisted branches of the banyan tree; scraped palm fronds against the roof tiles. Through the open window jalousies she could smell ozone mixed with the sweet fragrances of white ginger blooms. The new storm would be here soon in all its fury.

The wind kept her from hearing Tanner reenter the kitchen. She sensed his presence, looked up, and saw him standing there with his eyes on her like probes. He'd put on all of John's clothing and found a pair of Reeboks for his feet. In his left hand he held the waterproof belt that had been strapped around his waist.

"Shirt's a little snug," he said, "but a pretty good fit otherwise. Your husband's got nice taste."

Shea didn't answer.

"In clothing, in houses, and in women."

She sipped her coffee, not looking at him.

Tanner limped around the table and sat down across from her. When he laid the belt next to the bottle of rum, the pouch that bulged made a thunking sound. "Boats too," he said. "I'll bet he keeps his best designs for himself; he's the kind that would. Am I right, Shea?"

"Yes."

"How many boats does he own?"

"Two."

"One's bound to be big. Oceangoing yacht?"

"Seventy-foot custom schooner."

"What's her name?"

"Moneybags."

Tanner laughed. "Some sense of humor."

"If you say so."

"Where does he keep her? Here or Miami?"

"Miami."

"She there now?"

"Yes."

"And the other boat? That one berthed here?"

"The harbor at Merrywing."

"What kind is she?"

"A sloop," Shea said. *"Carib Princess."*

"How big?"

"Thirty-two feet."

"She been back and forth across the Stream?"

"Several times, in good weather."

"With you at the helm?"

"No."

"You ever take her out by yourself?"

"No. He wouldn't allow it."

"But you can handle her, right? You said you know boats. You can pilot that little sloop without any trouble?"

"Why do you want to know that? Why are you asking so many questions about John's boats?"

"John's boats, John's houses, John's third wife." Tanner laughed again, just a bark this time. The wolfish smile pulled his mouth out of shape. "Are you afraid of me, Shea?"

"No."

"Not even a little?"

"Why? Should I be?"

"What do you think?"

"I'm not afraid of you," she said.

"Then how come you lied to me?"

"Lied? About what?"

"Your husband. Old John Clifford."

"I don't know what you mean."

"You said he'd be home soon. But he won't be. He's not in town with friends, he's not even on the island."

She stared silently at the steam rising from her cup. Her fingers felt cramped, as if she might be losing circulation in them.

"Well, Shea? That's the truth, isn't it?"

"Yes. That's the truth."

"Where is he? Miami?"

She nodded.

"Went there on business and left you all by your lonesome."

"It isn't the first time."

"Might be the last, though." Tanner reached for the rum bottle, poured some of the dark liquid into his mug, drank, and then smacked his lips. "You want a shot of this?"

"No."

"Loosen you up a little."

"I don't need loosening up."

"You might after I tell you the truth about Henry Tanner."

"Does that mean you lied to me too?"

"I'm afraid so. But you fessed up and now it's my turn."

In the blackness outside, the wind gusted sharply, banging a loose shutter somewhere at the front of the house. Rain began to pelt down with open-faucet suddenness.

"Listen to that," Tanner said. "Sounds like we're in for a big blow this time."

"What did you lie about?"

"Well, let's see. For starters, about how I came to be

in the water tonight. My bugeye ketch didn't sink in the squall. No, *Wanderer*'s tied up at a dock in Charlotte Amalie."

She sat stiffly, waiting.

"Boat I was on didn't sink, either," Tanner said. "At least as far as I know it didn't. I jumped overboard. Not long after the squall hit us."

There was still nothing for her to say.

"If I hadn't gone overboard, the two guys I was with would've shot me dead. They tried to shoot me in the water but the ketch was pitching like crazy and they couldn't see me in the dark and the rain. I guess they figured I'd drown even with a life jacket on. Or the sharks or barracuda would get me."

Still nothing.

"We had a disagreement over money. That's what most things come down to these days—money. They thought I cheated them out of twenty thousand dollars down in Jamaica, and they were right, I did. They both put guns on me before I could do anything and I thought I was a dead man. The squall saved my bacon. Big swell almost broached us, knocked us all off our feet. I managed to scramble up the companionway and go over the side before they recovered."

The hard beat of the rain stopped as suddenly as it had begun. Momentary lull: the full brunt of the storm was minutes away yet.

"I'm not a single-hander," he said, "not a sea tramp. That's another thing I lied about. Ask me what it is I really am, Shea. Ask me how I make my living."

"I don't have to ask."

"No? Think you know?"

"Smuggling. You're a smuggler."

"That's right. Smart lady."

"Drugs, I suppose."

"Drugs, weapons, liquor, the wretched poor yearning to breathe free without benefit of a green card. You name it, I've handled it. Hell, smuggling's a tradition in these waters. Men have been doing it for three hundred years, since the days of the Spanish Main." He laughed. "A modern freebooter, that's what I am. Tanner the Pirate. Yo ho ho and a bottle of rum."

"Why are you telling me all this?"

"Why not? Don't you find it interesting?"

"No."

"Okay, I'll give it to you straight. I've got a problem—a big problem. I jumped off that ketch tonight with one thing besides the clothes on my back, and it wasn't money." He pulled the waterproof belt to him, unsnapped the pouch that bulged, and showed her what was inside. "Just this."

Her gaze registered the weapon—automatic, large-caliber, lightweight frame—and slid away. She was not surprised; she had known there was a gun in the pouch when it made the thunking sound.

Tanner set it on the table within easy reach. "My two partners got my share of a hundred thousand from the Jamaica run. I might be able to get it back from them and I might not; they're a couple of hard cases and I'm not sure it's worth the risk. But I can't do anything until I quit this island. And I can't leave the usual ways because my money and my passport are both on that damn ketch. You see my dilemma, Shea?"

"I see it."

"Sure you do. You're a smart lady, like I said. What else do you see? The solution?"

She shook her head.

"Well, I've got a dandy." The predatory grin again. "You know, this really is turning into my lucky night. I couldn't have washed up in a better spot if I'd planned it. John Clifford's house, John Clifford's smart and pretty wife. And not far away, John Clifford's little sloop, the *Carib Princess*."

The rain came again, wind-driven, with enough force to rattle the windows. Spray blew in through the screens behind the open jalousies. Shea made no move to get up and close the glass. Tanner didn't even seem to notice the moisture.

"Here's what we're going to do," he said. "At dawn we'll drive in to the harbor. You do have a car here? Sure you do; he wouldn't leave you isolated without wheels. Once we get there we go onboard the sloop and you take her out. If anybody you know sees us and says anything, you tell them I'm a friend or a relative and John said it was okay for us to go for a sail without him."

She asked dully, "Then what?"

"Once we're out to sea? I'm not going to kill you and dump your body overboard, if that's worrying you.

The only thing that's going to happen is we sail the
Carib Princess across the Stream to Florida. A little
place I know on the west coast up near Pavilion Key
where you can sneak a boat in at night and keep her
hidden for as long as you need to."

"And then?"

"Then I call your husband and we do some business.
How much do you think he'll pay to get his wife and
his sloop back safe and sound? Five hundred thousand? As much as a million?"

"My God," she said. "You're crazy."

"Like a fox."

"You couldn't get away with it. You *can't.*"

"I figure I can. You think he won't pay because the
marriage is on the rocks? You're wrong, Shea. He'll
pay, all right. He's the kind that can't stand losing anything that belongs to him, wife or boat, and sure as hell
not both at once. Plus he's had enough bad publicity;
ignoring a ransom demand would hurt his image and
his business and I'll make damned sure he knows it."

She shook her head again—a limp, rag-doll wob-
bling, as if it were coming loose from the stem of her
neck.

"Don't look so miserable," Tanner said cheerfully.
"I'm not such a bad guy when you get to know me, and
there'll be plenty of time for us to get acquainted. And
when old John pays off, I'll leave you with the sloop
and you can sail her back to Miami. Okay? Give you
my word on that."

He was lying: his word was worthless. He'd told her his name, the name of his ketch and where it was berthed; he wouldn't leave her alive to identify him. Not on the Florida coast. Not even here.

Automatically Shea picked up her mug, tilted it to her mouth. Dregs. Empty. She pushed back her chair, crossed to the counter, and poured the mug full again. Tanner sat relaxed, smiling, pleased with himself. The rising steam from the coffee formed a screen between them, so that she saw him as blurred, distorted. Not quite human, the way he had first seemed to her when he came out of the sea earlier.

Jumbee, she thought. Smiling evil.

The gale outside flung sheets of water at the house. The loose shutter chattered like a jackhammer until the wind slackened again.

Tanner said, "Going to be a long wet night." He made a noisy yawning sound. "Where do you sleep, Shea?"

The question sent a spasm through her body.

"Your bedroom—where is it?"

Oh God. "Why?"

"I told you, it's going to be a long night. And I'm tired and my foot hurts and I want to lie down. But I don't want to lie down alone. We might as well start getting to know each other the best way there is."

No, she thought. No, no, no.

"Well, Shea? Lead the way."

No, she thought again. But her legs worked as if with a will of their own, carried her back to the table.

Tanner sat forward as she drew abreast of him, started to lift himself out of the chair.

She threw the mug of hot coffee into his face.

She hadn't planned to do it, acted without thinking; it was almost as much of a surprise to her as it was to him. He yelled and pawed at his eyes, his body jerking so violently that both he and the chair toppled over sideways. Shea swept the automatic off the table and backed away with it extended at arm's length.

Tanner kicked the chair away and scrambled unsteadily to his feet. Bright red splotches stained his cheeks where the coffee had scalded him; his eyes were murderous. He took a step toward her, stopped when he realized she was pointing his own weapon at him. She watched him struggle to regain control of himself and the situation.

"You shouldn't have done that, Shea."

"Stay where you are."

"That gun isn't loaded."

"It's loaded. I know guns too."

"You won't shoot me." He took another step.

"I will. Don't come any closer."

"No you won't. You're not the type. I can pull the trigger on a person real easy. Have, more than once." Another step. "But not you. You don't have what it takes."

"Please don't make me shoot you. Please, please don't."

"See? You won't do it because you can't."

"Please."

"You won't shoot me, Shea."

On another night, any other night, he would have been right. But on this night—

He lunged at her.

And she shot him.

The impact of the high-caliber bullet brought him up short, as if he had walked into an invisible wall. A look of astonishment spread over his face. He took one last convulsive step before his hands came up to clutch at his chest and his knees buckled.

Shea didn't see him fall; she turned away. And the hue and the cry of the storm kept her from hearing him hit the floor. When she looked again, after several seconds, he lay facedown and unmoving on the tiles. She did not have to go any closer to tell that he was dead.

There was a hollow queasiness in her stomach. Otherwise she felt nothing. She turned again, and there was a blank space of time, and then she found herself sitting on one of the chairs in the living room. She would have wept then but she had no tears. She had cried herself dry on the terrace.

After a while she became aware that she still gripped Tanner's automatic. She set it down on an end table; hesitated, then picked it up again. The numbness was finally leaving her mind, a swift release that brought her thoughts into sharpening focus. When the wind and rain lulled again she stood, walked slowly down the hall to her bedroom. She steeled herself as she opened the door and turned on the lights.

From where he lay sprawled across the bed, John's

sightless eyes stared up at her. The stain of blood on his bare chest, drying now, gleamed darkly in the lamp glow.

Wild night, mad night.

She hadn't been through hell just once, she'd been through it twice. First in here and then in the kitchen.

But she hadn't shot John. She hadn't. He'd come home at nine, already drunk, and tried to make love to her, and when she denied him he'd slapped her, kept slapping her. After three long hellish years she couldn't take it anymore, not anymore. She'd managed to get the revolver out of her nightstand drawer . . . not to shoot him, just as a threat to make him leave her alone. But he'd lunged at her, in almost the same way Tanner had, and they'd struggled, and the gun had gone off. And John Clifford was dead.

She had started to call the police. Hadn't because she knew they would not believe it was an accident. John was well liked and highly respected on Salt Cay; his public image was untarnished and no one, not even his close friends, believed his second wife's divorce claim or that he could ever mistreat anyone. She had never really been accepted here—some of the cattier rich women thought she was a gold digger—and she had no friends of her own in whom she could confide. John had seen to that. There were no marks on her body to prove it, either; he'd always been very careful not to leave marks.

The island police would surely have claimed she'd killed him in cold blood. She'd have been arrested and tried and convicted and put in a prison much worse than the one in which she had lived the past three years. The prospect of that was unbearable. It was what had driven her out onto the terrace, to sit and think about the undertow at Windflaw Point. The sea, in those moments, had seemed her only way out.

Now there was another way.

Her revolver lay on the floor where it had fallen. John had given it to her when they were first married, because he was away so much; and he had taught her how to use it. It was one of three handguns he'd bought illegally in Miami.

Shea bent to pick it up. With a corner of the bedsheet she wiped the grip carefully, then did the same with Tanner's automatic. That gun too, she was certain, would not be registered anywhere.

Wearily she put the automatic in John's hand, closing his fingers around it. Then she retreated to the kitchen and knelt to place the revolver in Tanner's hand. The first aid kit was still on the table; she would use it once more, when she finished talking to the chief constable in Merrywing.

We tried to help Tanner, John and I, she would tell him. And he repaid our kindness by attempting to rob us at gunpoint. John told him we kept money in our bedroom; he took the gun out of the nightstand before I could stop him. They shot each other. John died instantly, but Tanner didn't believe his wound was as serious as it was. He made me bandage it and then kept me in the kitchen, threatening to kill me too. I managed to catch him off guard and throw coffee in his face. When he tried to come after me the strain aggravated his wound and he collapsed and died.

If this were Miami, or one of the larger Caribbean islands, she could not hope to get away with such a story. But here the native constabulary was unsophisticated and inexperienced because there was so little crime on Salt Cay. They were much more likely to overlook the fact that John had been shot two and a half hours before Harry Tanner. Much more likely, too, to credit a double homicide involving a stranger, particularly when they investigated Tanner's background, than the accidental shooting of a respected resident who had been abusing his wife. Yes, she might just get away with it. If there was any justice left for her in this world, she would—and one day she'd leave Salt Cay a free woman again.

Out of the depths, she thought as she picked up the phone. Out of the depths. . . .

Writers are notoriously poor judges of their own work, a phenomenon which may be operating in the present case. People who like "The Pattern" really like it. Ed Gorman and Cemetery Dance*'s editor and publisher, Rich Chizmar, for instance; both consider it among my half dozen best dark-suspense tales. Very gratifying, of course, and they may well be right. Still, while I obviously like the story myself or it wouldn't be included here, I'd rank it somewhere in the lower middle of the pack of the fifty or so that I've written. See what you think. The reader, as always, has the last word.*

The Pattern

At 11:23 P.M. on Saturday, the twenty-sixth of April, a small man wearing rimless glasses and a dark gray business suit walked into the detective squad room in San Francisco's Hall of Justice and confessed to the murders of three Bay Area housewives whose bodies had been found that afternoon and evening.

Inspector Glenn Rauxton, who first spoke to the small man, thought he might be a crank. Every major homicide in any large city draws its share of oddballs and mental cases, individuals who confess to crimes in order to attain public recognition in otherwise unsubstantial lives; or because of some secret desire for punishment; or for any number of reasons that can be found in the casebooks of police psychiatrists. But it wasn't up to Rauxton to make a decision either way. He left the small man in the company of his partner, Dan Tobias, and went in to talk to his immediate superior, Lieutenant Jack Sheffield.

"We've got a guy outside who says he's the killer of those three women today, Jack," Rauxton said. "Maybe a crank, maybe not."

Sheffield turned away from the portable typewriter at the side of his desk; he had been making out a report for the chief's office. "He come in of his own volition?"

Rauxton nodded. "Not three minutes ago."

"What's his name?"

"He says it's Andrew Franzen."

"And his story?"

"So far, just that he killed them," Rauxton said. "I didn't press him. He seems pretty calm about the whole thing."

"Well, run his name through the weirdo file, and then put him in one of the interrogation cubicles," Sheffield said. "I'll look through the reports again before we question him."

"You want me to get a stenographer?"

"It would probably be a good idea."

"Right," Rauxton said, and went out.

Sheffield rubbed his face wearily. He was a lean, sinewy man in his late forties, with thick graying hair and a falconic nose. He had dark brown eyes that had seen most everything there was to see, and been appalled by a good deal of it; they were tired, sad eyes. He wore a plain blue suit, and his shirt was open at the throat. The tie he had worn to work when his tour started at 4:00 P.M., which had been given to him by his wife and consisted of interlocking, psychedelic-colored concentric circles, was out of sight in the bottom drawer of his desk.

He picked up the folder with the preliminary information on the three slayings and opened it. Most of it was sketchy telephone communications from the involved police forces in the Bay Area, a precursory report from the local lab, a copy of the police telex that he had sent out statewide as a matter of course following the discovery of the first body, and that had later alerted the other authorities in whose areas the two subsequent corpses had been found. There was also an Inspector's Report on that first and only death in San Francisco, filled out and signed by Rauxton. The last piece of information had come in less than a half hour earlier, and he knew the facts of the case by memory; but Sheffield was a meticulous cop and he liked to have all the details fixed in his mind.

The first body was of a woman named Janet Flanders, who had been discovered by a neighbor at 4:15 that afternoon in her small duplex on 39th Avenue, near Golden Gate Park. She had been killed by several blows about the head with an as yet unidentified blunt instrument.

The second body, of one Viola Gordon, had also been found by a neighbor—shortly before 5:00 P.M.—in her neat, white frame cottage in South San Francisco. Cause of death: several blows about the head with an unidentified blunt instrument.

The third body, Elaine Dunhill, had been discovered at 6:37 P.M. by a casual acquaintance who had stopped by to return a borrowed book. Mrs. Dunhill lived in a modest cabin-style home clinging to the wooded hillside above Sausalito Harbor, just north of San Francisco. She, too, had died as a result of several blows about the head with an unidentified blunt instrument.

There were no witnesses, or apparent clues, in any of the killings. They would have, on the surface, appeared to be unrelated if it had not been for the fact that each of the three women had died on the same day, and in the same manner. But there were other cohesive factors as well—factors that, taken in conjunction with the surface similarities, undeniably linked the murders.

Item: each of the three women had been between the ages of thirty and thirty-five, on the plump side, and blond.

Item: each of them had been orphaned nonnatives of California, having come to the San Francisco Bay Area from different parts of the Midwest within the past six years.

Item: each of them had been married to traveling salesmen who were home only short periods each month, and who were all—according to the information garnered by investigating officers from neighbors and friends—currently somewhere on the road.

Patterns, Sheffield thought as he studied the folder's contents. Most cases had one, and this case was no exception. All you had to do was fit the scattered pieces of its particular pattern together, and you would have your answer. Yet the pieces here did not seem to join logically, unless you concluded that the killer of the women was a psychopath who murdered blond, thirtyish, orphaned wives of traveling salesmen for some perverted reason of his own.

That was the way the news media would see it, Sheffield knew, because that kind of slant always sold copies, and attracted viewers and listeners. They would try to make the case into another Zodiac thing. The radio newscast he had heard at the cafeteria across Bryant Street, when he had gone out for supper around nine, had presaged the discovery of still more bodies of Bay Area housewives and had advised all women whose husbands were away to remain behind locked doors. The announcer had repeatedly referred to the deaths as "the bludgeon slayings."

Sheffield had kept a strictly open mind. It was, for all practical purposes, his case—the first body had been found in San Francisco, during his tour, and that gave him jurisdiction in handling the investigation. The cops in the two other involved cities would be in constant touch with him, as they already had been. He would have been foolish to have made any premature speculations not based solely on fact, and Sheffield was anything but foolish. Anyway, psychopath or not, the case still promised a hell of a lot of not very pleasant work.

Now, however, there was Andrew Franzen.

Crank? Or multiple murderer? Was this going to be one of those blessed events—a simple case? Or was Franzen only the beginning of a long series of very large headaches?

Well, Sheffield thought, we'll find out soon enough. He closed the folder and got to his feet and crossed to the door of his office.

In the squad room, Rauxton was just finishing a computer check. He came over to Sheffield and said, "Nothing on Franzen in the weirdo file, Jack."

Sheffield inclined his head and looked off toward the row of glass-walled interrogation cubicles at the rear of the squad room. In the second one, he could see Dan Tobias propped on a corner of the bare metal desk inside; the man who had confessed, Andrew Franzen, was sitting with his back to the squad room, stiffly erect in his chair. Also waiting inside, stoically seated in the near corner, was one of the police stenographers.

Sheffield said, "Okay, Glenn, let's hear what he has to say."

He and Rauxton went over to the interrogation cubicle and stepped inside. Tobias stood, shook his head almost imperceptibly to let Sheffield and Rauxton know that Franzen hadn't said anything to him. Tobias was tall and muscular, with a slow smile and big hands and—like Rauxton—a strong dedication to the life's work he had chosen.

He moved to the right corner of the metal desk, and Rauxton to the left corner, assuming set positions like football halfbacks running a bread-and-butter play. Sheffield, the quarterback, walked behind the desk, cocked one hip against the edge, and leaned forward slightly, so that he was looking down at the small man sitting with his hands flat on his thighs.

Franzen had a round, inoffensive pink face with tiny-shelled ears and a Cupid's-bow mouth. His hair was brown and wavy, immaculately cut and shaped, and it saved him from being nondescript; it gave him a certain boyish character, even though Sheffield placed his age at around forty. His eyes were brown and liquid, like those of a spaniel, behind his rimless glasses.

Sheffield got a ballpoint pen out of his coat pocket and tapped it lightly against his front teeth; he liked to have something in his hands when he was conducting an interrogation. He broke the silence, finally, by saying, "My name is Sheffield. I'm the lieutenant in charge here. Now before you say anything, it's my duty to advise you of your rights."

He did so, quickly and tersely, concluding with, "You understand all of your rights as I've outlined them, Mr. Franzen?"

The small man sighed softly and nodded.

"Are you willing, then, to answer questions without the presence of counsel?"

217

"Yes, yes."

Sheffield continued to tap the ballpoint pen against his front teeth. "All right," he said at length. "Let's have your full name."

"Andrew Leonard Franzen."

"Where do you live?"

"Here in San Francisco."

"At what address?"

"Nine-oh-six Greenwich."

"Is that a private residence?"

"No, it's an apartment building."

"Are you employed?"

"Yes."

"Where?"

"I'm an independent consultant."

"What sort of consultant?"

"I design languages between computers."

Rauxton said, "You want to explain that?"

"It's very simple, really," Franzen said tonelessly. "If two business firms have different types of computers, and would like to set up a communication between them so that the information stored in the memory banks of each computer can be utilized by the other, they call me. I design the linking electronic connections between the two computers, so that each can understand the other; in effect, so that they can converse."

"That sounds like a very specialized job," Sheffield said.

"Yes."

"What kind of salary do you make?"

"Around eighty thousand a year."

Two thin, horizontal lines appeared in Sheffield's forehead. Franzen had the kind of vocation that bespoke intelligence and upper-class respectability; why would a man like that want to confess to the brutal murders of three simple-living housewives? Or an even more puzzling question: If his confession was genuine, what was his reason for the killings?

Sheffield said, "Why did you come here tonight, Mr. Franzen?"

"To confess." Franzen looked at Rauxton. "I told this man that when I walked in a few minutes ago."

"To confess to what?"

"The murders."

"What murders, specifically?"

Franzen sighed. "The three women in the Bay Area today."

"Just the three?"

"Yes."

"No others whose bodies maybe have not been discovered as yet?"

"No, no."

"Suppose you tell me why you decided to turn yourself in?"

"Why? Because I'm guilty. Because I killed them."

"And that's the only reason?"

Franzen was silent for a moment. Then slowly, he said, "No, I suppose not. I went walking in Aquatic Park when I came back to San Francisco this afternoon, just walking and thinking. The more I thought, the more I knew that it was hopeless. It was only a matter of time before you found out I was the one, a matter of a day or two. I guess I could have run, but I wouldn't know how to begin to do that. I've always done things on impulse, things I would never do if I stopped to think about them. That's how I killed them, on some insane impulse; if I had thought about it I never would have done it. It was so useless. . . ."

Sheffield exchanged glances with the two inspectors. Then he said, "You want to tell us how you did it, Mr. Franzen?"

"What?"

"How did you kill them?" Sheffield asked. "What kind of weapon did you use?"

"A tenderizing mallet. One of those big wooden things with serrated ends that women keep in the kitchen to tenderize a piece of steak."

It was silent in the cubicle now. Sheffield looked at Rauxton, and then at Tobias; they were all thinking the same thing: the police had released no details to the news media as to the kind of weapon involved in the slayings, other than the general information that it was a blunt instrument. But the initial lab report on the first victim—and the preliminary observations on the other two—stated the wounds of each had been made by a roughly square-shaped instrument, which had sharp "teeth" capable of making a series of deep indentations as it bit into the flesh. A mallet such as Franzen had just described fitted those characteristics exactly.

Sheffield asked, "What did you do with the mallet, Mr. Franzen?"

"I threw it away."

"Where?"

"In Sausalito, into some bushes along the road."

"Do you remember the location?"

"I think so."

"Then you can lead us there later on?"

"I suppose so, yes."

"Was Elaine Dunhill the last woman you killed?"

"Yes."

"What room did you kill her in?"

"The bedroom."

"Where in the bedroom?"

"Beside her vanity."

"Who was your first victim?" Rauxton asked.

"Janet Flanders."

"You killed her in the bathroom, is that right?"

"No, no, in the kitchen . . ."

"What was she wearing?"

"A flowered housecoat."

"Why did you strip her body?"

"I didn't. Why would I—"

"Mrs. Gordon was the middle victim, right?" Tobias asked.

"Yes."

"Where did you kill her?"

"The kitchen."

"She was sewing, wasn't she?"

"No, she was canning," Franzen said. "She was canning plum preserves. She had mason jars and boxes of plums and three big pressure cookers all over the table and stove . . ."

There was wetness in Franzen's eyes now. He stopped talking and took his rimless glasses off and wiped at the tears with the back of his left hand. He seemed to be swaying slightly on the chair.

Sheffield, watching him, felt a curious mixture of relief and sadness. The relief was due to the fact that there was no doubt in his mind—nor in the minds of Rauxton and Tobias; he could read their eyes—that Andrew Franzen was the slayer of the three women. They had thrown detail and "trip-up" questions at him, one right after another, and he had had all the right answers; he knew particulars that had also not been given to the news media, that no crank could possibly have known, that only the murderer could have been aware of. The case had turned out to be one of the simple ones, after all, and it was all but wrapped up now; there would be no more "bludgeon slayings," no public hue and cry, no attacks on police inefficiency in the press, no pressure from the commissioners or the mayor. The sadness was the result of twenty-six years of police work, of living with death and crime every day, of looking at a man who seemed to be the essence of normalcy and yet who was a cold-blooded multiple murderer.

Why? Sheffield thought. That was the big question. Why did he do it?

He said, "You want to tell us the reason, Mr. Franzen? Why you killed them?"

The small man moistened his lips. "I was very happy, you see. My life had some meaning, some challenge. I was fulfilled—but they were going to destroy everything." He stared at his hands. "One of them had found out the truth—I don't know how—and tracked down the other two. I had come to Janet this morning, and she told me that they were going to expose me, and I just lost my head and picked up the mallet and killed her. Then I went to the others and killed them. I couldn't stop myself; it was as if I were moving in a nightmare."

"What are you trying to say?" Sheffield asked. "What was your relationship with those three women?"

The tears in Andrew Franzen's eyes shone like tiny diamonds in the light from the overhead fluorescents.

"They were my wives," he said.

In the sixties and seventies I perpetrated a fair amount of fantasy and science fiction, much of it with Barry Malzberg and the majority of it eminently forgettable. Of all the s-f with my name on it, I like maybe six stories—four collaborations, including a 10,000-word satire on hack-writing called "Prose Bowl" that some critics consider a minor classic, and two solo efforts. "The Rec Field" is one of the solos, a blend of s-f and psychological suspense whose payoff line gave me a small chill when I wrote it in 1979. It surprised me with another when I reread it recently, hence its inclusion here.

The Rec Field

We'd been on Repair Outpost 217-C for thirty-four months when Renzo got the idea to build a rec field.

One of us should have thought of it long before that. Except for compu-disks, the only recreation we had was cards and chess and backgammon—indoor games that neither of us cared for much. The thing was, we'd both been raised on outdoor sports. Soccer was Renzo's game and baseball was mine; we would talk soccer and baseball for hours, the classic professional contests, the matchups we'd been involved in ourselves when we were kids back home. Funny how the mind works. All those hours of sports talk and it still took thirty-four months for one of us to suggest a rec field of our own.

But then, I guess maybe we'd both blocked off the idea because of the conditions we were working under. Like 217-C itself. It was an uninhabited dwarf planet located just outside the Company's C-Sector shipping lanes, most of it igneous rock and volcanic ash, with here and there little clusters of trees and patches of bright green grass. Gravity was within 2.3 of Earth's, axis rotation was 21.40 Earth hours, but the atmosphere was low in oxygen; you could breathe it without a life-pac, only not if you were doing anything strenuous and not for more than a couple of hours at a time. And the weather was bad; hot and dank all the time, day and night, with a dense cloud cover always hanging low overhead that made even the daylight a dark gray. We never once saw the planet's sun nor either of its two tiny moons.

Another thing was that we didn't have any equipment—balls, bats, things like that—and no way of getting any sent in. The Company refused to stock the drone supply ship that came from Sector Base every six months with what they called "frivolous material"; the compu-disks were the only concession they made. And we couldn't leave the outpost ourselves, because if we did we would forfeit all of our accumulated wages. We were aware of that when we signed on, of course; it was in the Company contract. They paid enormous salaries, but the catch was that you had to sign on for a full six years and they withheld all your credits until those six years were up.

If any other human beings had come to 217-C we *could* have asked them to bring us the stuff we needed on a return trip. But in all our thirty-four months the only other man we'd laid eyes on was Dietrich, the Sector Chief, who came in every fifteen months or so on a routine inspection tour. Each of the freighters that were forced to veer in from the lanes for refueling or repairs was a drone, which were cheaper to operate than manned ships. If the Company could have figured a way to run outposts like this with Mechanicals instead of skilled mechanics, I suppose they would have done it. But they hadn't and so here we were— Renzo and me.

We got along pretty well from the first, Renzo and me, but even two people with common interests—and we had plenty of them besides sports; that was why we'd been selected to work together as a team—can get on each other's nerves after a while. Particularly in a place like this, where there was no sunlight or moonlight and everything was colorless except for the trees and those beautiful patches of bright green grass. We might even have turned against each other if it hadn't been for the mind-psychs the Company performed on all of its employees. They said the mind-psychs were to keep you from thinking about women and sex and family ties back home, but they were also to keep you from fighting with your partner; they didn't tell you that because they didn't want you worrying about it going in.

As it was, we'd stopped talking to each other for days at a time when Renzo came up with the idea for the rec field. Then all the friction disappeared and we were as close as we'd been in the early months. It was almost like being reborn.

We went to work right away. The first thing we did was to draw up plans and then keep on redrafting them until we had the field laid out exactly the way we wanted it. It would be a hundred and fifty meters long and a hundred meters wide. It would be enclosed on three sides by a curving wooden fence three meters high; the fourth side would be four rows of spectators' seats, even though no spectators would ever sit in them, because we agreed the field should look as authentic as possible. It would be floored in that bright green grass, except for base paths and a pitching mound and home plate area for baseball, and it would have soccer goals and dugout benches and all the other necessary items.

It would be the best damn rec field anybody ever built spaceward of Earth.

Once we were satisfied with the plans, we went looking for the best possible site. It took us two days to settle on one that pleased both of us. The spot we picked was behind and to the east of the bubble we lived in, at the edge of the compound and right up close to the biggest cluster of trees and patch of grass.

We started construction the next day. We measured

distances, staked them out, and cleared the area of ash and rock. With laser tools from the repair hangar, we cut down trees and shaped them into boards and posts of different sizes. We dug holes for fence posts and the soccer goals and home plate on the baseball diamond. We used a thermosetting resin to bind joints and lock the bleacher sections together.

At the end of eight months—forty-two months altogether on Outpost 217-C—we had the field roughed out; the fence and bleachers built. We considered painting everything, but the only duropaint we had was gray, the color of the Company freighters and the color of the surroundings, and we weren't about to use that. Besides, the natural wood color looked fine. And it would look even better once we got the grass put in.

That was our next project, the grass. We dug up blocks of sod a half meter square and carried them to the field and laid them down carefully to form the baseball diamond and the soccer rectangle. When that job was finished we set to work on the dugout benches and the goals. And when they were done we laser-carved a rock into a replica of home plate, put it down, manufactured three bases and two goal nets out of supply material, and put those in place.

By that time we had been working on the field a few days short of eleven months. We weren't quite finished yet—there were a few small things to be taken care of, and one major problem to be solved, before we could begin to use it—but in essence it was done. And done right, just as we had planned it.

Renzo and I stood admiring it after we'd tied the last goal net into place. "You ever see anything so god-damn fine in all your life?" he said.

"No," I said, "never."

"All the work was worth it, Alex. If it hadn't been for the field, the past eleven months would've been rough—a hell of a lot rougher than the first thirty-four."

"I know," I said. "But we've got it made now; once we start the games, the next twenty-seven will be even easier."

"We'll play soccer first, when everything's ready," he said. "That all right with you?"

"Sure. Soccer it is."

A little while later, when the heat got to be unbearable, we went back to the bubble to rest and take some nourishment. And while we were eating a message came through from Sector Base, the first one we'd had since an outbound freighter was diverted in for airlock repairs three months ago: Sector Chief Dietrich was on his way to 217-C for another inspection and was scheduled to arrive in sixty-two hours. Renzo and I were to get everything ready for him, including the spare quarters; he was planning to stay at least overnight.

The news didn't interest either of us as much as it might have before we began building the rec field. It had been fifteen months since Dietrich's last visit—fifteen months since we had seen another human being—but we were still pretty excited about the way the field had turned out. And neither of us liked Dietrich much anyway. He was a strict Company man, the kind that let you know you were only a drone yourself, not much different than the fleet of ships that were under his supervision. He didn't like sports, either. I'd tried to talk to him about baseball the first time he'd come for inspection and he hadn't shown the slightest bit of interest.

But after we had acknowledged the message, Renzo said, "You know, the timing for Dietrich's visit isn't bad. Now we'll be able to show off the completed field to him."

"You think he'll approve of it?"

"Sure he will. Why wouldn't he approve of it?"

We spent most of the next three days getting the repair hangar and refueling station and rocket pit ready for Dietrich's inspection. Everything had to be clean, in its proper place, ready for any emergency; if he found anything at all out of line, which he wouldn't, the Company contract said we could get docked for it.

We did manage to do a little more work on the rec field, most of it cosmetic: trimming the grass, sanding rough edges off the fence and the bleacher seats, that sort of thing. Renzo and I had a lot of pride in that field and we wanted it to look as nice as possible for Dietrich.

As scheduled, the Sector Chief's small one-man shuttle vectored in at 0900 hours. When Dietrich had shut off his engines and locked down on the pad, Renzo and I went out and stood waiting near the hatch

231

for the forward airlock. It was another ten minutes before he came out, dressed in his silver-gray Company uniform.

It was good to see another human again, even Dietrich; and he was a pretty impressive figure, you had to admit that. Tall, ageless, big round head with a mat of hair the same silver-gray as his suit, face brown and so smooth it looked polished. Sharp green eyes, bright and cold—the only color anywhere about him. Like the grass and the tree leaves were the only color on 217-C.

The first thing he said was, "Good to see you again, men." But he didn't sound as if he meant it. And he didn't smile or offer to shake hands with either of us. "Everything cope here?"

"Yes, sir," Renzo said. "Everything cope."

Dietrich gave both of us long penetrating looks, like he was trying to establish a telepathic link so he could shuffle through our thoughts. Then he said, "Well, let's get moving," and we left the pad and went straight to the bubble.

But Dietrich didn't want to rest or eat or clean up in his quarters before beginning inspection; he never did. So right away it was through our living area, then into the supply section for an inventory check on the stores, then out to the hangar for another inventory check on the tool and supply bins there.

It was late afternoon before Dietrich finished with the hangar. He seemed satisfied that everything was in order—but not too happy about it, as if he'd *wanted* to find something out of line. He said, "We'll save the rest of the compound for tomorrow. Right now I could use some nourishment."

I said, "Whatever you say, Mr. Dietrich."

On the way back to the bubble Renzo caught my eye and grinned and nodded in the direction of the rec field. Then he said to the Chief, "If you don't mind, sir, there's something Alex and I'd like to show you before we go in."

"Show me?"

"Yes, sir. It won't take long."

"What is it?"

"Something we're kind of proud of."

I could see that Dietrich wasn't much interested in anything we would want to show him, but he shrugged and said, "All right, where is it?"

"Over behind the bubble," Renzo said, and we took him out there and right up near the fence beyond the bleachers, on the first base side of the baseball diamond. "Isn't that a fine-looking recreation field, Mr. Dietrich? Alex and me built it in our spare time over the last twelve months; we just finished it a few days ago."

Dietrich stood looking around at the field for a third of a minute. Then he turned and stared at us. There were wrinkles in his forehead and alongside his nose, and his cold eyes seemed even colder, like frozen green water. "Is this some kind of joke?" he said.

"Sir?"

"There's no recreation field here. There's *nothing* here except bare rock."

Renzo and I both frowned at him. "That's a lie," I said. "The field's right here in front of the trees."

"What trees?" Dietrich said. "There aren't any trees on 217-C. It's a dead world; nothing grows here."

"That's a lie too," Renzo said. "There *are* trees. That's how we built the field. With the trees and the grass."

Dietrich didn't say anything this time. Past him I saw the green field shimmer and seem to fade away for a second, leaving nothing but black and gray. But that was only a trick of the dark daylight, an optical illusion. It was there, all right. It was there.

I said, "You've got no right to say our field isn't here. It's all we've got; it's all we've had for eleven months. If it wasn't for that field we'd both have cracked up a long time ago."

"I think I've heard enough," Dietrich said coldly. He pushed past us and headed toward the bubble.

Renzo said, "Where're you going, Mr. Dietrich?"

"To call for a psych team," he said without looking back.

"Psych team? You think we *have* cracked up."

"It's not up to me to decide that."

"Well, you sure as hell did decide it if you're calling in a psych team." Renzo's face had gone all flushed and squeezed up with anger. I felt the same way; the dark gray things were jumping inside my mind again, the way they had before we started building the field. "Use the insanity clause in our contracts," he said, "to cheat us out of our wages. That's the idea, isn't it? I'd heard the Company did things like that but I never believed it until this minute."

Dietrich just kept on walking, a little faster now, toward the bubble.

I traded a glance with Renzo. Then I took out the laser tool I kept in my toolbelt, lined up, and cut Dietrich down with one clean slice; he didn't make a sound as he fell. Lasering all those trees to build the rec field had made me a pretty good marksman.

We went over and stood above the Sector Chief's body. Neither of us said anything; we didn't have to. After all this time together I was tuned in to Renzo's thoughts and he was tuned in to mine, almost as if we'd become symbiotes. What we were both thinking was that now our last major rec problem was solved.

So without wasting any time we got busy. And just before dark that night we went out onto the field, onto all that beautiful bright green grass, and played our first game of soccer.

We used Dietrich's head for the ball.

My first published story dealt with salmon fishermen plying their trade along the northern California coast, individuals whom I admire for their courage and resilience. "Deathwatch" is also about salmon fishermen—and, even more prominently, about levels of light and dark. This may be the darkest of all my stories, in fact, in more ways than one; an existential nightmare that has left some readers depressed, others annoyed or repelled or both, and still others thoughtful and with a disinclination to turn out the lights. Those in the last group are the ones for whom it was written.

Deathwatch

They just came and told me I'm dying.

I've got first- and second-degree burns over sixty percent of my body, and the doctors—two of them—said it's hopeless, there's nothing they can do. I don't care. It's better this way. Except for the pain. They gave me morphine but it doesn't help. It doesn't keep me from thinking either.

Before the doctors, there were two county cops. And Kjel. The cops told me Pete and Nicky are dead, both of them killed in the explosion. They said Kjel and me were thrown clear, and that he'd come out of it with just minor burns on his face and upper body. They said he hung on to me until another boat showed up and her crew pulled us out of the water. I don't understand that. After what I did, why would he try to save my life?

Kjel told them how it was. The cops didn't say much to me about it, just wanted to know if what Kjel said was the truth. I said it was. But it doesn't make any difference, why or how. I tried to tell them that, and something about the light and the dark, but I couldn't make the words come out. They wouldn't have understood anyway.

After the cops left, Kjel asked to see me. One of the doctors said he had something he wanted to say. But I wouldn't let him come in. I don't want to hear what he has to say. It doesn't matter, and I don't want to see him.

Lila is in the waiting room outside. The same doctor told me that, too. I wouldn't let her come in either. What good would it do to see her, talk to her? There's nothing she can say, nothing I can say—the same as with Kjel. She's been sitting out there sixteen hours, ever since they brought me here from the marina. All that time, sitting out there, waiting.

They have a word for it, what she's doing.

Deathwatch.

The pain . . . oh God, I've never hurt like this. Never. Is this how it feels to burn in hell? An eternity of fire and pain . . . and light? If that's what's in store for me, it won't be so bad if there's light. But what if it's dark down there? Christ, I'm so scared. What if the afterlife is dark, too?

Night Freight

I want to pray but I don't know how. I never went to church much, I never got to know God. The doctors asked if I wanted to see a minister. I said no. What could a minister do for me? Would a minister understand about the light and the dark? I don't think so. Not the way I understand.

The lights in this room are bright, real bright. I asked the doctors to turn the lights up as high as they would go and one of them said he would and he did. But outside, it's night—it's dark. I can see it, the dark, pressing against the window, if I look over that way. I don't look. Dying scares me even more when I look at the night—

I just looked. I couldn't stop myself. The dark, always the dark, trying to swallow the light. But not the black dark that comes with no moon, no stars. Gray dark, softened by fog. High fog tonight, high and heavy, blowing cold. It'll drop by morning, though. There won't be much visibility. But that won't stop the boats from going out. Never has, never will. Wouldn't have stopped us from going out—me and Kjel and Pete and Nicky. It's the season, and the big Kings are running. Christ, it's been a good salmon run this year. One of the best in the last ten. If it keeps up like this, Kjel said this morning, we'll have the mortgage on *The Kingfisher* paid off by the end of the year.

But he said that early this morning, while we were still fishing.

He said that before the dark came and swallowed the light.

It seems like so long ago, what happened this morning. And yet it also seems like it must have been just a minute or two . . .

We were six miles out, finished for the day and on our way in—made limit early, hit a big school of Kings. Whoo-ee! They were practically jumping into the boat. I was in the wheelhouse, working on the automatic depth finder because it'd been acting up a little, wishing we could afford a better one. Wishing, too, that we could afford a Loran navigation system like some of the other skippers had on their boats. Kjel and Pete and Nicky were working the outriggers, hauling in the lines by hand. We didn't have one of those hydraulic winches, either, the kind with an automatic trigger that pulls in a fish as soon as it hits the line. The kind that does all the work for you. We had to do it ourselves.

The big Jimmy diesel was rumbling and throbbing, loud, at three-quarters throttle. I shouldn't have been able to hear them talking out on deck. But I heard. Maybe it was the wind, a trick of the wind. I don't know. It doesn't matter. I heard.

I heard Nicky laugh, and Pete say something that had Lila's name in it, and Kjel said, "Shut up, you damned fool, he'll hear you!"

And Nicky said, "He can't hear inside. Besides, what if he does? He knows already, don't he?"

And Kjel said, "He doesn't know. I hope to Christ he never does."

And Pete said, "Hell, he's got to have an idea.

The whole village knows what a slut he's married to. . . ."

I had a box wrench in my hand. I put it down and walked out there and I said, "What're you talking about? What're you saying about Lila?"

None of them said anything. They all just looked at me. It was a gray morning, no sun. A dark morning, not much light. Getting darker, too. I could see clouds on the horizon, dark hazy things, swallowing the light—swallowing it fast.

I said, "Pete, you called my wife a slut. I heard you."

Kjel said, "Danny, take it easy, he didn't mean nothing—"

I said, "He meant something. He meant it." I reached out and caught Pete by the shirt and threw him up against the port outrigger. He tried to tear my hands loose; I wouldn't let go. "How come, Pete? What do you know about Lila?"

Kjel said, "For Christ's sake, Danny—"

"What do you know, goddamn you!"

Pete was mad. He didn't like me roughing him up like that. And he didn't give a damn if I knew—I guess that was it. He'd only been working for us a few months. He was a stranger in Camaroon Bay. He didn't know me and I didn't know him and he didn't give a damn.

"I know because I was with her," he said. "You poor sap, she's been screwing everybody in the village behind your back. Everybody! Me, Nicky, even Kjel here—"

241

Kjel hit him. He reached in past me and hit Pete and knocked him loose of my hands, almost knocked him overboard. Pete went down. Nicky backed away. Kjel backed away too, looking at me. His face was all twisted up. And dark—dark like the things on the horizon.

"It's true, then," I said. "It's true."

"Danny, listen to me—"

"No," I said.

"It only happened once with her and me. Only once. I tried not to, Danny, Jesus I tried not to but she . . . Danny, listen to me . . ."

"No," I said.

I turned around, I put my back to him and the other two and the dark things on the horizon and I went into the wheelhouse and shut the door and locked it. I didn't feel anything. I didn't think anything either. There was some gasoline in one of the cupboards, for the auxiliary engine. I got the can out and poured the gas on the deckboards and splashed it on the bulkheads.

Outside Kjel was pounding on the door, calling my name.

I lit a match and threw it down.

Nothing happened right away. So I unlocked the door and opened it, and Kjel started in, and I heard him say, "Oh my God!" and he caught hold of me and yanked me through the door.

That was when she blew.

There was a flash of blinding light, I remember that.

And I remember being in the water, I remember seeing flames, I remember the pain. I don't remember anything else until I woke up here in the hospital.

The county cops asked me if I was sorry I did it. I said I was. And I am, but not for the reason they thought. I couldn't tell them the real reason. They wouldn't have understood, because first they'd have had to understand about the light and the dark.

I close my eyes now and I can see my old man's face on the night *he* died. He was a drunk and the liquor killed him, but nobody ever knew why. Except me. He called me into his room that night, I was eleven years old, and he told me why.

"It's the dark, Danny," he said. "I let it swallow all the light." I thought he was babbling. But he wasn't. "Everything is light or dark," he said. "That's what you got to understand. People, places, everything, the whole world—light or dark. You got to reach for the light, Danny. Sunshine and smiles, everything that's light. If you don't you'll let the dark take over, like I did, and the dark will destroy you. Promise me you won't let that happen to you, boy. Promise me you won't."

I promised. And I tried—Christ, Pa, I *tried*. Thirty years I reached for the light. But I couldn't hold onto enough of it, just like you couldn't. The dark kept creeping in, creeping in.

Once I told Lila about the dark and the light. She just laughed. "Is that why you always want to make love with the light on, sleep with the light on?" she said. "You're crazy sometimes, Danny, you know that?" she said.

I should have known then. But I didn't. I thought *she* was light. I reached for her six years ago, and I held her and for a while she lit up my life . . . I thought she was light. But she wasn't, she isn't. Underneath she's the dark. She's always been the dark, swallowing the light piece by piece—with Nicky, with Pete, with all the others. Kjel, too, my best friend. Turning him dark too.

I did it all wrong, Pa. All of it, right to the end. And that's the real reason I'm sorry about what I did this morning.

I shouldn't have blown them up, blown me up. I should have blown *her* up, lit up the dark with the fire and light.

Too late now. I did it all wrong.

And she's still out there, waiting.

The dark out there, waiting.

Deathwatch.

The pain isn't so bad now, the fire on me doesn't burn so hot. The morphine working? No, it isn't the morphine.

Something cool touches my face. I'm not alone in the room anymore.

The bastard with the scythe is here.

But I won't look at him. I won't look at the dark of his clothes and the dark under his hood. I'll look at the light instead . . . up there on the ceiling, the big fluorescent tubes shining down, light shining down, look at the light, reach for the light, the light . . .

And the door opens, I hear it open, and from a long way off I hear Lila's voice say, "I cóuldn't stay away, Danny, I had to see you, I had to come—"

The dark!

A major social problem of our times is the stuff of this mordant little tale. The central premise strikes me as all too possible; if something like it hasn't happened yet, I for one won't be surprised to pick up my morning newspaper one day soon and find an account of a similar occurrence. It should probably be noted that my personal sympathies here are about equally divided between Rennert and Dain and their real-life counterparts. Victims both, victims all.

Home

Rennert unlocked the door to his apartment, thinking that it was good to be home. It had been a long day at the office and he was eager for a dry martini and a quiet dinner. He walked in, shut and relatched the door. The hall, five steps long, led into the living room; when he reached the end of it he stopped suddenly and stood gawping.

A man was sitting on his couch.

Just sitting there, completely at ease, one leg crossed over the other. Middle-aged, nondescript, wearing shabby clothing. And thin, so thin you could see the bones of his skull beneath sparse brown hair and a papery layer of skin and flesh.

It took Rennert a few seconds to recover from his shock. Then he demanded, "Who the hell are you?"

"My name is Dain. Raymond Dain."

"What're you doing in my apartment?"

"Waiting for you."

"For Christ's sake," Rennert said. "I don't know you. I've never seen you before in my life." Which wasn't quite true. There was something vaguely familiar about the man. "How did you get in here?"

"The same way you just came in."

"The door was locked. I locked it this morning—"

"I'm good with locks."

A thread of fear had begun to unwind in Rennert. He was a quiet, timid man who took pains to avoid any potentially dangerous situation. He had no experience with anything like this; he didn't know how to handle it.

"What's the idea?" he said. "What do you want?"

Dain was looking around the room. "This is a nice apartment. Really nice."

"I asked what you want."

"Comfortable. Warm. Everything in good taste."

"None of the furnishings is worth stealing," Rennert said. "There's nothing here worth stealing—you must know that by now. I have twenty dollars in my wallet and about two hundred in my checking account. I work for an insurance company, my salary isn't—"

"I'm not after your money, Mr. Rennert."

". . . So you know my name."

"From the mailbox downstairs."

"If you're not a thief, then what are you?"

"A salesman. That is, I used to be a salesman. Sporting goods. At one time I was the company's top man in California."

"I don't—"

"But then one of the bigger outfits bought us out and right away they began downsizing. They said my salary was too high and my commissions too low, so I was one of the first to be booted out."

"I'm sorry to hear that, but—"

"I couldn't get another job," Dain said. "Everywhere I went they said I was too old. Eventually I lost everything. My wife and I had been living high and on the edge and it didn't take long, less than a year. House, car, all my possessions of any value—everything went. Then my wife went too. I ended up with nothing."

Rennert couldn't think of anything to say. He felt as though he'd walked into the middle of somebody else's nightmare.

"You can't imagine how bad it was," Dain said. "The first year I tried twice to do away with myself. But gradually I came to terms with my situation. Developed a new outlook and started to put my life back together. A long, slow process, but it's going to work out. It's definitely going to work out."

"Well, I'm glad to hear it, but that doesn't explain what you're doing in my apartment. Or give you any right to be here."

Dain got slowly to his feet. Rennert stiffened, but Dain didn't come his way; instead he moved to the undraped picture window and stood peering out.

249

"Quite a view from here," he said. "You can see a lot of the park. On clear days I'll bet you can see the ocean, too."

Rennert said, "That's it, the park."

"What about the park?"

"That's where I've seen you before. Panhandling in the park."

"I don't do that," Dain said in an offended tone. "I've never once resorted to panhandling."

"All right. Wandering around over there then."

"I've seen you in the park too. Several times."

"How did you find out where I live?"

"I followed you the last time. Yesterday."

"Why? Why *me*?"

"You were always alone, whenever I saw you, and I wanted to find out if you lived alone."

"Well, now you know," Rennert said shakily. "I live alone and you live in one of the homeless camps in the park. So what? What's the idea if you don't intend to rob me?"

"I've been existing in one of the camps, yes. I hate it. I hate being homeless."

"I'm sure you do. It has to be rough—"

"You have no idea how rough, Mr. Rennert. Only those of us who've been through it really know."

"I believe that. And I'm sympathetic, I truly am. But I think you'd better leave now."

"Why?"

"Why? Because I don't want you here. Because

you're trespassing. Because you won't tell me why you broke in or what it is you want."

"I did tell you," Dain said. "You weren't listening."

"All you told me is that you've started to put your life back together, and I can't help you with that."

"But you can."

"How? How can I?"

"Isn't it obvious?"

"Not to me. Do you want me to call the police?"

"No."

"Then leave. Just leave, right now. I don't want any trouble with you."

Dain looked at him in silence. A sad, waiting look. No, not sad—hungry.

"Go away," Rennert said desperately, "leave me alone. Don't you understand? I can't do anything for you!"

Dain said, "You're the one who doesn't understand, Mr. Rennert. I told you I hate being homeless and I meant just that. A decent job, possessions, even a wife and family—I can manage without those. But I can't go on, I can't have any kind of life, without a home."

"For God's sake, what does that have to do with me? This is *my* apartment, *my* home—"

"Not anymore," Dain said.

Understanding came to Rennert in a thunderous jolt. Even before he recognized the object Dain took from his pocket, heard the faint snicking sound, and saw the shine of steel, he understood everything. Panic sent him running into the hall, his mouth coming open and a scream rising in his throat.

He didn't quite make it to the door. And the scream didn't quite make it all the way out.

Dain sighed, a deep and heartfelt sigh. "It's good to be home," he said, and went into his bathroom to wash the blood off his hands.

I like cats. Better than dogs and much better than some humans, in fact. You might not think so when you finish reading "Tom," but the story grew out of a wry glimmer of understanding of the cat psyche—my wife and I are owned by two and we've been owned by others over the years—rather than out of any aversion. I have no illusions about the cute and cuddly little buggers; if my cats could manage it, especially on those days when their food bowl doesn't get filled on time, Decker's fate could very well be mine. . . .

Tom

Decker was so absorbed in the collection of Fredric Brown stories he was reading that he didn't see the cat jump onto the balcony railing. He felt its presence after a while, and when he glanced up there it was, switching its tail and staring at him.

At first he was startled; it was as if the cat had materialized out of nowhere. Then he felt a small pleasure. Except for birds and two deer running in the woods, it was the first living creature he'd seen in two weeks. Not that he minded the solitude here; it was the main reason he'd come to this northern California wilderness—a welcome change from his high-pressure Silicon Valley computer job, and a chance to work uninterrupted on the novel he was trying to write. But after fourteen days he was ready for a little company, even if it was only a stray tomcat.

He closed the well-worn paperback and returned the cat's stare. "Well," he said, "hello there, Tom. Where'd you come from?"

The cat didn't move except for its switching tail. Continued to watch him with eyes that were an odd luminous yellow. Otherwise it was an ordinary *Felis catus*, a big butterscotch male with the unneutered tom's overlarge head. It might have been anywhere from three to ten years old.

A minute or so passed—and Decker's feeling of pleasure passed with it. There was something strange about those steady unblinking eyes, something in their depths that might have been malice . . .

No, that was silly. A product of his hyperactive imagination, nurtured for nearly twenty years now by a steady diet of mystery and horror fiction, his one passion other than microtechnology. A product too, he thought, of the coincidental fact that the cat's sudden appearance had coincided with his reading of a Brown story called "Aelurophobe," which was about a man who had a morbid fear of cats.

He had no such fear; at least he'd never been afraid of cats before today. And yet . . . those funny luminous eyes. He had never encountered a cat quite like this one before today.

His mind conjured up another Brown story he'd read, about an alien intelligence that had come to Earth and taken over the body of the protagonist's pet cat.

Then, in spite of himself, he remembered a succession of other stories by other writers about cats who were demons and sorcerers, about human beings who were werecats.

Decker suppressed a shiver. Shook himself and smiled a little sheepishly. "Come on," he said aloud, "that's all pure fantasy. Cats are just cats."

He got up and crossed to the railing. The tom seemed to tense without actually moving. Decker said, "So, guy, what're you doing way out here in the piney woods?" and reached out a hand to pat the animal's head.

Before he could touch it, the cat leaped gracefully to the floor and ran through the open doors into the cabin. He blinked after it for a few seconds, then followed it inside. Where he found it sitting on one arm of the wicker settee, flicking its tail and staring at him again.

For a reason he couldn't explain, Decker began to feel apprehensive. "Hell," he said, "what's the matter with me? Tom, you're nothing to be afraid of."

The apprehension did not go away. Neither did the cat. When Decker walked deliberately to the settee, with the intention of either shooing or carrying the tom outside, it bounded off again. Took up another watchful position on top of a battered old bookcase.

"All right now," Decker said, "what's the idea? You want something, is that it? You hungry, maybe?"

The fur along the cat's back rippled. Otherwise it sat motionless.

Decker nodded. "Sure, that must be it. Big old tom

like you, you need plenty of fuel. If I give you something to eat, you'll go away and let me get back to my reading."

He went into the kitchen, poured a little milk into a dish, tore two small strips of white meat from a leftover Swanson's chicken breast, and took the food back into the living room. He put it down on the floor near the bookcase, backed off half a dozen paces.

The cat did not move.

"Well, go ahead," Decker said. "Eat it and get out."

Ten seconds died away. Then the tom jumped off the bookcase, walked past the food without pausing even to sniff it, and sat down again in the bedroom doorway.

Okay, Decker thought uneasily, so you're not hungry. What else could you want?

He made an effort to recall what he knew about cats. Well, he knew they had been considered sacred by the ancient Egyptians, who worshiped them in temples, paraded them on feast days, embalmed and mummified them when they died and then buried them in holy ground. And that the Egyptian goddess Bast had supposedly endowed them with semidivine powers.

He knew that in the Middle Ages they had been linked to the Devil and the practice of Black Arts and were burned and tortured in religion-sanctioned witch hunts.

He knew that Henry James (whom he had read in

college) once said about them: "Cats and monkeys, monkeys and cats—all human life is there."

He knew that they were predators with a streak of cruelty: they liked to toy with their prey before devouring it.

And he knew they were independent, selfish, aloof, patient, cunning, mischievous, extra clean, and purred when they were contented.

In short, his knowledge was limited, fragmentary, and mostly trivial. And none of it offered a clue to this cat's presence or behavior.

"The hell with it," he said. "This has gone far enough. Tom, you're trespassing. Out you go, right now."

He advanced on the cat, slowly so as not to frighten it. It let him get within two steps, then darted away again. Decker went after it—and went after it, and went after it. It avoided him effortlessly, gliding from one point in the room to another without once taking its yellow-bright gaze from him.

After several minutes, winded and vaguely frightened himself, he gave up the chase. "Damn you," he said, "what do you *want* here?"

The tom stared, switching its tail.

Decker's imagination began to soar again. All sorts of fantastic explanations occurred to him. Suppose the cat was Satan in disguise, come after his soul? Suppose, as in George Langelaan's story "The Fly," a scientist somewhere had been experimenting with a matter transporter and a cat had gotten inside with an evil human subject? Suppose the tom was a kind of modern-day Medusa: look at it long enough and it drives you mad? Suppose—

The cat jumped off the couch and started toward him.

Decker felt a sharp surge of fear. Rigid with it, he watched the animal come to within a few feet and then sit again and glare up at him. Incoming sunlight reflected in its yellow eyes created an illusion of depth and flame that was almost hypnotic.

Compulsively, Decker turned and ran out of the room and slammed the door behind him.

In the kitchen he picked up the telephone—and immediately put it down again. Who was he going to call? The county sheriff's office? "I've got a strange cat in my rented cabin and I can't get rid of it. Can you send somebody right out?" Good Christ, they'd laugh themselves sick.

Decker poured a glass of red wine and tried to get a grip on himself. I'm not an aelurophobe, he thought, and I'm not paranoid or delusional, and I'm not—nice irony for you—a 'fraidy cat. Cats are just cats, damn it. So why am I letting this one upset me this way?

The wine calmed him, made him feel sheepish again. He went back into the living room.

The cat wasn't there.

He looked in the bedroom and the bathroom, the cabin's only other rooms. No cat. Gone, then. Grew tired of whatever game it had been playing, ran off through the balcony doors and back into the woods.

That made him feel even better—more relieved, he admitted to himself, than the situation warranted. He shut and locked the balcony doors, took the Fred Brown paperback to the couch, and tried to resume reading.

He couldn't concentrate. It was hot in the cabin with the doors and windows shut, and the cat was still on his mind. He decided to have another glass of wine. Maybe that would mellow him enough to restore his mental equilibrium, even get his creative juices flowing. He hadn't done as much work on his novel in the past two weeks as he'd planned.

He poured the wine, drank half of it in the kitchen. Took the rest into the bedroom, where he'd set up his laptop Macintosh.

The tomcat was sitting in the middle of the bed.

Fear and disbelief made Decker drop the glass; wine like blood spatters glistened across the redwood flooring. "How the hell did you get in here?" he shouted.

Switch. Switch.

He lunged at the bed, but the cat leapt down easily and raced out of the room. Decker ran after it, saw it dart into the kitchen. He ran in there—and the cat had vanished again. He searched the room, couldn't find it. Back to the living room. No cat. Bedroom, bathroom. No cat.

Fine, dandy, except for one thing. All the doors and windows were still tightly shut. The tom couldn't have gotten out; it *had* to still be inside the cabin.

Shaken, Decker stood looking around, listening to the silence. How had the cat gotten back inside in the first place? Where was it hiding?

What did it want from him?

He tried to tell himself again that he was overreacting. But he didn't believe it. His terror was real and so was the lingering aura of menace the tom had brought with it.

I've got to find it, he thought grimly. Find it and get rid of it once and for all.

Bedroom. Nightstand drawer. His .32 revolver.

Decker had never shot anything with the gun, for sport or otherwise; he'd only brought it along for security, since his nearest neighbor was half a mile away and the nearest town was another four miles beyond there. But he knew he would shoot the cat when he found it, irrational act or not. Just as he would have shot a human intruder who threatened him.

Once more he searched the cabin, forcing himself to do it slowly and methodically. He looked under and behind the furniture, inside the closets, under the sink, through cartons—every conceivable hiding place.

There was no sign of the tom.

His mouth and throat were sand-dry; he had to drink three glasses of water to ease the parching. The thought occurred to him then that he hadn't found the cat because the cat didn't exist; that it was a figment of his hyperactive imagination induced by the Brown story. Hallucination, paranoid obsession . . . maybe he was paranoid and delusional after all.

"Crap," he said aloud. "The damned cat's real."

He turned from the sink—and the cat was sitting on the kitchen table, glowing yellow eyes fixed on him, tail switching.

Decker made an involuntary sound, threw up his arm, and tried to aim the .32; but the arm shook so badly that he had to brace the gun with his free hand. The cat kept on staring at him. Except for the rhythmic flicks of its tail, it was as still as death.

His finger tightened on the trigger.

Switch.

And sudden doubts assailed him. What if the cat had telekinetic powers, and when he fired, it turned the bullet back at him? What if the cat was some monstrous freak of nature, endowed with superpowers, and before he could fire it willed him out of existence?

Supercat, he thought. Jesus, I am going crazy!

He pulled the trigger.

Nothing happened; the gun didn't fire.

The cat jumped down off the table, came toward him—not as it had earlier, but as if with a purpose.

Frantically Decker squeezed the trigger again, and again, and still the revolver failed to fire. The tom continued its advance. Decker backed away in terror, came up against the wall, then hurled the weapon at the cat, straight at the cat. It should have struck the cat squarely in the head, only at the last second it seemed to *loop around* the tom's head like a sharp-breaking curveball—

Vertigo seized him. The room began to spin, slowly,

then rapidly, and there was a gray mist in front of his eyes. He felt himself starting to fall, shut his eyes, put out his hands to the wall in an effort to brace his body—

—and the wall wasn't there—

—and he kept right on falling . . .

Decker opened his eyes. He was lying on a floor, only it was not the floor of his rented kitchen; it was the floor of a gray place, a place without furnishings or definition, a place where the gray mist floated and shimmied and everything—walls, floor, ceiling—was distorted, surreal.

A nonplace. A cat place?

Something made a noise nearby. A cat sound unlike any he had ever heard or could have imagined—a shrill mewling roar.

Decker jerked his head around. And the tom was there, the tom filled the nonplace as if it had grown to human size while he had been shrunk to feline dimensions. It loomed over him, its tail switching, its whiskers quivering. When he saw it like that he tried to stand and run . . . and it reached out one massive paw, almost lazily, and brought it down on his chest, pinned him to the floor. Its jaws opened wide, and he was looking up then into the wet cavern of its mouth, at the rows of sharp white spikes that gleamed there.

Cats are predators with a streak of cruelty: they like to toy with their prey before devouring it.

"No!"

Big old tom like you, you need plenty of fuel.

Decker opened his mouth to scream again, but all that came out was a mouselike squeak.

And then it was feeding time. . . .

Don't be fooled by the touristy background descriptions in the following. What we have here is dark and deadly things lurking beneath an innocuous surface, like piranha in the seemingly placid waters of a lake. They're the sneaky sort, too, in that they may just continue to nibble for a while after you've had your taste of paradise. The tale's basic premise was given to me by a bookseller friend, who swears he met the real-life counterparts of the Archersons on a trip to England a few years ago. Art (if my fictional interpretation can be called that) imitates the seamier side of life, for a change.

A Taste of Paradise

Jan and I met the Archersons at the Hotel Kolekole in Kailua Kona, on the first evening of our Hawaiian vacation. We'd booked four days on the Big Island, five on Maui, four on Kauai, and three and a half at Waikiki Beach on Oahu. It would mean a lot of shunting around, packing and unpacking, but it was our first and probably last visit to Hawaii and we had decided to see as many of the islands as we could. We'd saved three years for this trip—a second honeymoon we'd been promising ourselves for a long time—and we were determined to get the absolute most out of it.

Our room was small and faced inland; it was all we

could afford at a luxury hotel like the Kolekole. So in order to sit and look at the ocean, we had to go down to the rocky, black-sand beach or to a roofed but open-sided lanai bar that overlooked the beach. The lanai bar was where we met Larry and Brenda Archerson. They were at the next table when we sat down for drinks before dinner, and Brenda was sipping a pale green drink in a tall glass. Jan is naturally friendly and curious and she asked Brenda what the drink was— something called an Emerald Bay, a specialty of the hotel that contained rum and crème de menthe and half a dozen other ingredients—and before long the four of us were chatting back and forth. They were about our age, and easy to talk to, and when they invited us to join them we agreed without hesitation.

It was their first trip to Hawaii too, and the same sort of dream vacation as ours: "I've wanted to come here for thirty years," Brenda said, "ever since I first saw Elvis in *Blue Hawaii*." So we had that in common. But unlike us, they were traveling first-class. They'd spent a week in one of the most exclusive hotels on Maui, and had a suite here at the Kolekole, and would be staying in the islands for a total of five weeks. They were even going to spend a few days on Molokai, where Father Damien had founded his lepers' colony over a hundred years ago.

Larry told us all of this in an offhand, joking way— not at all flaunting the fact that they were obviously well-off. He was a tall, beefy fellow, losing his hair as I was and compensating for it with a thick brush moustache. Brenda was a big-boned blonde with pretty gray eyes. They both wore loud Hawaiian shirts and flower leis, and Brenda had a pale pink flower—a hibiscus blossom, she told Jan—in her hair. It was plain that they doted on each other and plain that they were having the time of their lives. They kept exchanging grins and winks, touching hands, kissing every now and then like newlyweds. It was infectious. We weren't with them ten minutes before Jan and I found ourselves holding hands too.

They were from Milwaukee, where they were about to open a luxury catering service. "Another lifelong dream," Brenda said. Which gave us something else in common, in an indirect way. Jan and I own a small restaurant in Coeur d'Alene, Carpenter's Steakhouse, which we'd built into a fairly successful business over the past twenty years. Our daughter Lynn was managing it for us while we were in Hawaii.

We talked with the Archersons about the pros and cons of the food business and had another round of drinks which Larry insisted on paying for. When the drinks arrived, he lifted his mai tai and said, "*Aloha nui kakou*, folks."

"That's an old Hawaiian toast," Brenda explained. "It means to your good health, or something like that. Larry is a magnet for Hawaiian words and phrases. I swear he'll be able to write a tourist phrasebook by the time we leave the islands."

"Maybe I will too, *kuu ipo*."

She wrinkled her nose at him, then leaned over and

nipped his ear. "*Kuu ipo* means sweetheart," she said to us.

When we finished our second round of drinks, Larry asked, "You folks haven't had dinner yet, have you?"

We said we hadn't.

"Well then, why don't you join us in the Garden Court? Their mahimahi is out of this world. Our treat—what do you say?"

Jan seemed willing, so I said, "Fine with us. But let's make it Dutch treat."

"Nonsense. I invited you, that makes you our guests. No arguments, now—I never argue on an empty stomach."

The food was outstanding. So was the wine Larry selected to go with it, a rich French chardonnay. The Garden Court was open-sided like the lanai bar, and the night breeze had a warm, velvety feel, heavy with the scents of hibiscus and plumeria. The moon, huge and near full, made the ocean look as though it were overlaid with a sheet of gold.

"Is this living or is this living?" Larry said over coffee and Kahlúa.

"It's a taste of paradise," Jan said.

"It *is* paradise. Great place, great food, great drinks, great company. What more could anybody want?"

"Well, I can think of one thing," Brenda said with a leer.

Larry winked at me. "That's another great thing about the tropics, Dick. It puts a new spark in your love life."

"I can use a spark," I said. "I think a couple of my plugs are shot."

Jan cracked me on the arm and we all laughed.

"So what are you folks doing tomorrow?" Larry asked. "Any plans?"

"Well, we thought we'd either drive down to the Volcanoes National Park or explore the northern part of the island."

"We're day-tripping up north ourselves—Waimea, Waipio Valley, the Kohala Cost. How about coming along with us?"

"Well . . ."

"Come on, it'll be fun. We rented a Caddy and there's plenty of room. You can both just sit back and relax and soak up the sights."

"Jan? Okay with you?"

She nodded, and Larry said, "Terrific. Let's get an early start—breakfast at seven, on the road by eight. That isn't too early for you folks? No? Good, then it's settled."

When the check came I offered again to pay half. He wouldn't hear of it. As we left the restaurant, Brenda said she felt like going dancing and Larry said that was a fine idea, how about making it a foursome? Jan and I begged off. It had been a long day, as travel days always are, and we were both ready for bed.

In our room, Jan asked, "What do you think of them?"

"Likable and fun to be with," I said. "But exhausting. Where do they get all their energy?"

"I wish I knew."

"Larry's a little pushy. We'll have to make sure he doesn't talk us into anything we don't want to do." I paused. "You know, there's something odd about the way they act together. It's more than just being on a dream vacation, having a good time, but I can't quite put my finger on it. . . ."

"They're like a couple of kids with a big secret," Jan said. "They're so excited they're ready to burst."

We've been married for nearly thirty years and we often have similar impressions and perceptions. Sometimes it amazes me just how closely our minds work.

"That's it," I said. "That's it exactly."

The trip to the northern part of the island was enjoyable, if wearying. Larry and Brenda did most of the talking, Larry playing tour guide and unraveling an endless string of facts about Hawaii's history, geography, flora, and fauna. We spent a good part of the morning in the rustic little town of Waimea, in the saddle between Kohala Mountain and the towering Mauna Kea—the seat of the Parker Ranch, the largest individually owned cattle ranch in the United States. It was lunchtime when we finished rubbing elbows with Hawaiian cowboys and shopping for native crafts, and Brenda suggested we buy sandwich fixings and a bottle of wine and find someplace to have a picnic.

Larry wanted to hike out to the rim of the Waipio Valley and picnic there, but the rest of us weren't up to a long walk. So we drove up into the mountains on the Kawaihae road. When the road leveled out across a long plateau, we might have been in California or the Pacific Northwest: rolling fields, cattle, thick stands of pine. In the middle of one of the wooded sections, Larry slowed and then pulled off onto the verge.

"Down there by that stream," he said. "Now that's a perfect spot for a picnic."

Brenda wasn't so sure. "You think it's safe? Looks like a lot of brush and grass to wade through . . ."

He laughed. "Don't worry, there aren't any wild animals up here to bother us."

"What about creepy-crawlies?"

"Nope. No poisonous snakes or spiders on any of the Hawaiian islands."

"You sure about that?"

"I'm sure, *kuu ipo*. The guidebooks never lie."

We had our picnic, and all through it Larry and Brenda nuzzled and necked and cast little knowing glances at each other. Once he whispered something in her ear that made her laugh raucously and say, "Oh, you're wicked!" Their behavior had seemed charming last night, but today it was making both Jan and me uncomfortable. Fifty-year-old adults who act like conspiratorial teenagers seem ludicrous after you've spent enough time in their company.

Kawaihae Bay was beautiful, and the clifftop view from Upolu Point was breathtaking. On the way back down the coast we stopped at a two-hundred-year-old temple built by King Kamehameha, and at the white-sand Hapuna Beach, where Jan fed the remains of our picnic to the dozens of stray cats that lived there. It was after five when we got back to Kailua Kona.

The Archersons insisted again that we have dinner with them and wouldn't take no for an answer. So we stayed at the Kolekole long enough to change clothes and then went out to a restaurant that specialized in luau-style roast pork. And when we were finished eating, back we went to the hotel and up to their suite. They had a private terrace and it was the perfect place, Brenda said, to watch one of the glorious Hawaiian sunsets.

Larry brought out a bottle of Kahlúa, and when he finished pouring drinks he raised his glass in another toast. "To our new *aikane*, Jan and Dick."

"*Aikane* means good friends," Brenda said.

Jan and I drank, but my heart wasn't in it and I could tell that hers wasn't either. The Archersons were wearing thin on both of us.

The evening was a reprise of yesterday's: not too hot, with a soft breeze carrying the scent of exotic flowers. Surfers played on the waves offshore. The sunset was spectacular, with fiery reds and oranges, but it didn't last long enough to suit me.

Brenda sighed elaborately as darkness closed down. "Almost the end of another perfect day. Time goes by so quickly out here, doesn't it, Jan?"

"Yes it does."

Larry said, "That's why you have to get the most out of each day in paradise. So what'll we do tomorrow? Head down to see the volcanoes, check out the lava flows?"

"There's a road called Chain of Craters that's wonderful," Brenda said. "It goes right out over the flows and at the end there's a place where you can actually walk on the lava. Parts of it are still *hot!*"

I said, "Yes, we've been looking forward to seeing the volcano area. But since you've already been there, I think we'll just drive down by ourselves in the morning—"

"No, no, we'll drive you down. We don't mind seeing it all again, do we, Brenda?"

"I sure don't. I'd love to see it again."

"Larry, I don't mean this to sound ungrateful, but Jan and I would really like some time to ourselves—"

"Look at that moon coming up, will you? It's as big as a Halloween pumpkin."

It was, but I couldn't enjoy it now. I tried again to say my piece, and again he interrupted me.

"Nothing like the moons we get back home in Wisconsin," he said. He put his arm around Brenda's shoulders and nuzzled her neck. "Is it, pet? Nothing at all like a Wisconsin moon."

She didn't answer. Surprisingly, her face scrunched up and her eyes glistened and I thought for a moment she would burst into tears.

Jan said, "Why, Brenda, what's the matter?"

273

"It's my fault," Larry said ruefully. "I used to call her that all the time, but since the accident . . . well, I try to remember not to, but sometimes it just slips out."

"Call her what? Pet?"

He nodded. "Makes her think of her babies."

"Babies? But I thought you didn't have children."

"We don't. Brenda, honey, I'm sorry. We'll talk about something else . . ."

"No, it's all right." She dried her eyes on a Kleenex and then said to Jan and me, "My babies were Lhasa apsos. Brother and sister—Hansel and Gretel."

"Oh," Jan said, "dogs."

"Not just dogs—the sweetest, most gentle . . ." Brenda snuffled again. "I miss them terribly, even after six months."

"What happened to them?"

"They died in the fire, the poor babies. We buried them at Shady Acres. That's a nice name for a pet cemetery, don't you think? Shady Acres?"

"What kind of fire was it?"

"That's right, we didn't tell you, did we? Our house burned down six months ago. Right to the ground while we were at a party at a friend's place."

"Oh, that's *awful*. A total loss?"

"Everything we owned," Larry said. "It's a good thing we had insurance."

"How did it happen?"

"Well, the official verdict was that Mrs. Cooley fell asleep with a lighted cigarette in her hand."

I said, "Oh, so there was someone in the house besides the dogs. She woke up in time and managed to get out safely, this Mrs. Cooley?"

"No, she died too."

Jan and I looked at each other.

"Smoke inhalation, they said. The way it looked, she woke up all right and tried to get out, but the smoke got her before she could. They found her by the front door."

"Hansel and Gretel were trapped in the kitchen," Brenda said. "She was so selfish—she just tried to save herself."

Jan made a throat-clearing sound. "You sound as though you didn't like this woman very much."

"We didn't. She was an old witch."

"Then why did you let her stay in your house?"

"She paid us rent. Not much, just a pittance."

"But if you didn't like her—"

"She was my mother," Brenda said.

Far below, on the lanai bar, the hotel musicians began to play ukuleles and sing a lilting Hawaiian song. Brenda leaned forward, listening, smiling dreamily. "That's 'Maui No Ka Oi,' " she said. "One of my all-time favorites."

Larry was watching Jan and me. He said, "Mrs. Cooley really was an awful woman, no kidding. Mean, carping—and stingy as hell. She knew how much we wanted to start our catering business but she just wouldn't let us have the money. If she hadn't died in

275

the fire . . . well, we wouldn't be here with you nice folks. Funny the way things happen sometimes, isn't it?"

Neither Jan nor I said anything. Instead we got to our feet, almost as one.

"Hey," Larry said, "you're not leaving?"

I said yes, we were leaving.

"But the night's young. I thought maybe we'd go dancing, take in one of the Polynesian revues—"

"It's been a long day."

"Sure, I understand. You folks still have some jet lag too, I'll bet. Get plenty of sleep and call us when you wake up, then we'll all go have breakfast before we head for the volcanoes."

They walked us to the door. Brenda said, "Sleep tight, you lovely people," and then we were alone in the hallway.

We didn't go to our room; instead we went to the small, quiet lobby bar for drinks we both badly needed. When the drinks came, Jan spoke for the first time since we'd left the Archersons. "My God," she said, "I had no idea they were like that—so cold and insensitive under all that bubbly charm. Crying over a pair of dogs and not even a kind word for her mother. They're actually glad the poor woman is dead."

"More than glad. And much worse than insensitive."

"What do you mean?"

"You know what I mean."

"You don't think they—"

"That's just what I think. What we both think."

"Her own mother?"

"Yes. They arranged that fire somehow so Mrs. Cooley would be caught in it, and sacrificed their dogs so it would look even more like an accident."

"For her money," Jan said slowly. "So they could start their catering business."

"Yes."

"Dick . . . we can't just ignore this. We've got to *do* something."

"What would you suggest?"

"I don't know, contact the police in Milwaukee . . ."

"And tell them what that can be proven? The Archersons didn't admit anything incriminating to us. Besides, there must have been an investigation at the time. If there'd been any evidence against them, they wouldn't have gotten Mrs. Cooley's money and they wouldn't be here celebrating."

"But that means they'll get away with it, with cold-blooded murder!"

"Jan, they already have. And they're proud of it, proud of their own cleverness. I think they contrived to tell us the story on purpose, with just enough hints so we'd figure out the truth."

"Why would they do that?"

"The same reason they latched onto us, convinced themselves we're kindred spirits. The same reason they're so damned eager. They're looking for somebody to share their secret with."

"Dear God."

We were silent after that. The tropical night was no

longer soft; the air had a close, sticky feel. The smell of hibiscus and plumeria had turned cloyingly sweet. I swallowed some of my drink, and it tasted bitter. Paradise tasted bitter now, the way it must have to Adam after Eve bit into the forbidden fruit.

The guidebooks do lie, I thought. There are serpents in this Eden, too.

Early the next morning, very early, we checked out of the Kolekole and took the first interisland flight to Honolulu and then the first plane home.

*Trains, like werewolves and a few dozen other wide-
ranging subjects, are a source of endless fascination
for me. A couple of my novels have railroading ele-
ments; and I've edited two anthologies of train stories,
one mystery/suspense* (Midnight Specials) *and one
traditional Western* (The Railroaders). *"Sweet Fever,"
the second of two short stories built around this theme
("Night Freight" being the other), is a mood piece
steeped in railroad and hoboing atmosphere, one reason why it is among the most anthologized of all my
short fiction. Parenthetically I'll add that, as was the
case with "The Monster," it came to me whole—title,
plot, setting, everything—and is essentially a first draft
written at white heat.*

Sweet Fever

Quarter before midnight, like on every evening except
the Sabbath or when it's storming or when my
rheumatism gets to paining too bad, me and Billy Bob
went down to the Chigger Mountain railroad tunnel to
wait for the night freight from St. Louis. This here was
a fine summer evening, with a big old fat yellow moon
hung above the pines on Hankers Ridge and mocking-
birds and cicadas and toads making a soft ruckus.
Nights like this, I have me a good feeling, hopeful, and
I know Billy Bob does too.

They's a bog hollow on the near side of the tunnel

opening, and beside it a woody slope, not too steep. Halfway down the slope is a big catalpa tree, and that was where we always set, side by side with our backs up against the trunk.

So we come on down to there, me hobbling some with my cane and Billy Bob holding onto my arm. That moon was so bright you could see the melons lying in Ferdie Johnson's patch over on the left, and the rail tracks had a sleek oiled look coming out of the tunnel mouth and leading off toward the Sabreville yards a mile up the line. On the far side of the tracks, the woods and the rundown shacks that used to be a hobo jungle before the county sheriff closed it off thirty years back had them a silvery cast, like they was all coated in winter frost.

We set down under the catalpa tree and I leaned my head back to catch my wind. Billy Bob said, "Granpa, you feeling right?"

"Fine, boy."

"Rheumatism ain't started paining you?"

"Not a bit."

He give me a grin. "Got a little surprise for you."

"The hell you do."

"Fresh plug of blackstrap," he said. He come out of his pocket with it. "Mr. Cotter got him in a shipment just today down at his store."

I was some pleased. But I said, "Now you hadn't ought to go spending your money on me, Billy Bob."

"Got nobody else I'd rather spend it on."

I took the plug and unwrapped it and had me a chew.

Old man like me ain't got many pleasures left, but fresh blackstrap's one; good corn's another. Billy Bob gets us all the corn we need from Ben Logan's boys. They got a pretty good sized still up on Hankers Ridge, and their corn is the best in this part of the hills. Not that either of us is a drinking man, now. A little touch after supper and on special days is all. I never did hold with drinking too much, or doing anything too much, and I taught Billy Bob the same.

He's a good boy. Man couldn't ask for a better grandson. But I raised him that way—in my own image, you might say—after both my own son Rufus and Billy Bob's ma got taken from us in 1947. I reckon I done a right job of it, and I couldn't be less proud of him than I was of his pa, or love him no less, either.

Well, we set there and I worked on the chew of blackstrap and had a spit every now and then, and neither of us said much. Pretty soon the first whistle come, way off on the other side of Chigger Mountain. Billy Bob cocked his head and said, "She's right on schedule."

"Mostly is," I said, "this time of year."

That sad lonesome hungry ache started up in me again—what my daddy used to call the "sweet fever." He was a railroad man, and I grew up around trains and spent a goodly part of my early years at the round-house in the Sabreville yards. Once, when I was ten, he let me take the throttle of the big 2-8-0 Mogul steam locomotive on his highballing run to Eulalia, and I can't recollect no more finer experience in my whole life. Later on I worked as a callboy, and then as a fireman on a 2-10-4, and put in some time as a yard tender engineer, and I expect I'd have gone on in railroading if it hadn't been for the Depression and getting myself married and having Rufus. My daddy's shortline company folded up in 1931, and half a dozen others too, and wasn't no work for either of us in Sabreville or Eulalia or anywheres else on the iron. That squeezed the will right out of him, and he took to ailing, and I had to accept a job on Mr. John Barnett's truck farm to support him and the rest of my family. Was my intention to go back into railroading, but the Depression dragged on, and my daddy died, and a year later my wife Amanda took sick and passed on, and by the time the war come it was just too late.

But Rufus got him the sweet fever too, and took a switchman's job in the Sabreville yards, and worked there right up until the night he died. Billy Bob was only three then; his own sweet fever comes most purely from me and what I taught him. Ain't no doubt trains been a major part of all our lives, good and bad, and ain't no doubt neither they get into a man's blood and maybe change him, too, in one way and another. I reckon they do.

The whistle come again, closer now, and I judged the St. Louis freight was just about to enter the tunnel on the other side of the mountain. You could hear the big wheels singing on the track, and if you listened close you could just about hear the banging of couplings and the hiss of air brakes as the engineer throttled down for the curve. The tunnel don't run straight through Chigger Mountain; she comes in from the north and angles to the east, so that a big freight like the St. Louis got to cut back to quarter speed coming through.

When she entered the tunnel, the tracks down below seemed to shimmy, and you could feel the vibration clear up where we was sitting under the catalpa tree. Billy Bob stood himself up and peered down toward the black tunnel mouth like a bird dog on a point. The whistle come again, and once more, from inside the tunnel, sounding hollow and miseried now. Every time I heard it like that, I thought of a body trapped and hurting and crying out for help that wouldn't come in the empty hours of the night. I swallowed and shifted the cud of blackstrap and worked up a spit to keep my mouth from drying. The sweet fever feeling was strong in my stomach.

The blackness around the tunnel opening commenced to lighten, and got brighter and brighter until the long white glow from the locomotive's headlamp spilled out onto the tracks beyond. Then she come through into my sight, her light shining like a giant's eye, and the engineer give another tug on the whistle, and the sound of her was a clattering rumble as loud to my ears as a mountain rockslide. But she wasn't moving fast, just kind of easing along, pulling herself out of that tunnel like a night crawler out of a mound of earth.

The locomotive clacked on past, and me and Billy

Bob watched her string slide along in front of us. Flats, boxcars, three tankers in a row, more flats loaded down with pine logs big around as a privy, a refrigerator car, five coal gondolas, another link of box cars. Fifty in the string already, I thought. She won't be dragging more than sixty, sixty-five. . . .

Billy Bob said suddenly, "Granpa, look yonder!"

He had his arm up, pointing. My eyes ain't so good no more, and it took me a couple of seconds to follow his point, over on our left and down at the door of the third boxcar in the last link. It was sliding open, and clear in the moonlight I saw a man's head come out, then his shoulders.

"It's a floater, Granpa," Billy Bob said, excited. "He's gonna jump. Look at him holding there—he's gonna jump."

I spit into the grass. "Help me up, boy."

He got a hand under my arm and lifted me up and held me until I was steady on my cane. Down there at the door of the boxcar, the floater was looking both ways along the string of cars and down at the ground beside the tracks. That ground was soft loam, and the train was going slow enough that there wasn't much chance he would hurt himself jumping off. He come to that same idea, and as soon as he did he flung himself off the car with his arms spread out and his hair and coattails flying in the slipstream. I saw him land solid and go down and roll over once. Then he knelt there, shaking his head a little, looking around.

Well, he was the first floater we'd seen in seven

months. The yard crews seal up the cars nowadays, and they ain't many ride the rails anyhow, even down in our part of the country. But every now and then a floater wants to ride bad enough to break a seal, or hides himself in a gondola or on a loaded flat. Kids, old-time hoboes, wanted men. They's still a few.

And some of 'em get off right down where this one had, because they know the St. Louis freight stops in Sabreville and they's yardmen there that check the string, or because they see the rundown shacks of the old hobo jungle or Ferdie Johnson's melon patch. Man rides a freight long enough, no provisions, he gets mighty hungry; the sight of a melon patch like Ferdie's is plenty enough to make him jump off.

"Billy Bob," I said.

"Yes, Granpa. You wait easy now."

He went off along the slope, running. I watched the floater, and he come up on his feet and got himself into a clump of bushes alongside the tracks to wait for the caboose to pass so's he wouldn't be seen. Pretty soon the last of the cars left the tunnel, and then the caboose with a signalman holding a red-eye lantern out on the platform. When she was down the tracks and just about beyond my sight, the floater showed himself again and had him another look around. Then, sure enough, he made straight for the melon patch.

Once he got into it I couldn't see him, because he was in close to the woods at the edge of the slope. I couldn't see Billy Bob neither. The whistle sounded one final time, mournful, as the lights of the caboose disappeared, and a chill come to my neck and set there like a cold dead hand. I closed my eyes and listened to the last singing of the wheels fade away.

It weren't long before I heard footfalls on the slope coming near, then the angry sound of a stranger's voice, but I kept my eyes shut until they walked up close and Billy Bob said, "Granpa." When I opened 'em the floater was standing three feet in front of me, white face shining in the moonlight—scared face, angry face, evil face.

"What the hell is this?" he said. "What you want with me?"

"Give me your gun, Billy Bob," I said.

He did it, and I held her tight and lifted the barrel. The ache in my stomach was so strong my knees felt weak and I could scarcely breathe. But my hand was steady.

The floater's eyes come wide open and he backed off a step. "Hey," he said, "hey, you can't—"

I shot him twice.

He fell over and rolled some and come up on his back. They wasn't no doubt he was dead, so I give the gun back to Billy Bob and he put it away in his belt. "All right, boy," I said.

Billy Bob nodded and went over and hoisted the dead floater onto his shoulder. I watched him trudge off toward the bog hollow, and in my mind I could hear the train whistle as she'd sounded from inside the tunnel. I thought again, as I had so many times, that it was the way my boy Rufus and Billy Bob's ma must have sounded that night in 1947, when the two floaters from the hobo jungle broke into their home and raped her and shot Rufus to death. She lived just long enough to tell us about the floaters, but they was never caught. So it was up to me, and then up to me and Billy Bob when he come of age.

Well, it ain't like it once was, and that saddens me. But they's still a few that ride the rails, still a few take it into their heads to jump off down there when the St. Louis freight slows coming through the Chigger Mountain tunnel.

Oh my yes, they'll *always* be a few for me and Billy Bob and the sweet fever inside us both.

That old standby, the ghost story, is one of the most difficult types to write effectively. The number of variations is finite and the best of them have been used—in some cases, used to, um, death. The only ones I've perpetrated with even the smallest claim to originality are "Peekaboo" (if you choose to consider same a ghost story; there is at least one other interpretation) and "Deathlove." You may be interested to know that another, less effective version of this story exists—a straight crime yarn without the supernatural twist, called "For Love." Some writers just can't help being shameless self-plagiarists. Me and Ray Chandler, among others.

Deathlove

I sit hunched forward in the taxi as it rushes through the dark, empty streets. It will not be long now, Judith, my love; a few hours, then a few short weeks until you and I are one. Forever.

And the truck comes out of nowhere

And we come into the quiet residential area six blocks from Lake Industrial Park. I tell the driver to stop at the next corner. A moment later I stand alone in the darkness. The night wind is cold; I turn up the collar on my overcoat as I watch the taxi's taillights fade and disappear. Then I walk rapidly toward the park, my hand touching the gun in my coat pocket.

The industrial development is deserted when I arrive; there is no sign of the night security patrols which make periodic checks of the area. I pause to look at my watch. Just past nine. Then I make my way to the squat stone building that houses McAnally's firm, Ajax Plumbing Supply. A light burns in the office, behind blind-covered windows—the only light in the park. As always on Friday evenings, McAnally is working late and alone.

I move to the rear of the building, to the shadowed parking area. McAnally's car is the only one there. I know it well; I have seen it every day for the past four years, in the driveway of his house across the street from my own, and I have written the insurance policy on it.

I allow myself a small smile as I walk to the base of the high fence that rings the supply yard, blend into the blackness there. All is progressing as I've planned. I'm confident that there will be no problems of any kind.

This isn't right, the truck

As I wait I concentrate on the visual image of Judith that lingers in my mind. Long auburn hair, gentle green eyes, the smooth sensuous lines of her body. Judith smiling, Judith laughing, Judith in all her moods from pensive to gay to kittenish. Every night I dream of her. Every night I long to hold her, touch her, possess her. There is no love greater than mine for Judith; it has become the one and only purpose of my existence.

"Soon now, darling," I whisper in the cold stillness. "Soon . . ."

I do not have long to wait. McAnally, punctual as always, leaves the building at exactly nine-thirty. I tense in anticipation as he crosses the darkened parking area. He reaches the car, but I wait until he unlocks it before I step out and approach him.

He hears my footsteps and glances up, startled. I stop in front of him.

"Hello, Fred," I say.

Recognition smooths his nervous frown. "Why . . . hello, Martin. You gave me a jolt, coming out of the dark like that. What're you doing *here*, of all places?"

"Waiting for you."

"What on earth for?"

"Because I'm going to kill you."

He stares at me incredulously. "What did you say?"

"I'm going to kill you, Fred."

"Hey, that's not funny. Are you drunk?"

I take out the gun. "Now do you believe me?"

For the first time, his eyes show fear. "Martin, for God's sake. What's the matter with you? Why would you want to kill *me*?"

"For love," I say.

"For . . . what?"

"Love, pure and simple love. You're in the way, Fred. You stand between Judith and me."

"You and . . . Judith?"

I smile at him.

"No!" McAnally says. He shakes his head in disbelief. "It's not true. My wife loves me, she's devoted to me."

"Is she?"

"Of course she is! She'd never be a party to—"

"To what I'm planning? Are you really so sure?"

Another head shake. He *isn't* sure, not any longer.

I am enjoying this; I smile again. "Have you ever wondered about the perfect murder? Whether or not it's possible? I have, and I believe it is. Soon now I'm going to prove it."

"This is . . . insane. You're insane, Martin!"

"Not at all. I'm merely in love. Of course I do have my practical side. There's the hundred-thousand-dollar double indemnity policy on your life with my company. Once Judith and I are married, after a decent interval of mourning, it will take care of our needs nicely."

"You can't do this," McAnally says. "I won't *let* you do it!" And he makes a sudden jump forward, clawing at the gun.

But I've expected this, even anticipated how clumsy his fear makes him. I move aside easily, bring the barrel down on the side of his head. He falls moaning to the pavement. I hit him again, then finish opening the car door and drag him onto the floor in back. I slip in under the wheel.

* * *

Night Freight

There is something wrong with all this

As I drive out of Lake Industrial I am watchful for one of the night patrols, but I see no one. Observing the speed limit, I follow the route that McAnally habitually takes home—a route that includes a one-mile stretch through Old Mill Canyon. The canyon road is little used since the construction of a bypassing freeway; McAnally takes it because it is the shortest way to the suburban development where we both live.

At the top of the canyon road is a sharp curve, with a bluff wall on the left and a wide shoulder with a guardrail along its outer edge. Beyond the rail is a two-hundred-foot drop into the canyon below. There are no lights behind me as I take McAnally's car to the crest. From there I can see for a quarter mile or so past the curve. That part of the road is also deserted.

I stop the car a hundred feet below the shoulder, take a few deep breaths before I press down hard on the accelerator and twist the wheel until the car is headed straight for the guardrail. While the car is still on the road I brake sharply; the tires burn and shriek on the asphalt, providing the skid marks that will confirm McAnally's death as a tragic accident.

The truck

I manage to fight the car to a halt a dozen feet from the guardrail. I rub sweat from my forehead, reverse to the road again. When I've set the emergency brake, I get out to make certain we're still alone. Then I pull McAnally from the rear floor, prop him behind the wheel, wedge his foot against the accelerator pedal. The engine roars and the car begins to rock. I grasp the release lever for the emergency brake, prepare myself, jerk the brake off, and fling my body out of the way.

The car hurtles forward. An edge of the open driver's door slaps against my hip, knocking me down, but I'm not hurt. McAnally's car crashes into the guardrail, splintering it, and goes through; it seems to hang in space for a long moment, amid a shower of wood fragments, then plunges downward. The darkness is filled with the thunderous rending of metal as the machine bounces and rolls into the canyon.

I go to the edge and look over. There is no fire, but I can make out the shape of the wreckage far below. I say aloud, "I'm sorry, Fred. It's not that I hated you, or even disliked you. It's just that you were in the way."

Then I turn, keeping to shadow along the side of the road, and begin the long three-mile walk home.

What is it that's so wrong

And late the following morning I stand on the porch of the home that now belongs only to Judith, my Judith. I ring the bell, my chest constricted with excitement as I wait for her to answer.

The door opens at last, and my love looks out at me.

My ardor swells inside me until it is almost like physical pain.

"Hello, Judith," I say gravely. "I just heard about Fred, and of course I came right over."

Her grief-swollen mouth trembles. "Thank you, Martin. It was such a terrible accident, so . . . so *sudden*. I guess you know how much Fred and I cared for each other. I feel lost and alone without him."

"You're not alone," I tell her, and silently add the words *my love.* "It's true we've never been any more than casual neighbors, but I want you to know that there isn't anything I wouldn't do for you. Not *anything* I wouldn't do . . ."

The truck!

I know what it is now. I know what's wrong.

None of this happened.

It was planned to happen just this way, a thousand times I envisioned it, it was like a Technicolor film in my mind as I rode in the taxi. But something else took place, something interfered. The truck, the taxi—

An accident.

I remember it now. The taxi rushing through the dark, empty streets, and the truck coming out of nowhere, barreling through the red light at the intersection, and the impact, and the spinning, and the pain. And then . . . nothing.

Where am I?

Utter blackness. No pain now, no feeling at all.

Vague bodiless sensation of floating, drifting. Coma? Hospital? No, something else, somewhere else. Thoughts, the sudden remembering, the drifting and I am beginning to understand, to realize that I was killed in that accident.

I'm dead.

Fred McAnally is alive and it is Martin Hammond who is dead.

. . . and the door opens at last, and my love looks out at me. My ardor swells inside me until it is almost like physical pain . . .

No, not dead. Not as I've always understood death to be.

Even though I was killed in that accident, part of me remains alive.

Increasing awareness now. I think, I comprehend, therefore I *am*. The essence, the intellect, of Martin Hammond has somehow survived.

Why?

And the answer comes: My love for Judith, the depth and power of my love for her. Too strong even for death. Transcending death. My love lives, therefore I live.

And where I am must be
the netherworld.

Yes. Drifting—spirit drifting. I *am* spirit.

The blackness is beginning to lighten, to become a soft gray; and as it does my awareness increases and I realize with sudden joy that soon I will be capable of vision, corporeality, mobility through time and space. I will be able to return to the mortal world, to Judith. I will be able to

bring my love to my love in the warm silent hours of a night when she is alone . . .

. . . and all at once—there is no temporality where I exist—I find myself standing in her bedroom, that place where I longed so often and so desperately to be. She is there, wearing a pale blue dressing gown, sitting before her vanity mirror while she brushes her hair. Her face is radiant, smiling, and I know it is a Friday night and she is waiting for McAnally. I accept this, it does not disturb me. Nothing can disturb me now that I am in the presence of my love.

Her voice whispers in the quiet, counting each brush stroke. "Eighty-nine, ninety, ninety-one . . ." But she might be counting the minutes until we are together at last, and that is how I choose to hear her words. "Ninety-eight, ninety-nine, one hundred . . ."

Reflected in the mirror, her beauty is so flawless that it is as if I am looking at a priceless painting that must not be seen by anyone else, must belong to no one else but me. I no longer have a heart, but if I did it would be hammering like the beat of drums. I no longer have loins, but if I did they would be aflame with the purity of my desire.

"One hundred nineteen, one hundred twenty . . ."

The need to go to her, touch her, is exquisite. But

how will she react when she sees me? I mustn't frighten her.

Slowly I cross the room. Yet as I draw near, the image of myself that I expect to see behind hers does not materialize. Then I am standing close to her, closer than ever before—and still she is alone in the glass.

"One hundred forty-eight, one hundred forty—"

Abruptly she stops counting, holding the brush against the silkiness of her hair. Her smile fades; small ridge lines appear on her forehead.

"Judith," I whisper. "Judith, my love."

She frowns at the mirror, puts down the brush.

"I'm here, darling."

And I reach out with trembling fingers, touch the softness of her shoulder.

She shivers, as though it were not I but a sudden chill draft that caressed her. She turns, looks around the bedroom—and it is then I accept the truth. She can't see me, or hear me, or feel the gentle pressure of my hand. Perhaps it is because I am not strong enough yet. And perhaps

it is McAnally.

I know then that this is so. He is still alive, he still stands between us—now like a wall between our two worlds.

Always, always, that bastard McAnally!

Judith rises from her chair, crosses to the window, secures the lock. Then she sheds her dressing gown, and the silhouette of her body beneath her thin night-dress fills me with rapture. I watch her put out the lights, get into bed, and lie with the coverlet drawn up to her chin.

After a time, the rhythm of her breathing grows regular. When I am certain she is asleep I walk to the bed and sit down beside her.

She stirs but does not open her eyes.

With great care I lift the coverlet. This is the moment I have ached for most of all, the moment that makes even my death inconsequential.

I take her in my arms.

She moans softly, shivers, tries to turn away in her sleep. I continue to hold her in a tender embrace. "Judith," I whisper in her ear, "it's all right. I'm growing stronger, and when I'm strong enough I'll find another way to kill Fred. A push down the basement steps, a falling object from the platform in the garage—I'll find a way."

More moans come from her, but I hear them now as murmurs of love. I kiss the warm hollow of her throat, and my hand finds her breast, and in ecstasy I lie there with her, waiting.

Waiting.

First, for McAnally.

But most of all for that time when my love will come awake and see and hear and feel me at last, lying beside her in the warm silent hours of the night . . .

The simplest ideas are often the best ones, a truism I think is demonstrated by several stories in this collection. "Black Wind," like the others, therefore depends for its effects on mood and character. And thus another truism: It's all in the handling. The story, incidentally, was the basis for a pretty good short-subject film several years ago. As far as I know, my luck and the movie industry being what they are, the only people who ever saw it, besides members of the production company, were me and my immediate family.

Black Wind

It was one of those freezing late-November nights, just before the winter snows, when a funny east wind comes howling down out of the mountains and across Woodbine Lake a quarter mile from the village. The sound that wind makes is something hellish, full of screams and wailings that can raise the hackles on your neck if you're not used to it. In the old days the Indians who used to live around here called it a "black wind"; they believed that it carried the voices of evil spirits, and that if you listened to it long enough it could drive you mad.

Well, there are a lot of superstitions in our part of upstate New York; nobody pays much mind to them in this modern age. Or if they do, they won't admit it even to themselves. The fact is, though, that when the black wind blows, the local folks stay pretty close to home, and the village, like as not, is deserted after dusk.

That was the way it was on this night. I hadn't had a customer in my diner in more than an hour, since just before seven o'clock, and I had about decided to close up early and go on home. To a glass of brandy and a good hot fire.

I was pouring myself a last cup of coffee when the headlights swung into the diner's parking lot.

They whipped in fast, off the county highway, and I heard the squeal of brakes on the gravel just out front. Kids, I thought, because that was the way a lot of them drove, even around here—fast and a little reckless. But it wasn't kids. It turned out instead to be a man and a woman in their late thirties, strangers, both of them bundled up in winter coats and mufflers, the woman carrying a big fancy alligator purse.

The wind came in with them, shrieking and swirling. I could feel the numbing chill of it even in the few seconds the door was open; it cuts through you like the blade of a knife, that wind, right straight to the bone.

The man clumped immediately to where I was standing behind the counter, letting the woman close the door. He was handsome in a suave, barbered city way; but his face was closed up into a mask of controlled rage.

"Coffee," he said. The word came out in a voice that matched his expression—hard and angry, like a threat.

"Sure thing. Two coffees."

"One coffee," he said. "Let her order her own."

The woman had come up on his left, but not close to him—one stool between them. She was nice-looking in the same kind of made-up, city way. Or she would have been if her face wasn't pinched up worse than his; the skin across her cheekbones was stretched so tight it seemed ready to split. Her eyes glistened like a pair of wet stones and didn't blink at all.

"Black coffee," she said to me.

I looked at her, at him, and I started to feel a little uneasy. There was a kind of savage tension between them, thick and crackling; I could feel it like static electricity. I wet my lips, not saying anything, and reached behind me for the coffeepot and two mugs.

The man said, "I'll have a ham-and-cheese sandwich on rye bread. No mustard, no mayonnaise; just butter. Make it to go."

"Yes, sir. How about you, ma'am?"

"Tuna fish on white," she said thinly. She had close-cropped blond hair, wind-tangled under a loose scarf; she kept brushing at it with an agitated hand. "I'll eat it here."

"No, she won't," the man said to me. "Make it to go, just like mine."

She threw him an ugly look. "I want to eat here."

"Fine," he said—to me again; it was as if she

303

weren't there. "But I'm leaving in five minutes, as soon as I drink my coffee. I want that ham-and-cheese ready by then."

"Yes sir."

I finished pouring out the coffee and set the two mugs on the counter. The man took his, swung around, and stomped over to one of the tables. He sat down and stared at the door, blowing into the mug, using it to warm his hands.

"All right," the woman said, "all right, all right. All right." Four times like that, all to herself. Her eyes had cold little lights in them now, like spots of fox fire.

I said hesitantly, "Ma'am? You still want the tuna sandwich to eat here?"

She blinked then, for the first time, and focused on me. "No. To hell with it. I don't want anything to eat." She caught up her mug and took it to another of the tables, two away from the one he was sitting at.

I went down to the sandwich board and got out two pieces of rye bread and spread them with butter. The stillness in there had a strained feel, made almost eerie by the constant wailing outside. I could feel myself getting more jittery as the seconds passed.

While I sliced ham I watched the two of them at the tables—him still staring at the door, drinking his coffee in quick angry sips; her facing the other way, her hands fisted in her lap, the steam from her cup spiraling up around her face. Well-off married couple from New York City, I thought: they were both wearing the same type of expensive wedding ring. On their way to

304

a weekend in the mountains, maybe, or up to Canada for a few days. And they'd had a hell of a fight over something, the way married people do on long tiring drives; that was all there was to it.

Except that that *wasn't* all there was to it.

I've owned this diner thirty years and I've seen a lot of folks come and go in that time; a lot of tourists from the city, with all sorts of marital problems. But I'd never seen any like these two. That tension between them wasn't anything fresh-born, wasn't just the brief and meaningless aftermath of a squabble. No, there was real hatred on both sides—the kind that builds and builds, seething, over long bitter weeks or months or even years. The kind that's liable to explode some day.

Well, it wasn't really any of my business. Not unless the blowup happened in here, it wasn't, and that wasn't likely. Or so I kept telling myself. But I was a little worried just the same. On a night like this, with that damned black wind blowing and playing hell with people's nerves, anything could happen. Anything at all.

I finished making the sandwich, cut it in half, and plastic-bagged it. Just as I slid it into a paper sack, there was a loud banging noise from across the room that made me jump half a foot; it sounded like a pistol shot. But it had only been the man slamming his empty mug down on the table.

I took a breath, let it out silently. He scraped back his chair as I did that, stood up, and jammed his hands into his coat pockets. Without looking at her, he said to the woman, "You pay for the food," and started past her table toward the restrooms in the rear.

She said, "Why the hell should I pay for it?"

He paused and glared back at her. "You've got all the money."

"I've got all the money? Oh, that's a laugh. *I've* got all the money!"

"Go on, keep it up." Then in a louder voice, as if he wanted to make sure I heard, he said, "Bitch." And stalked away from her.

She watched him until he was gone inside the corridor leading to the rest rooms; she was as rigid as a chunk of wood. She sat that way for another five or six seconds, until the wind gusted outside, thudded against the door and the window like something trying to break in. Jerkily she got to her feet and came over to where I was at the sandwich board. Those cold lights still glowed in her eyes.

"Is his sandwich ready?"

I nodded and made myself smile. "Will that be all, ma'am?"

"No. I've changed my mind. I want something to eat too." She leaned forward and stared at the glass pastry container on the back counter. "What kind of pie is that?"

"Cinnamon apple."

"I'll have a piece of it."

"Okay—sure. Just one?"

"Yes. Just one."

I turned back there, got the pie out, cut a slice, and wrapped it in waxed paper. When I came around with it she was rummaging in her purse, getting her wallet out. Back in the rest room area, I heard the man's hard, heavy steps; in the next second he appeared and headed straight for the door.

The woman said, "How much do I owe you?"

I put the pie into the paper sack with the sandwich, and the sack on the counter. "That'll be three-eighty."

The man opened the door; the wind came shrieking in, eddying drafts of icy air. He went right on out, not even glancing at the woman or me, and slammed the door shut behind him.

She laid a five-dollar bill on the counter. Caught up the sack, pivoted, and started for the door.

"Ma'am?" I said. "You've got change coming."

She must have heard me, but she didn't look back and she didn't slow up. The pair of headlights came on out front, slicing pale wedges from the darkness; through the front window I could see the evergreens at the far edge of the lot, thick swaying shadows bent almost double by the wind. The shrieking rose again for two or three seconds, then fell back to a muted whine; she was gone.

I had never been gladder or more relieved to see customers go. I let out another breath, picked up the fiver, and moved over to the cash register. Outside, above the thrumming and wailing, the car engine revved up to a roar and there was the ratcheting noise

307

of tires spinning on gravel. The headlights shot around and probed out toward the county highway.

Time now to close up and go home, all right; I wanted a glass of brandy and a good hot fire more than ever. I went around to the tables they'd used, to gather up the coffee cups. But as much as I wanted to forget the two of them, I couldn't seem to get them out of my mind. Especially the woman.

I kept seeing those eyes of hers, cold and hateful like the wind, as if there was a black wind blowing inside her, too, and she'd been listening to it too long. I kept seeing her lean forward across the counter and stare at the pastry container. And I kept seeing her rummage in that big alligator purse when I turned around with the slice of pie. Something funny about the way she'd been doing that. As if she hadn't just been getting her wallet out to pay me. As if she'd been—

Oh my God, I thought.

I ran back behind the counter. Then I ran out again to the door, threw it open, and stumbled onto the gravel lot. But they were long gone; the night was a solid ebony wall.

I didn't know what to do. What could I do? Maybe she'd done what I suspicioned, and maybe she hadn't; I couldn't be sure because I don't keep an inventory on the slots of utensils behind the sandwich board. And I didn't know who they were or where they were going. I didn't even know what kind of car they were riding in.

I kept on standing there, chills racing up and down my back, listening to that black wind scream and scream around me. Feeling the cold sharp edge of it cut into my bare flesh, cut straight to the bone.

Just like the blade of a knife . . .

The editor who commissioned this story, Peter Crowther, specifically requested a horror tale set in the Old West which deals with a little-known superstition. I had a devil of a time (no pun intended) coming up with a suitable idea until I happened to be paging through a book on nineteenth-century village life, hunting inspiration. One of the chapters was entitled "The Coffin Trimmer"—a pleasant piece of nostalgia about a gentle, benign spinster who worked for a mortician in the author's hometown. My coffin trimmer, naturally, is anything but gentle, the superstition she represents is anything but benign, and what happens after her arrival in the village of Little River is anything but pleasant. . . .

The Coffin Trimmer

I'm scared.

I have never been so scared.

No one in Little River shares my terror. They refuse to listen to me, to open their eyes to the terrible truth. They call me a superstitious fool. Or tetched, or downright deranged. One day they will realize how blind they've been—the ones that are left. But by then it will be too late.

Lord have mercy on us all.

It doesn't make sense that Little River was chosen. Ours is no worse nor different than any other small

northern California town. Dairy and beef cattle is what
supports us; agricultural crops such as alfalfa, too. We
have six saloons, a gambling house, and a whore-
house, compared to only three churches, but that
doesn't mean there is much sin or even much impiety.
There isn't. We haven't had a killing or any other
major crime in nearly twenty years. Rowdyism is con-
fined to Independence Day and once in a while when a
cowhand off one of the ranches gets liquored up of a
Saturday night. We're a God-fearing town of thirteen
hundred and sixty-eight souls, according to the 1892
census. Good souls, with no more than a bucketful
destined for a handshake with Satan on their judgment
day.

Doesn't make sense, either, that it would start
when Abe Bedford put up his new undertaking
building. But it did, and no mistake. I used to believe
everything that happened in this life had its clear-cut
purpose and meaning, and if you studied on it long
enough, looked at it in just the right way, you'd
come to know or at least suspect what it was. Not
this, though. No one can figure out the cause or reason for this—no one mortal, anyhow. And perhaps
that's a blessing. I know too much already; I'm too
scared as it is. I reckon I couldn't stand to know the
rest of it too.

Abe Bedford buys all his rough pine boxes and
fancier coffins from a casketmaker in the county seat.
He used to store them in the barn back of his house on
Oak Street. Had the coffins trimmed there, as well, by

his wife Maude before she passed away and then by the Widow Brantley; he buys them without lining because it's thriftier that way. His embalming room and viewing parlor were in a rented building down on lower Main, near the train depot. He'd been the only undertaker in town for some while, but Little River was growing and Abe took to fretting that before long some other mortician would move in and open a fancy establishment and take away a good portion of his business. He came to the idea that what he had to do was build his own fancy establishment first, in a better location than lower Main—a place that was big enough for embalming and viewing, and to show off and store his caskets and rough boxes.

So he had a new building put up on the other side of his Oak Street property, close to the street. It had a large plate glass window in front so folks walking or riding by could look in and see the trimmed display coffins with their satin linings and silk pillows and shiny brass fittings. Abe also laid in shrubbery and a lawn and a brick walk and a wide brick drive to accommodate his black hearse and team of four. When it was all done, everybody agreed the new undertaking parlor was a worthy addition to the community.

Abe had been open for business in the new place less than a week when the woman who called herself Grace Selkirk came to town.

No one knew where she came from, or even how she arrived in Little River. She simply appeared one day, and took a room overnight at the hotel where the

313

drummers and railroad men always stayed; and the next day she was living in Abe Bedford's house, keeping it for him and working in the Widow Brantley's stead as his coffin trimmer.

Tongues started to wag right off. Gossip's a major industry in any small town, and in Little River the women and members of the Hot Stove League in Cranmer's General Merchandise Store work harder at it than most. I hear more gossip, I reckon, than just about anyone in town. Cranmer's General Merchandise Store is mine, inherited from my daddy when he passed on fifteen years ago. George Cranmer is my name.

Abe Bedford is a widower and reasonable handsome for a man in his late forties. Grace Selkirk looked to be about thirty-five and was not too hard on the eye, in a chilly sort of way. Before long, folks had Abe and the Selkirk woman sharing a bed. Some even went so far as to claim he had met her on one of his trips to San Francisco, where his son lived, and brought her back with him on the sly so they could live together in sin.

I didn't believe any of it. I've known Abe for four decades; there is no more moral and God-fearing man in this state. He'd heard the gossip, too, and it hurt him. He wouldn't have anything to do with Grace Selkirk, he said to me one night, not that way, not if she was the only woman in a thousand miles. She made him shiver just to look at her, he said.

I asked him why he hired her and he said he didn't rightly know. She'd showed up on his doorstep the morning after she arrived in town and asked him for the work; he was about to refuse her, for he'd had no trouble doing for himself since Maude died, but he couldn't seem to find the words. Couldn't bring himself to let her go since, either. She was a good cook and housekeeper, he said, and the fact was, she trimmed coffins better than Maude or the Widow Brantley ever had. Why, some of her finished caskets were funerary works of art.

Nobody liked Grace Selkirk much. She never made any effort to be neighborly and little enough to be civil. Stayed close to Abe's home and undertaking parlor, and on the few occasions she came down to Main Street and into my store, she hardly spoke a word. I could surely understand why she made Abe shiver. She was the coldest woman I'd ever laid eyes on. Ice and snow weren't any colder.

One blustery day when she walked into the store, old Mead Downey was occupying his usual stool by the white-bellied stove, and he tried to make conversation with her. She wouldn't have any of it. Went about her business and then walked out as if old Mead wasn't even there. He spit against the hot side of the stove, waited for it to sizzle, and allowed as how he'd never believed those rumors about her and Abe and now he knowed for a fact they weren't true.

"Why's that?" one of the other loafers asked him.

315

"He's still alive, ain't he?" Mead said. "First time he stuck his pizzle in that woman, him and it would of froze solid."

All the boys laughed fit to choke. I laughed too. I thought it was a pretty funny remark then.

It isn't funny now.

The one thing about Grace Selkirk that you couldn't fault was her coffin-trimming. As Abe had said, she was an artist with silk and satin, taking pains to get the folds in the lining and the fluff of the pillows just so. She did her work right there in the showroom, in plain sight behind the plate glass window. Most any time of day, and late some evenings, you'd see her at it. She spent twice as much time working in the undertaking building as she did keeping Abe's house for him.

It wasn't that she was readying caskets for future use. No, all the ones she trimmed were for fresh business. More folks than usual had commenced dying in Little River. Nobody worried about the increase in fatalities; births and deaths run that way, in high-low cycles. A feeble joke even got started that Abe had done such a bang-up job on his new establishment, people were dying to get into it.

Grace Selkirk had been in town about six weeks when Charley Bluegrass came rushing into my store one night. It was a chilly fall night with a touch of rain in the air. I'd stayed open late, as I often do, because I am a confirmed bachelor and I'd rather be in the store playing checkers and dominoes and shooting the breeze with members of the Hot Stove League than sitting alone in my dusty parlor.

Bluegrass wasn't Charley's true last name. Everyone called him that on account of he'd planted a Kentucky Bluegrass lawn for Miss Edna Tolliver a few years back and it had come up so rich and green, half the women in the county took after him to do the same job for them. Which he did. He'd given up his handyman chores and taken to working as a gardener fulltime. Charley was a half-breed Miwok and liked his liquor more than most men. He'd been liking it pretty well on this night; you could smell it on him when he blew in.

He was all het up, his eyes sparkly with drink and excitement. "That new woman, that Grace Selkirk—she's dead!"

The Hot Stove League and I all came to attention. I said, "Dead? You sure, Charley?"

"I'm sure. I seen her through the window at the undertaker's. All laid out in one of them coffins, deader than a doornail."

Frank McGee crossed himself. He was new in town and a freshman member of the League, a young clerk in the Argonaut Drugstore who drove his wagon all the way to the county seat of a Sunday so he and his wife could attend what he called Mass in the Catholic Church over there. Old Mead said, "What killed her? Frostbite?" and commenced to cackling like a hen with a half-stuck egg. Nobody paid him any mind.

"I don't know what killed her," Charley Bluegrass said. "I didn't see no marks, no blood or nothing, but I didn't stop to look close."

"Some of you gents better go on over to the undertaking parlor and have a look," I said. "And then tell Abe."

Toby Harper and Evan Millhauser volunteered and hurried out. Charley Bluegrass stayed behind to warm himself at the stove and sneak another drink from the flask he carried in his hip pocket. I don't usually allow the imbibing of spirits on the premises—I don't drink nor smoke myself; chewing sassafras root is my only vice—but under the circumstances I figured Charley was entitled.

We all thought Toby and Evan would be gone awhile, but they were back in ten minutes. And laughing when they walked in. "False alarm," Toby said. "That Selkirk woman ain't dead. She's walking around over there livelier than any gent in this room."

Charley Bluegrass jumped to his feet. "That can't be. She's dead, I saw her laid out in that coffin."

"Well, she just got resurrected," Evan said. "You better change the brand of panther piss you're drinking, Charley. It's making you see things that aren't there."

Charley shook his head. "I tell you, she was dead. The lamplight was real bright. Her face . . . it was all white and waxy. Something strange, too, like it wasn't—" He bit the last word off and swallowed the ones that would have come next. A shiver went through him; he reached for his flask.

"Like it wasn't what?" I asked him.

"No," he said, "no, I ain't going to say."

Toby said, "I'll bet she was lining the coffin and laid down in it to try it for a fit. You know how she is with her trimming. Everything's got to be just so."

"Tired too, probably, hard as she works," one of the others said. "Felt so good, stretched out on all that silk and satin, she fell asleep. That's what you saw, Charley. Her sleeping in that box."

"She wasn't sleeping," Charley Bluegrass said, "she was dead." And nobody could convince him otherwise.

The next morning *he* was the one who was dead.

Heart failure, Doc Miller said. Charley Bluegrass was thirty-seven years old and never sick a day in his life.

Citizens of Little River kept right on dying. Old folks, middle-aged, young; even kids and infants. More all the time, though not so many more that it was alarming. Wasn't like a plague or an epidemic. No, what they died of was the same ailments and frailties and carelessness as always. Pneumonia, whooping cough, diphtheria, coronary thrombosis, consumption, cancer, colic, heart failure, old age; accident and misadventure too. Only odd fact was that more deaths than usual seemed to be sudden, of people like Charley Bluegrass that hadn't been sick or frail. Old Mead was one who just up and died. The young Catholic clerk, Frank McGee, was another.

When I heard about Frank I took over to the undertaking parlor to pay my respects. Mrs. McGee was there, grieving next to the casket. I told her how sorry I was, and she said, "Thank you, Mr. Cranmer. It was so sudden . . . I just don't understand it. Last night my Frank was fine. Why, he even laughed about dying before his time."

"Laughed?"

"Well, you recollect what happened to that half-breed Indian, Charley Bluegrass? The night before *he* died?"

"I surely do."

"Same curious thing happened to my Frank. He went out for a walk after supper and chanced over here to Oak Street. When he looked in through Mr. Bedford's show window he saw the very same as Charley Bluegrass."

"You mean Grace Selkirk lying in one of the coffins?"

"I do," Mrs. McGee said. "Frank thought she was dead. There was something peculiar about her face, he said."

"Peculiar how?"

"He wouldn't tell me. Whatever it was, it bothered him some."

Charley Bluegrass, I recalled, had also remarked about Grace Selkirk's face. And he hadn't wanted to talk about what it was, either.

"Frank was solemn and quiet for a time. But not long; you know how cheerful he always was, Mr. Cranmer. He rallied and said he must've been wrong and she was asleep. Either that, or he'd had a delusion—and him not even a drinking man. Then he laughed and said he hoped he wouldn't end up dead before his time like poor Charley Bluegrass . . ." She broke off weeping.

Right then, I began to get a glimmer of the truth.

Almost everyone in Little River visited my store of a week. Whenever a spouse or relative or close acquaintance of the recent deceased came in, I took the lady or gent aside and asked questions. Three told me the same as Frank McGee's widow: Their dead had also chanced by the undertaking parlor not long before they drew their last breaths, and through the show window saw Grace Selkirk lying in one of the coffins, dead or asleep. Two of the deceased had mentioned her face, too—something not quite right about it that had disturbed them but that they wouldn't discuss.

Five was too many for coincidence. If there was that many admitted what they'd seen, it was likely an equal number—and perhaps quite a few more than that— had kept it to themselves, taken it with them to their graves.

That was when I knew for certain.

My first impulse was to rush over and confront Grace Selkirk straight out. But it would have been pure folly and I came to my senses before I gave in to it. I went to see Abe Bedford instead. He was my best friend and I thought if anybody in town would listen to me, it was Abe.

I was wrong. He backed off from me same as if I'd just told him I was a leper. Why, it was the most ridiculous thing he'd ever heard, he said. I must be deranged to put stock in such an evil notion. Drive her out of town? Take a rope or a gun to her? "You go around urging such violence against a poor spinster, George Cranmer," he said, "and *you'll* be the one driven out of town."

He was nearly right, too. The ministers of our three churches wouldn't listen, nor would the mayor or the town council or anyone else in Little River. The truth was too dreadful for them to credit; they shut their minds to it. Folks stopped trading at my store, commenced to shunning me on the street. Wasn't anything I could do or say to turn even one person to my way of thinking.

Finally I quit trying and put pen to paper and wrote it all out here. I pray someone will read it later on, someone outside Little River, and believe it for the pure gospel truth it is. I have no other hope left than that.

She calls herself Grace Selkirk but that isn't her name. She has no name, Christian or otherwise. She isn't a mortal woman. And coffin-trimming isn't just work she's good at—it's her true work, it's what she is. The Coffin Trimmer.

The Angel of Death.

I don't know if she's after the whole town, every last soul in Little River, but I suspect she is. Might get them too. One other fact I do know: This isn't the first town she's come to and it won't be the last. Makes a body tremble to think how many must have come before, all over the country, all over the world, and how many will come after.

But that is not the real reason I'm so scared. No, not even that. Last night I worked late and walked home by way of Oak Street. Couldn't help myself, any more than I could help glancing through Abe Bedford's show window. And there she was in a fresh-trimmed coffin, the silk and satin draped just so around her, face all pale and waxy and dead. But the face wasn't hers; I looked at it close to make sure.

It was mine. A shadow vision of my own fresh corpse waiting to be put into the ground.

I'm next.

This little tale of psychosexual obsession brought yelps of protest from more than one faithful reader when it first appeared. The story seems to push some people's buttons, and not because of the act referred to in the final sentence; the phrase containing reference to said act was left out of the originally published version. The yelps pleased me. I hope there'll be more from readers who catch "Funeral Day" here for the first time. Pushing buttons, after all, is what fiction is all about—from the writer's point of view, anyway.

Funeral Day

It was a nice funeral. And easier to get through than he'd imagined it would be, thanks to Margo and Reverend Baxter. They had kept it small, just a few friends; Katy had had no siblings others than Margo, no other living relatives. And the casket had been closed, of course. A fall from a two-hundred-foot cliff . . . it made him shudder to think what poor Katy must have looked like when they found her. He hadn't had to view the body, thank God. Margo had attended to the formal identification.

The flowers were the worst part of the service. Gardenias, Katy's favorite. Dozens and dozens of gardenias, their petals like dead white flesh, their cloyingly sweet perfume filling the chapel and making him a little dizzy after a while, so that he couldn't concentrate on Reverend Baxter's mercifully brief eulogy.

At least *he* hadn't been pressed to stand up next to the bier and speak. He couldn't have done it. And besides, what could he have said about a woman he had been married to for six years and stopped loving— if he had ever really loved her—after two? It wasn't that he'd grown to hate or even dislike her. No, it was just that he had stopped caring, that she had become a stranger. Because she was so weak . . . that was the crux of it. A weak, helpless stranger.

Afterward, he couldn't remember much of the ride to the cemetery. Tearful words of comfort from Jane Riley, who had been Katy's closest friend; someone patting his hand—Margo?—and urging him to bear up. And later, at the gravesite . . . "We therefore commit her body to the ground, earth to earth, ashes to ashes, dust to dust . . ." and Reverend Baxter sprinkling a handful of dirt onto the coffin while intoning something about subduing all things unto Himself, amen. He had cried then, not for the first time, surely not for the last.

The ride home, to the small two-story house he had shared with Katy a half mile from the college, was a complete blank to him. One moment he was at the gravesite, crying; the next, it seemed, he was in his living room, surrounded by his books and the specimen cases full of the insects he had collected during his entomological researches. Odd, he realized then, how little of Katy had gone into this room, into any of the rooms in the house. Even the furniture was to his taste. The only contributions of hers that he could remember were frilly bits of lace and a bright seascape she had bought at a crafts fair. And those were gone now, along with her clothing and personal effects; Margo had already boxed them up so that he wouldn't have to suffer the task, and had had them taken away for charity.

Nine or ten people were there, Katy's and his friends, mostly from the college. Mourners who had attended the funeral and also been to the cemetery. Jane Riley and Evelyn Something—Dawson? Rawson? a woman he didn't know well that Katy had met at some benefit or other—had provided food, and there were liquor and wine and hot beverages. Margo and the Reverend had referred to the gathering as a "final tribute"; he called it a wake. But Katy wouldn't have minded. Knowing that, he hadn't objected.

Katy. Poor, weak, sentimental Katy . . .

The mourners ate and drank, they talked, they comforted and consoled. He ate and drank nothing; his stomach would have disgorged it immediately. And he talked little, and listened only when it seemed an answer was required.

"You *are* taking a few more days off, aren't you, George?" Alvin Corliss, another professor at the college. English Lit.

"Yes."

"Take a couple of weeks. Longer, if you need it. Go

327

on a trip, someplace you've always wanted to visit. It'll do you a world of good."

"Yes. I think I might . . ."

"Is Margo staying on awhile longer, George?" Helen Vernon, another of Katy's friends. They had gone walking together often, along the cliffs and elsewhere. But she hadn't been with Katy on the day of her fall. No, not on that day.

"Yes, Helen, she is."

"Good. You shouldn't be alone at a time like this."

"I don't mind being alone."

"A man needs a woman to do for him in his time of grief. Believe me, I know . . ."

On and on, on and on. Why didn't they leave? Couldn't they see how much he wanted them to go? He felt that if they stayed much longer he would break down—but of course he didn't break down. He endured. When his legs grew weak and his head began to throb, he sank into a chair and stared out through a window at his garden. And waited. And endured.

Dusk came, then full dark. And finally—but slowly, so damned slowly—they began to leave by ones and twos. It was necessary that he stand by the door and see them out. Somehow, he managed it.

"You've held up so well, George . . ."

"You're so brave, George . . ."

"If you need anything, George, don't hesitate to call . . ."

An interminable time later, the door closed behind

the last of them. Not a moment too soon; he was quite literally on the verge of collapse.

Margo sensed it. She said, "Why don't you go upstairs and get into bed? I'll clean up here."

"Are you sure? I can help—"

"No, I don't need any help. Go on upstairs."

He obeyed, holding onto the bannister for support. He and Katy had not shared a bedroom for the past three years; there had been no physical side to their marriage in almost four, and he had liked to read at night, and she had liked to listen to her radio. He was grateful, now that she was gone, that he did not have to occupy a bed he had shared with her. That would have been intolerable.

He undressed, avoided looking at himself in the mirror while he brushed his teeth, and crawled into bed in the dark. His heart was pounding. Downstairs in the kitchen, Margo made small sounds as she cleaned up after the mourners.

You're so brave, George . . .

No, he thought, I'm not. I'm weak—much weaker than poor Katy. Much, much weaker.

He forced himself to stop thinking, willed his mind blank.

Time passed; he had no idea how many minutes. The house was still now. Margo had finished her chores.

He lay rigidly, listening. Waiting.

A long while later, he heard Margo's steps in the

hall. They approached, grew louder . . . and went on past. The door of her room opened, shut again with a soft click.

He released the breath he had been holding in a ragged sigh. Not tonight, then. He hadn't expected it to be tonight, not this night. Tomorrow? The need in him was so strong it was an exquisite torture. How he yearned to feel her arms around him, to be drawn fiercely, possessively against the hard nakedness of her body, to succumb to the strength of her, the overpowering dominant *strength* of her! She had killed Katy for him; he had no doubt of it. When would she come to claim her prize?

Tomorrow?

Please, he thought as he began to masturbate, please let it be tomorrow. . . .

Some titles are irresistible. Or rather, from a writer's perspective, some lines and phrases are such perfect titles that they cry out for stories to be created for them. "Skeleton Rattle Your Mouldy Leg," for instance, a don marquis quote that inspired a "Nameless Detective" novelette. "The Mayor of Asshole Valley"—I haven't found the right story for that one yet, but I will eventually. And "I Think I Will Not Hang Myself Today," all thanks to G. K. Chesterton. As I wrote in an earlier headnote, fictioneers are notoriously poor judges of their own work; so I realize I'm inviting disagreement when I say that this little title-generated tale is among the two or three best, if not the best, of the three-hundred-plus shorts I've written. So be it. That's the reason I've saved it as the final entry in these pages.

I Think I Will Not Hang Myself Today

The leaves on the trees were dying.

She had noted that before, of course; neither her mind nor her powers of observation had been eroded by the passing years. But this morning, seen from her bedroom window, it seemed somehow a sudden thing, as if the maples and Japanese elms had changed color overnight, from bright green to red and brittle gold.

Just yesterday it had been summer, now all at once it was autumn.

John had been taken from her on an October afternoon. It would be fitting if autumn were her time, too.

Perhaps today, she thought. Why not today?

For a while longer Miranda stood looking out at the cold morning, the sky more gray than blue. Wind rattled the frail leaves, now and then tore one loose and swirled it to the ground. Even from a distance the maple leaves resembled withered hands, their veins and skeletal bone structure clearly visible. The wind, blowing from east to west, sent the fallen ones skittering across the lawn and its bordering flower beds, piled them in heaps along the wall of the old barn.

Looking at the barn this morning filled her with sadness. Once, when John was alive, the skirling whine of his power saws and the fine, fresh smells of sawdust and wood stain and lemon oil made the barn seem alive, as sturdy and indestructible as the beautiful furniture that came from his workshop. Now it was a sagging shell, a lonely place of drafts and shadows and ghosts, its high center beam like the crosspiece of a gallows.

So little left, she thought as she turned from the window. John gone these many years. Moira gone—no family left at all. Lord Byron gone six months, and as much as she missed the little Sealyham's companionship, she hadn't the heart to replace him with another pet. Gone, too, were most of her friends. And the pleasures of teaching grammar and classic English literature, the satisfaction that came from helping to shape young minds. ("We're sorry, Mrs. Halliday, but you know the mandatory retirement age in our district is sixty-five.") For a time there had been a few students to privately tutor, but none had come since last spring. County library cutbacks had ended her volunteer work at the local branch. The arthritis made it all but impossible for her to continue her sewing projects for homeless children. Even Mrs. Boyer in the next block had found someone younger and stronger to baby-sit her two preschoolers.

The loneliness had been endurable when she was needed, really needed. Being able to help others had given some meaning and purpose to her life. Now, though, she had become the needy one, requiring help with the cleaning, the yardwork, her weekly grocery shopping. All too soon, she would no longer be able to drive her car, and then she would be housebound, totally dependent on others. If that happened . . .

No, she thought, it mustn't. I'm sorry, John, but it mustn't.

She thought again of the old barn, his workshop, the long, high rafter beam. When it had become clear and irrefutable what she must one day do, there had never been any question as to the method. Mr.

Gilbert Chesterton had seen to that. She had bought the rope that very day, and it was still out there waiting. She would have to stand on a ladder in order to loop it around the beam—not an easy task, even though the knot had long ago been tied. But she would manage. She had always managed, hadn't she? Supremely capable, John had called her. That, and the most determined woman he had ever known; once her mind was made up, nothing would change it. Yes, and the end would be quick and she would not suffer. No one should ever have to suffer when the time came.

Chesterton's lines ran through her mind again:

The strangest whim has seized me
    . . . After all
I think I will not hang myself today.

She had first come across "A Ballade of Suicide," one of his minor works, when she was a girl, and there had been something so haunting in those three lines that she had never forgotten them. One day, she would alter the last of the lines by deleting the word *not*. This day, perhaps . . .

Miranda bathed and dressed and brushed her hair, which she kept short and wavy in the fashion John had liked. Satisfied with her appearance, she made her way downstairs and fixed a somewhat larger breakfast than usual—a soft-boiled egg to go with her habitual tea and toast. Then she washed the dishes—her hands were not paining too badly this morning—and entered the living room.

John had built every stick of furniture in there, of cherrywood and walnut. Tables, chairs, sofa and loveseat, sideboard, the tall cabinet that contained his collection of rifles and handguns. (She hated guns, but she had been unable to bring herself to rid the house of anything that had belonged to him.) Handcrafted furniture had been both his vocation and his hobby. An artist with wood, John Halliday. Everyone said so. She had loved to watch him work, to help him in his shop and to learn from him some of the finer points of his craft.

The photograph of John in his Navy uniform was centered on the fireplace mantel. She picked it up, looked at it until his lean, dark face began to blur, then replaced it. She dried her eyes and peered at the other framed photos that flanked his.

Mother, so slender and fragile, the black velvet-banded cameo she'd always worn hiding the grease burn on her throat. Father in cap and gown at one of his college graduation ceremonies, looking as young as one of his students. Moira and herself at ages four and seven, all dressed up for some occasion or other, and wasn't it odd how much prettier she had been as a child, when it was Moira who had grown into such a beautiful woman? Uncle Leon, his mouth full of the foul pipe he favored, and Aunt Gwen as round and white as the Pillsbury Doughboy. Gone, all gone. Dust. Sweet-sad memories and scattered specks of dust.

Miranda moved to the bookcases on the near side of the fireplace. Her domain; John had never been much of a reader, despite her best efforts. Plato, Thomas Aquinas, Shakespeare, Chaucer. Scott, Dickens, Hawthorne, the Brontë sisters, Stevenson. Browning and Byron and Eliot and Edna St. Vincent Millay. Nearly a dozen volumes of fiction and nonfiction by Chesterton, always her favorite. Oscar Wilde, so amusing and ironic—

The phone was ringing.

She may have heard the first ring or the bell may have sounded two or three times before she grew aware of it; she wasn't quite sure. She went to answer it.

"Miranda, dear, how are you?"

"Oh, hello, Patrice."

"You sound a bit melancholy this morning. Is everything all right?"

"Yes. You mustn't worry about me."

"But I do. You know I do."

Miranda knew it all too well. Patrice was one of her oldest friends, but their closeness was neither deep nor confiding. Patrice's life had been one long, smooth sail, empty of tragedy of any kind; she had never needed anyone outside her immediate family. And ever since Miranda's own tragic loss, Patrice's friendship and concern had been tinged with thinly concealed pity.

"I called to invite you to lunch tomorrow," Patrice said. "You need to get out more, and lunch at the Shady Grove Inn is just the ticket. My treat."

"That's good of you, but I don't believe I'll be able to accept."

"Other plans, dear?"

"I . . . may not be here tomorrow."

"Oh? Going away somewhere?"

"Possibly. It's not quite certain yet."

"May I ask where and with whom?"

"I'd rather not say."

"Of course, I understand. But talking about something in advance really doesn't prevent it from happening, you know."

"It can," Miranda said. "Sometimes it can."

"Well, you must tell me all about it afterward."

"It won't be a secret, Patrice. I can promise you that."

They talked a few minutes longer. Or rather Patrice talked, mostly about her grandchildren. Miranda only half listened. It seemed quite cold in the house now, despite the fact that she had turned up the heat when she came downstairs. Imagination? No, she could hear the wind in the eaves, gusting more strongly than before, and when that happened the house always felt drafty.

When Patrice finally said good-bye, Miranda returned to the living room and put on the gas-log flame in the

337

fireplace. She sat in front of it with a copy of Wilde's *The Importance of Being Earnest* open on her lap, and tried to read. She couldn't seem to concentrate. I wish I had something else to do, she thought, something useful or important.

Well, she thought then, there is something, isn't there? Out in the barn?

But she was not ready to go out there yet. Not just yet. She picked up Wilde and tried again to focus on his words.

She was dozing when the doorbell rang. Dreaming about something pleasant, something to do with John and their honeymoon in the Caribbean, but the jarring sound of the bell drove it away. A visitor? She so seldom had visitors these days. The prospect hurried her steps to the door.

But it wasn't a visitor; it was Dwayne, the mailman, on the porch outside. "Morning, Miz Halliday," he said. "More mail than usual today so I thought I'd bring it up, save you the trouble."

"That was good of you, Dwayne."

"Catalogues, mostly. Not even the end of October and already we got piles of Christmas catalogues. Seems like they start sending 'em out earlier every year."

"Yes, it does."

He handed over the thick stack, being cautious about it because he knew of her arthritis. "You going out today, Miz Halliday?"

"I may, yes. Why do you ask?"

"Well, it's pretty cold out. Wind's got ice in it, first breath of winter. Real pneumonia weather. Better bundle up warm if you do go out."

"I will, thank you."

He wished her a good morning and left her alone again.

Miranda sifted through her mail. No personal letters, of course. Just two bills and three solicitations, one of the solicitations addressed to "Maranda Holiday." She laid the bills, unopened, on the kitchen table, put the solicitations in the trash and the catalogues in the recycle box.

Except for the wind, the house was very quiet.

And still unwarm.

And so empty.

In her sewing room, she removed the letter—three pages, carefully folded—from the bottom drawer of her desk. She had written it quite a long time ago, but she could have quoted it verbatim. The wind gusted noisily as she started out with it, rattling shingles and shutters, and she remembered what Dwayne had said about bundling up warm. The front hall closet yielded her heaviest wool coat and a pair of fleece-lined gloves. She had the coat over her shoulders, the letter tucked into one of the pockets, when the phone rang again.

"Mrs. Halliday? This is Sally Boyer?"

"Yes, Mrs. Boyer."

"I wonder if I could ask a big favor? I know it's short notice and I haven't been in touch in a while, but if you could help us out I'd really appreciate it?" Mrs. Boyer was one of those individuals who turn statements into questions by a rising interrogative inflection on the last few words of a sentence. More than once Miranda had been tempted to help her correct this irritating habit, but it would have been impolite to bring it up herself.

"What is the favor?"

"Could you baby-sit for us tonight? My husband has a business dinner, a client and his wife from Los Angeles who showed up without any advance warning? Well, he thinks it's important for me to join them, and our regular sitter has band practice tonight and so I thought you . . . ?"

"I'm afraid I have another commitment," Miranda said firmly.

"You do? You couldn't possibly break it?"

"I don't see how I can, now."

"But I thought you, of all people . . . I mean . . ."

"Yes, Mrs. Boyer, I understand. And I'm sorry."

"I don't know who else to call," Mrs. Boyer said. "Can you think of anyone? You must know someone, some other elder . . . some other person?"

"I don't know anyone," Miranda said. "No one at all."

She said good-bye and replaced the receiver. She buttoned her coat, worked her gnarled fingers into the gloves, then crossed the rear porch and stepped outside.

The wind was blustery and very cold, but she didn't

hurry. It would not do to hurry at a time like this. She walked at a steady, measured pace across the leaf-strewn yard to the barn.

The front half was mostly a dusty catchall storage area, as it had been when John was alive. On the right side was a cleared section just large enough for her car; the remaining floor space was packed with trunks, boxes, discarded appliances, gardening equipment, and the like. Some of the cartons had been there for so long Miranda no longer had any idea what they contained. She made her way along the passenger side of the car to the doorway in the center partition; opened it and passed through into John's workshop.

His last few woodworking projects, finished and unfinished, were bulky mounds under the dustcloths she had placed over them. His workbench, lathe, table saws, and such were also shrouded. The bench was where the coiled rope lay, but Miranda did not go in that direction. Nor did she glance up at the ceiling beam in the shadows above.

At the workshop's far end, more shadows crowded the alcove where John had kept his cot and tiny refrigerator. On those long-ago summer nights when he had been deep into one of his projects, he had slept out here to avoid disturbing her. Now there was nothing inside the alcove, only the bare wood floor over packed earth.

Miranda knelt and raised the cunningly hidden hinged section. Underneath, the flowers she had placed there last week were already withered and crumbling, dust and petals scattered across the pair of old graves.

So many years since she'd found John and Moira together here that night. So many years since the strangest whim had seized her and she'd done what she felt she must—shot them both with one of John's handguns, quickly and efficiently, for no one should have to suffer when the time came. So many years since she had, in her supremely capable fashion, dug for each of them a final resting place and then, using the woodworking skills John had taught her, rebuilt the flooring to cover the graves.

No one had ever suspected. John Halliday had run off with his wife's beautiful younger sister—that was what everyone believed. Such a terrible tragedy for poor Miranda, they all said. But no one except her could know how terrible it really was to be left all alone with nobody to love except a little dog and fewer and fewer and fewer ways in which to atone for her sin.

It would be quite a shock when the citizens of Shady Grove learned the truth. And learn it they must; she had kept the secret too long and she could not carry it with her to her own grave—in the words of the poet Andrew Marvell, that "fine and private place." She had explained everything in the three-page letter; it would be her final act of atonement.

John and Moira knew all about the rope and the letter. Over and over she had told them that one day she must again do what she felt was necessary. Yet they were so reluctant to let her go. She could feel their reluctance now. Selfish. Even in death, they cared only for themselves.

"John," she said, "this is the proper day. Can't you understand how I feel?"

The wind mourned outside.

"Moira? We've hurt each other enough. Isn't it time we were together again?"

The last of the flowers suddenly trembled and broke apart. The earth seemed to tremble, too, as if there were stirrings within. It was only a draft caused by the wind, she knew it could be nothing else, yet it was as if they had caused it. As if they were beseeching and mocking her, saying quite clearly: "You can't leave us, Miranda. Who will tend to us once you're gone? Who will bring flowers and keep the weeds from growing up around us?

"*We* need you, Miranda. You know that, don't you?"

She did not argue; it never did any good to argue. She sighed and got slowly to her feet. "After all," she said, "I think I will not hang myself today."

She lowered the hinged section, thinking that she must buy fresh flowers to replace the withered ones because it was autumn and there were none left in the garden. But before she called the florist, she would ring up Mrs. Boyer and tell her she would be able to baby-sit tonight after all.

"Stacked Deck." Copyright © 1987 by Bill Pronzini. First published in *The New Black Mask #8*.

"Angel of Mercy." Copyright © 1996 by Bill Pronzini. First published in *Diagnosis: Terminal*.

"Night Freight." Copyright © 1967 by Renown Publications, Inc. Revised version copyright © 1991 by Bill Pronzini. First published in *Mike Shayne Mystery Magazine*.

"Liar's Dice." Copyright © 1992 by Bill Pronzini. First published in *Ellery Queen's Mystery Magazine*.

"Out Behind the Shed." Copyright © 1991 by Bill Pronzini. First published in *Final Shadows*.

"Souls Burning." Copyright © 1991 by Bill Pronzini. First published in *New Crimes 3*.

"Strangers in the Fog." Copyright © 1978 by Bill Pronzini. First published in *Ellery Queen's Mystery Magazine*.

"Peekaboo." Copyright © 1979 by Charles L. Grant. First published in *Nightmares*.

"Thirst." Copyright © 1973 by Mercury Press, Inc. Revised version copyright © 1988 by Bill Pronzini. First published in *The Magazine of Fantasy & Science Fiction*.

"Wishful Thinking." Copyright © 1999 by the Pronzini-Muller Family Trust. First published in *Irreconcilable Differences*.

"Ancient Evil." Copyright © 1993 by Bill Pronzini. First published in *The Ultimate Werewolf*.

"The Monster." Copyright © 1996 by Bill Pronzini. First published in *Ellery Queen's Mystery Magazine*.

"His Name Was Legion." Copyright © 1978 by Renown Publications, Inc. First Published in *Mike Shayne Mystery Magazine*.

"Out of the Depths." Copyright © 1994 by Bill Pronzini. First published in *Ellery Queen's Mystery Magazine*.

"The Pattern." Copyright © 1971 by H. S. D. Publications, Inc. First published in *Alfred Hitchcock's Mystery Magazine*.

"The Rec Field." Copyright © 1979 by Bill Pronzini. First published in *Chrysalis 6*.

"Deathwatch." Copyright © 1987 by Bill Pronzini. First published in *The Mystery Scene Reader*.

"Home." Copyright © 2000 by the Pronzini-Muller Family Trust.

"Tom." Copyright © 1992 by Bill Pronzini. First published in *Cat Crimes II*.

"A Taste of Paradise." Copyright © 1994 by Bill Pronzini. First published in *Ellery Queen's Mystery Magazine*.

"Sweet Fever." Copyright © 1976 by Bill Pronzini. First published in *Ellery Queen's Mystery Magazine*.

"Deathlove." Copyright © 1978 by Charles L. Grant. Revised version copyright © 2000 by the Pronzini-Muller Family Trust. First published in *Shadows*.

"Black Wind." Copyright © 1979 by Bill Pronzini. First published in *Ellery Queen's Mystery Magazine*.

"The Coffin Trimmer." Copyright © 1993 by Bill Pronzini. First published in *Touch Wood*.

"Funeral Day." Copyright © 1989 by Bill Pronzini. First published in *New Crimes*.

"I Think I Will Not Hang Myself Today." Copyright © 2000 by the Pronzini-Muller Family Trust. First published in *Ellery Queen's Mystery Magazine*.

THE NIGHTMARE CHRONICLES

DOUGLAS CLEGG

It begins in an old tenement with a horrifying crime. It continues after midnight, when a young boy, held captive in a basement, is filled with unearthly visions of fantastic and frightening worlds. How could his kidnappers know that the ransom would be their own souls? For as the hours pass, the boy's nightmares invade his captors like parasites—and soon, they become real. Thirteen nightmares unfold: A young man searches for his dead wife among the crumbling buildings of Manhattan... A journalist seeks the ultimate evil in a plague-ridden outpost of India... Ancient rituals begin anew with the mystery of a teenage girl's disappearance... In a hospital for the criminally insane, there is only one doorway to salvation... But the night is not yet over, and the real nightmare has just begun. Thirteen chilling tales of terror from one of the masters of the horror story.

___4580-X $5.50 US/$6.50 CAN

Dorchester Publishing Co., Inc.
P.O. Box 6640
Wayne, PA 19087-8640

Please add $1.75 for shipping and handling for the first book and $.50 for each book thereafter. NY, NYC, and PA residents, please add appropriate sales tax. No cash, stamps, or C.O.D.s. All orders shipped within 6 weeks via postal service book rate. Canadian orders require $2.00 extra postage and must be paid in U.S. dollars through a U.S. banking facility.

Name_____
Address_____
City_____State_____Zip_____
I have enclosed $_____ in payment for the checked book(s).
Payment <u>must</u> accompany all orders. ❑ Please send a free catalog.
   CHECK OUT OUR WEBSITE! www.dorchesterpub.com

MASQUES

BILL PRONZINI

Mardi Gras is a time of madness when an entire city seems to lose its mind. But for Steve Giroux, the madness has become all too real. A mysterious voice on the phone wants something from him—evidence of an unspeakable murder—and will use all the forces it commands to get it. Suddenly Steve is cast into a swirling nightmare of voodoo, black magic, and blood, a nightmare that can only get worse until he delivers what the voice wants. But how can Steve deliver what he's never had?

___4451-X $4.99 US/$5.99 CAN

Dorchester Publishing Co., Inc.
P.O. Box 6640
Wayne, PA 19087-8640

Please add $1.75 for shipping and handling for the first book and $.50 for each book thereafter. NY, NYC, and PA residents, please add appropriate sales tax. No cash, stamps, or C.O.D.s. All orders shipped within 6 weeks via postal service book rate. Canadian orders require $2.00 extra postage and must be paid in U.S. dollars through a U.S. banking facility.

Name_____

Address_____

City_____State_____Zip_____

I have enclosed $_____ in payment for the checked book(s).

Payment <u>must</u> accompany all orders. ☐ Please send a free catalog.

CHECK OUT OUR WEBSITE! www.dorchesterpub.com

BLOODLINES

J. N. WILLIAMSON

Marshall Madison disappeared the night his wife committed suicide. She saw the horrible things Madison did to their son, Thad, and couldn't deal with the knowledge that their daughter, Caroline, was next. Caroline is taken in by a kind, hardworking family, and Thad runs off to live by his wits on the streets of New York. But Madison means to make good on his promise to come for his children. And as he gets closer and closer, the trail of bodies in his wake gets longer and longer. No one will keep him from his flesh and blood.

___4468-4 $4.99 US/$5.99 CAN

Dorchester Publishing Co., Inc.
P.O. Box 6640
Wayne, PA 19087-8640

Please add $1.75 for shipping and handling for the first book and $.50 for each book thereafter. NY, NYC, and PA residents, please add appropriate sales tax. No cash, stamps, or C.O.D.s. All orders shipped within 6 weeks via postal service book rate. Canadian orders require $2.00 extra postage and must be paid in U.S. dollars through a U.S. banking facility.

Name_____
Address_____
City_____State_____Zip_____
I have enclosed $_____ in payment for the checked book(s).
Payment <u>must</u> accompany all orders. ❑ Please send a free catalog.

DRAWN TO THE GRAVE — MARY ANN MITCHELL

"A tight, taut dark fantasy with surprising plot twists and a lot of spooky atmosphere."
—Ed Gorman

Beverly thinks that she has found something special with Carl, until she realizes that he has stolen from her. But he doesn't just steal her money and her property—he steals her very life. Suddenly she is helpless and alone, able only to watch in growing despair as her flesh begins to decay and each day transforms her more and more into a corpse—a corpse without the release of death.

But Beverly is not truly alone, for Carl is always nearby, watching her and waiting. He knows that soon he will need another unknowing victim, another beautiful woman he can seduce...and destroy. And when lovely young Megan walks into his web, he knows he has found his next lover. For what can possibly go wrong with his plan, a plan he has practiced to perfection so many times before?

___4290-8 $4.99 US/$5.99 CAN

Dorchester Publishing Co., Inc.
P.O. Box 6640
Wayne, PA 19087-8640

Please add $1.75 for shipping and handling for the first book and $.50 for each book thereafter. NY, NYC, and PA residents, please add appropriate sales tax. No cash, stamps, or C.O.D.s. All orders shipped within 6 weeks via postal service book rate. Canadian orders require $2.00 extra postage and must be paid in U.S. dollars through a U.S. banking facility.

Name_____
Address_____
City_____ State_____ Zip_____
I have enclosed $_____ in payment for the checked book(s).
Payment <u>must</u> accompany all orders. ❏ Please send a free catalog.

Sips of Blood

MARY ANN MITCHELL

The Marquis de Sade. The very name conjures images of
decadence, torture, and dark desires. But even the worst
rumors of his evil deeds are mere shades of the truth, for the
world doesn't know what the Marquis became—they don't
suspect he is one of the undead. And that he lives among us
still. His tastes remain the same, only more pronounced.
And his desire for blood has become a hunger. Let Mary
Ann Mitchell take you into the Marquis's dark world of
bondage and sadism, a world where pain and pleasure
become one, where domination can lead to damnation. And
where enslavement can be forever.

___4555-9 $5.50 US/$6.50 CAN

Dorchester Publishing Co., Inc.
P.O. Box 6640
Wayne, PA 19087-8640

Please add $1.75 for shipping and handling for the first book and
$.50 for each book thereafter. NY, NYC, and PA residents,
please add appropriate sales tax. No cash, stamps, or C.O.D.s. All
orders shipped within 6 weeks via postal service book rate.
Canadian orders require $2.00 extra postage and must be paid in
U.S. dollars through a U.S. banking facility.

Name_____

Address_____

City_____ State_____ Zip_____

I have enclosed $_____ in payment for the checked book(s).

Payment <u>must</u> accompany all orders. ❑ Please send a free catalog.

   CHECK OUT OUR WEBSITE! www.dorchesterpub.com

UNGRATEFUL DEAD

GARY L. HOLLEMAN

When Alana Magnus first comes to Luther Shea's office, he thinks she is crazy. Her claim that her mother is interfering in her life sounds normal enough—except that her mother is dead. Bit by bit, Alana sees herself taking on the physical characteristics, even distinguishing marks, of her mother. And the more Luther looks into her claims, the more he comes to believe she is right.

___4472-2 $5.99 US/$6.99 CAN

Dorchester Publishing Co., Inc.
P.O. Box 6640
Wayne, PA 19087-8640

Please add $1.75 for shipping and handling for the first book and $.50 for each book thereafter. NY, NYC, and PA residents, please add appropriate sales tax. No cash, stamps, or C.O.D.s. All orders shipped within 6 weeks via postal service book rate. Canadian orders require $2.00 extra postage and must be paid in U.S. dollars through a U.S. banking facility.

Name_____
Address_____
City_____ State_____ Zip_____
I have enclosed $_____ in payment for the checked book(s).
Payment <u>must</u> accompany all orders. ☐ Please send a free catalog.
CHECK OUT OUR WEBSITE! www.dorchesterpub.com

MARC LAIDLAW
THE 37th MANDALA

"Genuinely creepy! This book has enough to keep the reader checking the corners"
—Stephen King

The mandalas have always been among us, unseen and uncalled. Those few occult masters who have encountered them have known to leave them alone, for to these unholy forces we are mere playthings, insignificant tools to be used, fed upon—and eventually discarded. When New-Age charlatan Derek Crowe learns the secrets of the mandalas he sees only the opportunity for easy money. He ignores the warnings, alters the mystical texts to make the dreaded mandalas seem benevolent to a gullible public, then publishes his book and waits for the profits to roll in. But Crowe is all too successful. For he has inadvertently released upon the earth a horror that is beyond all understanding or control—a horror both infinite and hungry.

___4658-X $4.99 US/$5.99 CAN

Dorchester Publishing Co., Inc.
P.O. Box 6640
Wayne, PA 19087-8640

Please add $1.75 for shipping and handling for the first book and $.50 for each book thereafter. NY, NYC, and PA residents, please add appropriate sales tax. No cash, stamps, or C.O.D.s. All orders shipped within 6 weeks via postal service book rate. Canadian orders require $2.00 extra postage and must be paid in U.S. dollars through a U.S. banking facility.

Name_____
Address_____
City_____State_____Zip_____
I have enclosed $_____ in payment for the checked book(s).
Payment <u>must</u> accompany all orders. ❑ Please send a free catalog.
        CHECK OUT OUR WEBSITE! www.dorchesterpub.com

Elizabeth Massie
Sineater

According to legend, the sineater is a dark and mysterious figure of the night, condemned to live alone in the woods, who devours food from the chests of the dead to absorb their sins into his own soul. To look upon the face of the sineater is to see the face of all the evil he has eaten. But in a small Virginia town, the order is broken. With the violated taboo comes a rash of horrifying events. But does the evil emanate from the sineater...or from an even darker force?

___4407-2 $5.99 US/$6.99 CAN

Dorchester Publishing Co., Inc.
P.O. Box 6640
Wayne, PA 19087-8640

Please add $1.75 for shipping and handling for the first book and $.50 for each book thereafter. NY, NYC, and PA residents, please add appropriate sales tax. No cash, stamps, or C.O.D.s. All orders shipped within 6 weeks via postal service book rate. Canadian orders require $2.00 extra postage and must be paid in U.S. dollars through a U.S. banking facility.

Name_____
Address_____
City_____ State_____ Zip_____
I have enclosed $_____ in payment for the checked book(s).
Payment <u>must</u> accompany all orders. ☐ Please send a free catalog.
CHECK OUT OUR WEBSITE! www.dorchesterpub.com

ATTENTION HORROR CUSTOMERS!

SPECIAL
TOLL-FREE NUMBER
1-800-481-9191

Call Monday through Friday
10 a.m. to 9 p.m.
Eastern Time
Get a free catalogue,
join the Horror Book Club,
and order books using your
Visa, MasterCard,
or Discover®

Leisure
Books

GO ONLINE WITH US AT DORCHESTERPUB.COM